The Return of The

THIN MAN

DASHIELL HAMMETT

The Original Screen Stories

AFTER THE THIN MAN
ANOTHER THIN MAN
SEQUEL TO THE THIN MAN

Edited by Richard Layman and Julie M. Rivett

A Mysterious Press Book
for Head of Zeus

First published in 2012 by Mysterious Press,
an imprint of Grove/Atlantic Inc, New York.

This edition first published in the UK in 2012 by Head of Zeus Ltd.
This paperback edition published in the UK in 2013 by Head of Zeus Ltd.

A CIP catalogue record for this book is available from the British Library.

Paperback ISBN: 9781908800626
eBook ISBN: 9781781850442

Printed and bound by CPI Group (UK) Ltd,
Croydon, CR0 4YY.

Head of Zeus Ltd
Clerkenwell House
45-47 Clerkenwell Green
London EC1R 0HT

www.headofzeus.com

CONTENTS

CONTENTS

Introduction

Dashiell Hammett's original screen stories for *After the Thin Man* and *Another Thin Man*, the second and third of the six movies in the *Thin Man* series starring William Powell and Myrna Loy, are the last long pieces of fiction Hammett ever wrote. He completed those stories in 1935 and 1938, respectively, when he was at the peak of his power as a writer and his authority as a literary figure. By 1934, in the space of four years, he had completed *The Maltese Falcon*, *The Glass Key*, and *The Thin Man*. He was hailed internationally as a literary celebrity and, while he responded with a celebrity's flamboyance, he was regarded by his peers as among the most accomplished American writers of his generation. He had the wit to be entertaining, the confidence to be irreverent, and the talent to satisfy not only the book-buying but the moviegoing audiences. He was a valuable commodity to MGM, which had an unexpected hit with its more or less faithful movie adaptation of *The Thin Man* in 1934, and it allowed him the extraordinary leeway afforded a stylish moneymaker. Hunt Stromberg may have been the producer, but he needed Hammett to make the particular kind of films the early *Thin Man* movies were. In a November 11, 1934, interview movie critic Philip K. Scheuer asked Hammett what the formula was for a successful mystery comedy. Hammett replied, "There is no formula." So he created one.

By 1934 Hammett was well known in Hollywood. He excelled at the tight, intriguing plots and sharp dialogue that moviemakers desperately sought in the early days of talkies. He had written original stories for Republic Studios, Paramount, Warner Brothers, and Howard Hughes's Caddo Company, and four of his novels had been optioned by major studios. He was prized for his ability to write authentic, witty dialogue and for his talent as a scenarist. He was able to command top dollar as a screenwriter, the only caveat being that he was unreliable and personally undisciplined. He was an alcoholic: when he applied himself, he was first-rate; when he was drinking, he was lazy and uncooperative. Beginning with *The Thin Man* Hammett took a pioneering approach to the crime novel by mixing comedy with intrigue, social fiction with crime fiction, and a hedonistic hero with a disciplined professional detective. That formula paid off handsomely for him even as the financial fortunes of the nation were crumbling. Hammett got a star's billing at the beginning—in important respects, he was Nick Charles—and MGM made him a rich man. It took Hammett to capture that character, and William Powell acted the part flawlessly.

Hammett's fifth, last, and most commercially successful novel, *The Thin Man*, was published on January 8, 1934. Two weeks later, he wrote his wife:

> "The book is going swell. It got very fine reviews—as you can see from the enclosed clippings—and last week sold better than any other book in New York, Philadelphia, and San Francisco, besides being near the top of the list in most other cities.
>
> "Second, MGM is buying the movie rights for $21,000, which is $4,000 less than Paramount paid for *The Glass Key*, but a pretty good price this year at that."

Indeed. It was the worst year of the Depression, and $21,000 was the equivalent of some $350,000 in present-day money.

In fact the *Los Angeles Times* reported that MGM, acting on the advice offered by Alexander Woollcott on his radio program, purchased movie rights eight days after the book was published. The studio set a budget of $250,000 for the first movie and assigned it to director W. S. Van Dyke, known as "one-shot Woody" for his efficiency in managing production budgets, suggesting that the studio had moderate expectations for the movie's success. They were wrong. *The Thin Man*, starring William Powell, Myrna Loy, and the wire fox terrier Asta, was released on May 25, 1934, to rave reviews (having been shot in sixteen days, according to *The Hollywood Reporter*). The National Board of Review named it one of the top ten movies of the year. More important, it was also one of the top ten moneymakers of 1934 and won four Academy Award nominations: Best Picture, Best Adapted Screenplay (Albert Hackett and Frances Goodrich), Best Director (Van Dyke), and Best Actor (William Powell). *The Thin Man* was regarded as the prototype for a new type of crime movie, softening the subject matter with witty comedy and romance. Van Dyke thought its success came from the depiction of a happily married couple, a strange oversimplification of Hammett's achievement in creating Nick and Nora Charles. Hammett commented: "They made a pretty funny picture out of it and it seems to be doing good business wherever it is shown." *The Thin Man* begged for a sequel.

Immediately after *The Thin Man* was released, producer Hunt Stromberg began thinking about a second Nick and Nora Charles movie. On August 29, 1934, he dictated his thoughts: "The treatment that we can give Nick and Nora is so plentiful that it will be comparatively easy to write the intimate story as soon as we get the crime element. Maybe we would want Nick to be dragged into a case that happens in San Francisco. I personally favor the New York idea, however, because it would give us the opportunity to bring back all those swell characters of the original—and there would be a large amount of humor in any idea that would demand Nick's presence back in New York. . . . The main object of this *second crime element* is to make it even more mysterious and ingenious than the first, for the millions who have seen *The Thin Man* will be smarter now in spotting suspects or guilty ones than they were in the first picture. . . . I'm not being any too clear, but we will discuss it later." It is clear enough that Stromberg needed help.

Late in September the Culver City office of MGM wrote to the New York office asking that they contact Hammett, who was on the East Coast at the time, to negotiate a contract for a sequel to *The Thin Man*. On October 1, New York replied that Hammett was inaccessible—he was moving between Florida and various stopping places in Manhattan—and that in any event it would not be possible to get any work from him. On October 19, Louis B. Mayer wrote from New York warning that Hammett suffered from "irregular habits." Nonetheless, on October 23, 1934, Hammett signed an agreement with MGM that stipulated, in part:

1. You are to leave for our Studios at Culver City, California, either October 24th or 25th, 1934. We will furnish you railroad transportation and compartment.
2. On arrival at our Studios you will begin writing for us, under our supervision and in accordance with our suggestions, a full and complete original story, which will be a sequel to The Thin Man and its characters and action previously written by you, and of substantially the same length, and will continue your services to us until such story is fully completed by you and accepted by us. You will comply with reasonable studio regulations while so employed by us.
3. For these services we will pay you at the rate of two thousand dollars ($2,000) weekly for each week (but not in excess of ten weeks) you so fully perform such services for us.

Hammett left the next day for Los Angeles, where he took a suite at the Beverly Wilshire Hotel and began work the following Monday, the twenty-eighth. That evening he wrote to his confidante Lillian Hellman: "And so passed the first day laboring in the picture-galleries. I think it's going to be all right. I like the people thus far, and I have a comfortable office."

Two days later he wrote Hellman again: "After the party [at Herbert Asbury's house] broke up Mrs. Joel Sayre and I did a little town roaming until nearly 5 this a.m., but I was up at 10 and so to work on my Thin Man sequel, but still without the exact murder hookup I want." And so it went. Writing on November 1: "I took Thyra [Samter Winslow, a Hollywood writer] to dinner last night and so I got very—not to say disgracefully—drunk . . . and so home at what hour I don't know and too hungovery to go to the studio today." Four days later:

> I went back on the booze pretty heavily until Saturday night—neglecting studio, dignity, and so on. And I was sick Sunday and today! This morning I showed up at M.G.M. for the first time since last Tuesday and squared myself, but didn't get much work done, since the publicity department took up most of my time, what with photographs, interviews and the like.
>
> "I'm still surprised at the fuss *The Thin Man* made out here. People bring the Joan Crawfords and Gables over to meet me instead of the usual vice versa. Hot-cha!

On November 26: "I'm off for another crack at the thinmansequel, on which I'm pretty cold at the time, but will probably be highpressured by Hunt Stromberg into the wildest enthusiasm before long."

Despite the drinking and carousing, Hammett managed to complete the first draft for *After the Thin Man: Thin Man Sequel* on January 8, 1935, on time—ten weeks after he had signed his contract. He promptly left Hollywood for New York. He had impressed his bosses with a first-rate screen story and his punctuality.

On June 19, 1935, MGM called him back into service, this time with the title of "motion picture executive." His contract stipulated: "Your services hereunder shall include, but not be limited to, such services as we may require of you as a general editorial aide and/or as an assistant and/or advisor not only in connection with the preparation of stories and/or continuities, but as well in connection with the actual production of photoplays. You agree to attend conferences and assist in the preparation and/or developing of ideas which may be submitted or contributed by us or others." The new agreement further stipulated that if Hammett was required to "write the complete continuity including dialogue for any photoplay" then during that period he would earn $1,750 per week. That was Depression money, the present-day equivalent of some $29,000 (using the scale of increase in the consumer price index). The next week Hammett wrote to his publisher Alfred Knopf (whom, by contract, he owed a sixth novel): "If you've anything coming out that looks like picture stuff, you might shoot it to me, as we are hunting for some material." In November Hammett signed a contract to adapt the proletarian novel *The Foundry* by Albert Halper for the screen for $5,000. That interest is the earliest indication of Hammett's active pursuit of the political agenda of the Communist Party USA.

Meanwhile, he completed his screen story for *After the Thin Man*, dated September 17, 1935, and promptly called, then wrote, Lillian Hellman: "After I called you I took a drink of Scotch, the first I've had since when was it?" It was a drunken letter, marking another long alcoholic binge. That fall Hammett was back and forth between Los Angeles and New York, partying and womanizing as if he were enjoying his last pleasures. Very nearly he was. Early in January 1936, he collapsed while traveling to New York and on January 17 he entered a private pavilion at Lenox Hill Hospital in Manhattan to be treated for gonorrhea, alcoholism, and exhaustion. He stayed on the East Coast, in Manhattan, Tavern Island, and Princeton, recuperating for the rest of the year, and so was not present at story conferences as Stromberg and the respected married team of Albert Hackett and Frances Goodrich, who had written the first *Thin Man* movie script, developed the screenplay for *After the Thin Man*.

After the Thin Man was produced between late September and October 31, 1936. Van Dyke directed, and William Powell and Myrna Loy starred again, as they did in all of the *Thin Man* movies; the tyro Jimmy Stewart was a featured actor. (Stewart appeared in nine movies made in 1936, his first full year as a movie actor.) The *Hollywood Reporter* revealed that the studio planned to feature Hammett in a small role in *After the Thin Man*, but he was recovering in New York during the filming and thus unavailable.

Hammett's screen story, punctuated with drinking and packed with sexual innuendo, was guaranteed to annoy Joseph I. Breen, head of the Production Code Administration, an arm of the Motion Picture Producers and Distributors of America, established in 1934 to enforce the industry's code of moral decency for movies. Breen was a prig, and it is not hard to imagine that Hammett's stories were often calculated to irritate him and other censors. Despite Breen's objection that "Throughout the story, there is an excessive amount of drinking, sufficient to constitute a violation of the special regulation governing drinking," booze remained integral to Nick and Nora Charles's characters, and there is plenty of playful sexuality. But it was up to Stromberg and the Hacketts to sanitize Hammett's story. He had little interest in the final script.

After the Thin Man was released on Christmas Day, 1936, and reviews were excellent. Writing in *The New York Times* on Christmas Day, Frank Nugent said, "If *After the Thin Man* is not quite the delight *The Thin Man* was, it is, at the very least, one of the most urbane comedies of the season. . . . Sequels commonly are disappointing and Metro-Goldwyn-Mayer was borrowing trouble when it dared advance a companion piece to one of the best pictures of 1934. But Dashiell Hammett's sense of humor has endured." Louella Parsons in the *Los Angeles Examiner* called it "a great feather in Metro-Goldwyn-Mayer's cap." When the movie opened, Hammett was in Princeton, New Jersey. He wrote Hellman five days later: "Powell I hear is fighting with MGM over a new contract, holding out for $200,000 a picture. MGM's recent statement that there will be no more sequels to *The Thin Man*, no matter how well this one does, is, I suppose, just a piece of iron pipe to slug him with."

"This one" did very well, almost as well as the first, bringing MGM a seven-figure profit in a Depression economy, and MGM needed Hammett as much as it needed Powell, Loy, and Asta for another sequel.

Hammett stayed in Princeton until March 15, 1937, and when he left, he went on the wagon. He wrote Hellman that Bea Kaufmann, Goldwyn's East Coast story editor, had asked him to do an original movie story, "which as you know I have no intention of doing. . . . By this time everybody ought to know that if I want to work in pictures I'll work with Hunt Stromberg, but even Leland Hayward [Hammett's agent] agrees with me—against his pocketbook—that I've got no business working in pictures at all." Hammett seems to have decided to leave Hollywood behind in February 1937 when he sold MGM all rights in perpetuity to Nick and Nora Charles and Asta for $40,000 (about $625,000 in 2011 dollars). He later wrote: "Maybe there are better writers in the world but nobody ever invented a more insufferably smug pair of characters. They can't take that away from me, even for $40,000."

Denials aside, Hammett was back in Hollywood at the Beverly Wilshire by September 1937, partying heavily, though, by his own testimony, soberly. He energetically served on the board of directors for the Screen Writers Guild (SWG), the writers' collective bargaining organization—vigorously opposed by the studios, particularly MGM—which sought to strengthen the rights of screenwriters in the movie business. Hammett's work for the SWG, combined with his erratic personal behavior, infuriated those in the front office at MGM. But *The Thin Man* movies were making MGM millions, and Hammett had strong advocates in Stromberg and his friends the Hacketts. (Oddly, MGM maintained interest in *The Foundry*, a Marxist novel about labor disputes among the workers at a Chicago electrotype foundry that ends with the workers realizing "the dumb thick wonder of their labor," and gave the screenplay assignment to Noel Langley, who two years later collaborated on the screenplay for *The Wizard of Oz*. Presumably no one in the front office at MGM had read Halper.)

On December 26, Hammett wrote Hellman that he was "in the middle of the usual so-the-script-is-done battles with my own dear producer, who insists that it's all right, but it's not exactly like the two previous scripts. The Hacketts sit on the sidelines and tremble while Hunt and I pace the floor and yell at one another. My latest line of attack is to point out that since he doesn't seem to know what was good and what bad in the two previous pictures they were so far as he is concerned just lucky flukes. It's good clean fun and can't lead to anything more serious than blows." On January 15, 1938 he wrote Hellman that it was his "tenth month without a drink."

By May, Hammett had a screen story and he had come to a parting of the ways with MGM. On May 12, he wrote to Hellman, "MGM and I are still at odds over the price of the new story. So I told my agent to say goodbye to Hunt for me and begin talking to Dave Selznick and maybe Sam the Good [both independent producers, at Selznick International and Samuel Goldwyn Productions, respectively]. Some little technicality about $5,000 I owe the studio on the Foundry deal a couple of years ago is holding up my check, but I dare say that will be straightened out in a day or two." Presumably the matter was resolved the next day, the date on the typescript for his *Another Thin Man* screen story. Hammett was paid a total of $35,000 for the job—$5,000 for the synopsis, $10,000 for the story idea, and $20,000 for the complete story. And the day after that, Hammett fell off the wagon hard. He had been growing progressively sicker and weaker since he had been in Hollywood last, and by late spring he became reclusive. He took to his bed, fearing he was losing his sanity. The Hacketts, alarmed at his insularity, visited him at the Beverly Wilshire and called Hellman for advice. She promised to care for him. On May 23, bottle in hand, Hammett flew to New York, where he was met by Hellman, who had arranged for an ambulance to take him to Lenox Hill Hospital. He weighed 125 pounds; the diagnosis was neurosis and pituitary hypofunction. He was in the hospital for twenty-two days, after which he went to Tavern Island, a private island off the coast of Connecticut where Lillian Hellman was writing *The Little Foxes*, to recuperate.

The day Hammett flew to the hospital Stromberg complained that the Hacketts were at a standstill on the script "owing to lack of knowledge of that last situation with its needed motivation for the whole treatment." When Hammett had recovered sufficiently to begin work again, MGM tried to re-sign him to a contract, but Hammett resisted. He was insulted by what he called "the tiny piece of bait on Hunt's hook" and he planned to resume work on an unfinished novel called *My Brother Felix*.

After further negotiation, Hammett and MGM came to reluctant terms. On July 15, 1938, he sold MGM a one-year option on all his writings for $5,000, a deal that seems to have included canceling the $5,000 he owed for nondelivery of *The Foundry*. He cleared up "that last situation" in *Another Thin Man* and produced an eight-page story idea, hard to take seriously, for a third *Thin Man* sequel on December 7, 1938, but continuation of the *Thin Man* series seemed uncertain then. William Powell was on leave, suffering from colon cancer and mourning the death of his lover, Jean Harlow. It was unclear whether he could continue the series, and Myrna Loy was reluctant to tackle another sequel. With the future of the *Thin Man* series in doubt, the studio rejected Hammett's eight-page story idea for a fourth Nick and Nora Charles movie and canceled his contract for the last time on Christmas Day. He was done with MGM, and they had had their fill of him. His "irregular habits" combined with his political opposition to the studio in his work for the Screen Writers Guild created a gulf too wide to bridge. Evidence of the studio's annoyance with their star writer is provided in the trailer for *Another Thin Man*. Hammett's name does not appear, though he was given credit for the original story in the credits for the full movie—as required by the contract SWG had forced on the studios.

Another Thin Man was released on November 17, 1939, to respectful but qualified reviews. Frank Nugent in *The New York Times* wrote:

> Some of the bloom is off the rose. A few of the running gags are beginning to show signs of pulling up lame. All this is bound to happen when a *Thin Man* leads to *After the Thin Man* and develops *Another Thin Man*. The law of diminishing returns tends to put any comedy on a reducing diet and it may, unless his next script is considerably brighter, confound us with a *Thin Man* thinned to emaciation. It hasn't

happened yet, mark! We're merely getting in our warning early, notifying Metro-Goldwyn-Mayer that there's a limit to everything—including the charm of the delightful Mr. and Mrs. Charles.

It wasn't Hammett's story that concerned Nugent but rather the formula imposed by Stromberg and the Hacketts that was growing stale.

Another Thin Man marks a clear break in the development of the series. Without Hammett and without the Hacketts, who had grown tired of the *Thin Man* formula, too, Stromberg was severely handicapped. He produced three more *Thin Man* movies—*Shadow of the Thin Man* (1941), *The Thin Man Goes Home* (1944), and *Song of the Thin Man* (1947)—but the screenplays written by new writers lacked the Hammett spark and attracted less and less favorable attention. Production on *The Thin Man Goes Home* was delayed when Myrna Loy refused to play Nora, instead doing Red Cross work at the beginning of World War II. She ultimately changed her mind, but regretted her decision. *Song of the Thin Man* was Myrna Loy's last movie for MGM. She said she hated the movie; it was a "lackluster finish to a great series."

Hammett never looked back. There is no record of his having even viewed the late *Thin Man* movies. He had more compelling interests by the end of 1938.

R. L.

AFTER THE THIN MAN

Headnote

Hammett submitted his initial screen story for *The Thin Man's* first sequel on January 8, 1935, and straight away left Hollywood for New York. The thirty-four-page tale he entrusted to producer Hunt Stromberg and screenwriters Albert Hackett and his wife Frances Goodrich was markedly different from his ultimate story, which he completed nine months later. In the first version, Nora sneaked out to play sleuth and was knocked cold, drugged, and kidnapped by Chinese hoodlums. Pedro the ex-gardener was not present to be shot to death on the Charleses' doorstep. David was not Selma's jilted suitor, but her younger brother. And Nick discovered that Polly's husband, Phil, was the murderer. There are enough similarities in scenes and characters to tie together the two proposed stories, but the plots differ dramatically.

During the spring of 1935, with Hammett absent from Hollywood and the *Thin Man* sequel's story conferences, MGM's development team foundered. Stromberg and the Hacketts toyed with alternative and additional plot points—narcotics and forgery rings, Oriental gangs, even a machine-gun massacre. In March, Stromberg boasted that the team was "purposefully complicating things" and he speculated on the possibility of running two or three plots, "tracks on this highway of crime," which would converge on Nick, who would solve them in "a single frame of story development and construction." By April the group knew that motives were a key problem, especially since, as Stromberg said, "the motive for the killing was FAR DIFFERENT than any motive previously credited to the case by anyone, including myself." Shortly after, director W. S. Van Dyke added more confusion to the mix with his own screenplay attempt, most notable for Nick's lackluster dialogue.

Amid and despite the maelstrom, the Hacketts produced a seventy-two-page temporary screenplay, dated April 29, 1935. But they still needed help. MGM rehired Hammett in June and by mid-July he crafted a new partial draft, twenty-nine pages that mark the beginnings of his final screen story for *After the Thin Man*. Hammett brought Nick and Nora back into focus and eliminated Stromberg's more fanciful digressions. He salvaged both the Hacketts' and his own best elements, then recombined and leavened them with new scenes and conflicts.

Hammett began his final screen story for *After the Thin Man*, dated September 17, 1935, on page 1, at scene 30, by stipulating a doorbell in place of what had been a telephone bell. The film's opening sequence is absent. The action picks up in midstream with the bell's ring and the sound of gunfire. There, and in five additional passages over the next twenty-two pages, Hammett calls for cuts or dissolves to particular scenes, with returns to his text afterward. He was operating, of course, without modern cut-and-paste conveniences. Hammett clearly intended his screen story to integrate specific passages from the Hacketts' April 29 screenplay. Their work was both appropriate to the revised narrative and in keeping with Hammett's own vision of Nick, Nora, and their supporting cast. Dashiell Hammett's screen story for *After the Thin Man* is presented here as he intended it, with the Hacketts' work incorporated according to his own instructions.

J. M. R.

AFTER THE THIN MAN

Dashiell Hammett

September 17, 1935

A train whistle sounds as the Chief arrives slowly in the Santa Fe Station in San Francisco. A stateroom on the train is stacked high with hatboxes, and suitcases, books, flowers, magazines, half-empty baskets of fruit. Although it is afternoon the stateroom is not yet made up. The top berth is down, piled high with bed-covers and sheets. On the lower berth is an array of White Rock bottles, glasses, bowls of ice, and a glass cocktail shaker propped against a pillow, almost full. There is also a half-packed bag open. Nick Charles standing before a mirror in the lavatory trying to shave. He is dressed except for his collar and coat. He has an old-fashioned open razor in his hand. He is swaying with the motion of the car, trying to balance himself on his widespread feet. Suddenly the car lurches, and he is thrown forward against the mirror, just missing by a fraction cutting off an ear. He looks reproachfully at the mirror, and then decides to go out into the stateroom to shave. Precariously he makes his way to the mirror behind the outer door, leading to the corridor. As he has the razor poised at his throat, the door is thrown open from the outside, pushing him back behind it, out of sight. Nora Charles, his wife, bursts in. She is in a negligee and slippers, fresh from her shower, with her toilet things in her hand. She is excited. She looks for Nick in the stateroom as she comes in.

Nora: "Nickie! Nickie! Where are you?"

She shuts the door after her and sees Nick behind the door, jammed up against the wall, his razor still at his throat, his eyes fixed in a glassy stare.

Nick, with the sickly sweet grin of a man who has just escaped death: "Hello, darling."

Nora, amazed at his position: "What are you trying to do?"

Nick: "Just having a little fun, darling."

Nora goes quickly to the lower berth, putting her toilet things in an open bag.

Nora: "You'd better hurry. We're getting into San Francisco in five minutes."

She takes a dress down from a hook. There is another hanging underneath it. Then she opens up a big hatbox, starting to pull a hat from it. She looks down, amazed and indignant.

Nora: "Asta!"

He is comfortably curled up in the hatbox on a large hat. He looks up and wiggles with delight.

Nora: "My best Sunday-go-to-meeting hat."

Asta jumps quickly out of the hatbox. Nora pulls out the hat and puts it on her head, making a very ridiculous appearance with her negligee, talking to Nick as she does so. Nick is leaning under the berth, pouring a drink from the cocktail shaker.

Nora: "I thought you were going to pack."

Nick: "I am. I've been putting away this likker."

As he throws his head back to drink the cocktail his skull cracks against the upper berth.

Nora: "You know, if you break that, they can sue you."

She goes quickly into the lavatory.

Nick: "I'm going to miss this little room of ours. It's left some lasting impressions on me."

He feels his head ruefully, then pours himself another drink.

Nora: "Pack these, will you, Nickie?"

Her filmy nightgown and negligee come flying at him from the bathroom. He extricates himself from them.

Nick: "Delighted."

He rolls them casually into a ball and stuffs them into the open bag. He picks up the cocktail shaker, still three-quarters full, and looks at it lovingly.

Nick: "I hate to leave this."

Nora, anxiously, from the lavatory: "Oh, don't leave anything."

Nick puts the top of the cocktail shaker on, and looks around for something to wrap it in. He catches sight of Nora's dress hanging on the wall. He puts his hand out toward it.

Nick: "Going to wear this dress?"

Nora's voice: "No. You can put that in."

Nick: "Fine."

He takes down the dress, wraps the cocktail shaker lovingly in it, and stuffs it into the bag, enthusiastically viewing the result.

The photographers and reporters are standing on the station platform looking into the distance, watching for the train. One of the men, looking off-scene, calls:

"Here she comes!"

In a body they all start to run toward the train.

Porters are hurrying out. Baggage men stand waiting. The train pulls in. The reporters and photographers who ran to meet it are now running back beside the train, trying to catch up with the Pullmans. The train comes to a stop, and a porter jumps off. The reporters rush up to him.

One of the reporters: "Nick Charles on this car?"

Porter: "Two cars back." The reporters and cameramen start to run back.

The porter puts down his little stepping block as Nick and Nora appear at the top of the steps. The reporters and photographers come running up. Asta is straining on the leash in Nick's hand.

1st Photographer: "Hold it there, Mr. Charles."

He snaps his picture and prepares to take another. Meanwhile the reporters are all talking at once, and the other photographers are taking pictures.

Reporters: "Hello, Nick." "How does it feel to be home?"

"How are you, Mrs. Charles? I'm from the *Chronicle*."

"Going to stay with us for a while?"

"Got a story for the *Examiner*, Nick?"

Nick, as Asta pulls him in a frenzy of excitement: "Gangway, boys! Gangway!"

Asta pulls Nick down the stairs. Nora follows, clinging to her purse and a little jewel case.

1st Reporter: "Going to keep on with the detective work, Nick?"

Nick: "No. I've retired. Just going to take care of my wife's money so I'll have something in my old age."

2nd Reporter: "You took that Wynant case in New York."

Nick: "I just did that for my wife. She wanted some excitement."

1st Reporter, turning to Nora: "I guess you had some excitement all right."

Nora: "It was wonderful. Two men tried to kill him."

Nick gives Nora a look. A big ex-prizefighter pushes his way through the crowd. He is Harold, the Charleses' chauffeur. He is very correctly dressed in uniform, and chewing gum as fast as his jaws will let him.

Nora: "Oh, Harold!"

Harold, grinning: "How are you, Mrs. Charles?"

Then with a change to a tone of utter familiarity: "Hi'yer, Nick."

He grasps Nick's hand and almost crushes it. Nick pulls it away, shaking it to get the circulation going.

Nick: "A little out of condition."

Harold starts to collect the bags belonging to Nick and Nora. The reporters are still hanging around, hoping for a story.

1st Reporter: "Come on, Nick. Give us a break. What are your plans?"

Nick: "My immediate plans?"

1st Reporter, eagerly: "Yes."

Nick: "Just a hot bath."

He looks at Asta, and speaks reproachfully: "Asta!"

The reporter looks down, and shakes his trouser leg.

Nick: "You'll have to forgive us. We've been cooped up for four days."

As Harold is picking up the bag that we saw Nick pack, Nora is horrified to see a stream of liquid pouring out.

Nora: "Oh, Nick, look! Something's leaked."

Nick sniffs at it, apprehensive, and then turns with relief.

Nick: "Thank Heaven. I thought it was the cocktails!"

Nora: "Cocktails! Oh, Nick!"

1st Photographer: "Just one more picture, Mr. Charles. Would you mind getting up on the steps again?"

Nick, pleasantly: "Certainly not."

He takes Nora's arm as they go up on the steps again.

2nd Photographer: "I'd like that, too."

All of the photographers look down into their cameras, ready to snap Nick and Nora. Then look up puzzled.

Nick and Nora are just disappearing out of sight, down the steps on the other side of the train. As they come through the crowd at the station, followed by porters and Harold, a little inconspicuous man bumps against Nora, who is trying to manage Asta on his leash. Nora stops, and pleasantly acknowledges the man's mumbled words of apology. The man is about to go on, when Nick sees him and recognizes him.

Nick, cordially: "Hello, Fingers."

Fingers turns, startled at the sound of Nick's voice. Then he sees who it is. He doesn't realize that Nick is with Nora.

Fingers: "Well, Nick! How are you?"

Nick: "How's business?"

Fingers: "Oh, I quit that racket."

Suddenly Nora, standing at one side, looks down and sees that her purse is gone . . . she is grasping only the strap of it in her hand. She turns excitedly to Nick.

Nora: "Nick . . . my purse. It's gone!"

But Nick takes it very easily.

Nick: "Oh, that's a shame."

He turns to Fingers: "Nora, I want you to meet Fingers."

Then, to Fingers: "This is the wife."

Fingers looks abashed and embarrassed. Nora, her mind on her lost purse, acknowledges the introduction a little distractedly.

Fingers: "Your wife. Well, gee! I'm sorry about your purse, Mrs. Charles."

Nora: "What'll I do, Nick? I know I had it with me."

Nick: "It'll turn up . . . won't it, Fingers?"

Fingers: "I certainly hope so."

He shakes hands with Nick, patting him affectionately with the other hand. Fingers: "Well, so long, Nick. Glad I bumped into you. Goodbye, Mrs. Charles. Happy New Year to you."

He goes off. Nick starts to walk Nora toward their car.

Nick, to Nora: "Come on."

But she is pulling back, wanting to go look for her purse.

Nora: "I can't just go off and . . ."

Nick, soothingly: "Come on. Come on. You don't want to embarrass him.

Nora: "What do you mean?"

Nick: "He's a purse snatcher. Think of his feelings."

He begins to feel in his pocket, on the side where Fingers gave him an affectionate pat.

Nora: "A purse snatcher! He must have taken it!"

She tries to turn back, but Nick holds her firmly. Nick's fingers have found something in his pocket. He turns and waves a genial goodbye and "all's well" to Fingers.

Nick: "So long, Fingers."

He pulls the purse out of his pocket and hands it to Nora: "He said it would turn up."

Nora: "You do know the nicest people!"

The car comes to a stop in front of the Charleses' house. Nick gets out of the car, pulled by Asta. The dog is straining at his leash, frantically excited at being home again. Nick bends down, trying to undo the leash.

Nick: "Just a minute, Asta. There you are."

He lets Asta loose and the dog starts to tear in and out around the trees, rushing back and forth . . . rolling on the ground, delighted to be home again. Suddenly he stops and looks off toward the backyard, then goes scurrying around the corner of the house.

There is a dog run and a little kennel in it, in the foreground. Asta comes tearing around the corner of the house, and pulls up short in front of the dog run.

A wirehaired female, just like Asta, is lying surrounded by about five puppies, all like her. She is looking up at Asta, and gently wagging her tail.

He barks delightedly at his wife. His tail seems to be wagging his whole body.

As Asta's excited bark continues, a little black Scottie puppy, of the same age as the others, comes waddling out of the kennel and makes his way to Mrs. Asta. Asta's bark suddenly stops.

As he looks at this black intruder, his high spirits suddenly evaporate. Asta turns toward the sound of a short bark.

The black Scottie is halfway through a hole he has dug under the fence separating the next-door yard from the Charleses'. He is very evidently the father of the little black puppy with Mrs. Asta. He is looking belligerently over at Asta. Asta bounds into the yard. The Scottie immediately drops his belligerent attitude, and backs hurriedly through the hole into his own backyard, and flees ignominiously. Asta bristles for a second, then turns his back and starts to dig furiously, filling up the tunnel underneath the fence.

Nick and Nora are standing at the front door of their house. Nick has his hand on the doorbell.

Nora: "All I want is a hot bath."

Nick: "I'll take a hot bath and a cold drink."

The door is flung open, letting out a blare of sound.

A man in the doorway is slightly drunk and very good-naturedly hospitable. He evidently has not the slightest idea of who Nick and Nora are. He is acting the part of the genial host. From behind him comes a din . . . a piano playing, voices shrieking with laughter, a girl's voice singing, a trap drum being played with more enthusiasm than skill.

The Man: "Come in! Come in! Make yourself at home!"

He steps back into the house, holding the door open.

Nick and Nora are looking amazed at the man. Nick steps back and looks at the number of the house.

Nick: "It's our house all right!"

Nora: "Let's go in. He says it's all right."

They start into the house.

The din is worse inside. Nick and Nora come slowly in. They look around them. Through different doorways we see crowds of people at the bar . . . and in the living room, surrounding the piano. A crap game is going on in another room.

The Man: "There's the bar right in there. Help yourself."

Nick: "Thanks."

The Man: "Okay."

Nora: "What's the celebration?"

The Man: "We're giving a surprise party to Nick and Nora."

Nick: "Nick and Nora?"

The Man: "Don't you know Nick and Nora?"

Nora: "No."

The Man: "Neither do I. But that's not going to spoil my fun. It's New Year's . . . so what's the odds? Go on in. Fake it. It's a cinch."

Nick: "Thanks for the tip."

The Man: "Get in there . . . and get some of that Napoleon brandy before it's all gone. See you later."

Nick, turning formally to Nora: "May I have this dance?"

Nora goes into his arms, smiling, and starts dancing toward the living room. A nice group of young people are crowded around the piano, most of them Nora's age, friends of hers when she was a debutante, men with whom she played around, before she married Nick. Some of them are in evening clothes, ready to go on to other parties; the rest are in street clothes. A man is sitting playing the piano, and beside him, a girl is trying to play a trap drum. Several couples are dancing. Nick and Nora dance in from the hallway. The guests are so absorbed that they don't pay any attention to them. There is a hum of conversation. The inevitable girl who knows all the words of the songs wants to sing, and couples call to the girl at the trap drum to keep better time. One couple is doing very complicated steps, and the rest are watching them, cheering them on.

About six men and girls are clustered around one man in a corner. He is talking earnestly, if a little drunkenly, to them.

The Man: "Listen, boys and girls. This is supposed to be a surprise party. So when they come in the door, we want to hide. Don't let them know there's a soul here."

One Girl: "That's a great idea!"

Another Girl: "You'd better tell the rest of them, Jerry."

Jerry: "You're right."

He steps out of the huddled group.

Nick and Nora are looking around, amused at their not being recognized.

Jerry: "Listen, everybody. This is supposed to be a surprise party. Let's get together on this."

A Girl: "Well, I'm acting surprised."

Nick gently steers Nora into the dining room.

A couple is dancing in the dining room.

The man is the one who greeted Nick and Nora at the door. He is dancing with a very lovely girl. Nick and Nora come in, still dancing. For a minute, the man and girl sway in position, as the man speaks to Nick. The girl's back is toward Nick and Nora.

The Man, indicating the girl with him: "Not bad, eh?"

Nick: "Not a-tall bad."

The Man: "How are you doing? Anyone wise to you yet?"

Nora, amused: "No."

The Man: "What'd I tell you?"

He dances away with his girl. Nick and Nora laugh, and make a sudden dash for the pantry door.

There is bedlam in the kitchen behind the scenes. The fat cook, Rose, is trying to make sandwiches and hors d'oeuvres for the unexpected guests. She is, at any other time, a good-natured individual . . . a heritage from Nora's mother. She is being helped by a pretty young maid, Ethel. The butler is getting in the way, trying to get some ice cubes out of a tray. They are all absorbed in their various occupations. Nick and Nora come in through the pantry, but the three servants are too busy to notice them.

Nick, softly, so that he will not be heard by the party inside: "Hey, there!"

Rose, thinking it is some hungry guest: "Coming! Coming!"

She turns with a plate of hors d'oeuvres in her hand, and suddenly sees that it is Nick and Nora. Her attitude changes immediately. She is delighted to see them: "Miss Nora! And Mr. Charles!"

The other two servants turn and eagerly smile at them.

Ethel: "Happy New Year, ma'am."

Nick, in a whisper: "Shush! Don't spoil their fun. They haven't surprised us yet."

Nora, in a whisper: "How are you, Rose?"

Then to the maid and butler: "Hello, Ethel . . . Peters."

The maid and the butler smile at them and whisper.

Ethel: "Nice to see you, ma'am."

Rose, also in a whisper: "We missed you something fierce."

From this time on they all speak in whispers.

Nora: "We missed *you* something fierce."

Nora sees the sandwiches and picks up one of them. She is about to eat it, when Nick takes it from her.

Nick: "You can't have that. It's for the guests."

He puts the whole sandwich into his mouth. Nora gives him a look, and then goes snooping over toward the stove. The butler starts into the dining room with a bucket of ice cubes.

Nora: "What're we going to have for dinner, Rose? I'm hungry."

Rose: "Your aunt telephoned, Miss Nora. She expects you there."

Nora looks at Nick, appalled. This is evidently the last place she wants to go.

Nora: "My aunt!"

But she gets no help from Nick. He leans over and kisses her.

Nick: "Goodbye, darling. See you next year."

Rose: "She expects you, too, Mr. Charles."

Nick looks around at Rose, unable to believe his ears.

Nick: "Me?"

Rose: "Yes, sir."

Nick, turning back to Nora: "What have your family got against me?"

Nora: "It's that annual family dinner."

Nick, picking up another sandwich: "Remind me not to go."

There is the sound of a doorbell. Nora: "What excuse'll I make?"

Nick: "Tell her I left a collar button in New York, and we have to go back for it."

Three pistol reports from the front door are followed by the sound of a door crashing back against a wall, and a man's hoarse exclamation.

Nick, followed by Nora, goes to the front door. The man who admitted them to the house—sober now—is standing at the door staring down with horrified face at a dead man huddled on the vestibule floor at his feet. The man at the door turns his frightened face to Nick and gasps: "I opened the door—bang, bang—he said, 'Mees Selma Young,' and fell down like that."

Nick corrects him mechanically—"Bang, bang, bang"—while kneeling to examine the man on the floor. He rises again almost immediately, saying: "Dead." By now guests and servants are crowding around them. Nora, craning her neck to look past Nick at the dead man's face, exclaims: "Nick, it's Pedro!"

Nick: "Who is Pedro?"

Nora: "You remember. Pedro Dominges—used to be Papa's gardener."

Nick says: "Oh, yes," doubtfully, looking at Pedro again. Pedro is a lanky Portuguese of fifty-five, with a pleasant, swarthy face and gray handlebar mustache. Nick addresses the butler: "Phone the police, Peters." Then he turns to discover that the man who opened the door has tiptoed past the corpse and is now going down the steps to the street. "Wait a minute," Nick calls. The man turns around on the bottom step and says very earnestly:

"Listen, I—I—this kind of thing upsets me. I got to go home and lay down."

Nick looks at the man without saying anything and the man reluctantly comes back up the steps, complaining: "All right, brother, but you're going to have a sick man on your hands."

A little man, obviously a crook of some sort, plucks at Nick's elbow and whines: "You got to let *me* out, Nick. You know I'm in no spot to be messing with coppers right now."

Nick says: "You should have thought of that before you shot him."

The little man jumps as if he had been kicked.

During this scene a crowd has been gradually assembling in the street around the door: first a grocer's delivery boy, then a taxi driver, pedestrians, etc. Now a policeman pushes his way through the crowd, saying: "What's going on here?" and comes up the steps. He salutes Nick respectfully, says: "How do you do, Mr. Charles? Glad to see you back," then sees the dead man and goggles at him.

Nick says: "We called in."

The policeman goes down the steps and begins to push the crowd around, growling: "Get back there! Get back there!" In the distance a police siren can be heard.

Indoors, a few minutes later, Lieutenant Abrams of the Police Homicide Detail—who looks somewhat like an older version of Arthur Caesar—is saying to Nora: "You're sure of the identification, Mrs. Charles? He's the Pedro Dominges that used to be your gardener?"

Nora: "Absolutely sure."

Abrams: "How long ago was that?"

Nora: "Six years at least. He left a little before my father died."

Abrams: "Why'd he leave?"

Nora: "I don't know."

Abrams: "Ever see him since?"

Nora: "No."

Abrams: "What did he want here?"

Nora: "I don't know. I—"

Abrams: "All right. Thanks." He speaks to one of his men: "See what you can get." The man goes to a phone in another room. (In this scene, the impression to be conveyed is that Abrams has already asked his preliminary questions and is now patiently going over the same ground again, checking up, filling in details.)

Abrams turns to the guests: "And none of you admit you know him, huh?" Several of them shake their heads, the others remain quiet.

Abrams: "And none of you know a Miss Selma Young?"

There is the same response.

Abrams: "All right." Then, more sharply: "Mullen, have you remembered anything else?"

The man who had opened the door runs his tongue over his lips and says: "No, sir. It's just like I told you. I went to the door when it rang, thinking it was maybe some more guests, or maybe them"—nodding at Nick and Nora—"and then there was the shots and he kind of gasped what sounded to me like 'Mees Selma Young' and fell down dead like that. I guess there was an automobile passing maybe—I don't know."

Abrams, aside to Nick: "Who is he?"

Nick: "Search me."

Abrams to Mullen: "Who are you? What were you doing here?"

Mullen, hesitantly: "I come to see about buying a puppy and somebody give me a drink and—" His face lights up and he says with enthusiasm: "It was a *swell* party. I never—"

Abrams interrupts him: "What are you doing answering the doorbell if you just chiseled in?"

Mullen, sheepishly: "Well, I guess I had a few drinks and was kind of entering in the spirit of the thing."

Abrams addresses one of his men: "Take good-time Charlie out to where he says he lives and works and find out about him." The man takes Mullen and goes out.

In another room, the detective at the phone is saying: "Right, Mack. I got it." He hangs up. As he reaches the door, the phone rings. He glances around, goes softly back to it.

In the hallway, the butler answers the phone: "Mr. Charles's residence . . . Yes, Mrs. Landis . . . Yes, ma'am." He goes into the room where the others are and speaks aside to Nora: "Mrs. Landis is on the telephone, ma'am."

Nora goes to the phone, says: "Hello, Selma. How are you, dear?"

Selma, in hat and street clothes, her face wild, cries hysterically: "Nora, you and Nick have simply got to come tonight! Something terrible has happened! I don't know what to—I'll kill myself if—you've got to! If you don't, I'll—" She breaks off as she sees Aunt Katherine standing in the doorway looking sternly at her. Aunt Katherine is very old, but still big-boned and powerful, with a grim, iron-jawed face. She, too, is in hat and street clothes and leans on a thick cane. Selma catches her breath in a sob, and says weakly: "Please come."

Nora, alarmed: "Certainly we'll come, dear. We'll do—"

Selma says hastily: "Thanks," and hangs up, avoiding Aunt Katherine's eyes. Aunt Katherine, not taking her eyes from Selma, puts out a hand and rings a bell, saying, when a servant comes in: "A glass of water." Both women remain as they are in silence until the servant returns with the water. Then Aunt Katherine takes the water from the servant, takes a tablet from a small bottle in her own handbag, and with water in one hand, tablet in the other, goes to Selma and says: "Take this and lie down until time for dinner."

Selma objects timidly: "No, Aunt Katherine, please. I'm all right. I'll be quite all right."

Aunt Katherine: "Do as I say—or I shall call Dr. Kammer."

Selma slowly takes the tablet and water.

The detective at Nick's who has been listening on the extension quickly puts down the phone and, returning to the room where the others are, calls Abrams aside and whispers into his ear, telling him what he overheard. While this is going on, Nora returns and tells Nick: "You're in for it, my boy. I promised Selma we'd come to Aunt Katherine's for dinner tonight. I had to. She's so upset she—"

Nick says: "That means outside of putting up with the rest of your family, we'll have to listen to her troubles with Robert. I won't—"

Nora says coaxingly: "But you like Selma."

Nick: "Not that much."

Nora: "Please, Nickie."

Nick: "I won't go sober."

Nora pats his cheek, saying: "You're a darling."

Abrams comes back from his whispered conference with the other detective and says: "Mrs. Charles, I'll have to ask you who you were talking to on the phone."

Nora, puzzled: "My cousin, Selma Landis."

Abrams: "She married?"

Nora: "Yes."

Abrams: "What was her last name before she was married?"

Nora: "Forrest, the same as mine."

Abrams: "She ever go by the name of Young?"

Nora: "Why no! Surely you don't think—" She looks at Nick.

Abrams: What was she so excited about?"

Nora, indignantly: "You listened?"

Abrams, patiently: "We're policemen, Mrs. Charles, and a man's been killed here. We got to try to find out what goes on the best way we can. Now is there any connection between what she was saying and what happened here?"

Nora: "Of course not. It's probably her husband."

Abrams: "You mean this fellow that was killed?"

Nick: "That's a thought!" He asks Nora solemnly: "Do you suppose Selma was ever married to Pedro?"

Nora: "Stop it, Nick." Then, to Abrams: "No, no—it's her husband she was talking about."

Abrams nods, says: "Maybe that's right. I can see that. I'm a married man myself." After a moment's thought he asks: "Did she know this fellow that was killed?"

Nora: "I suppose so. She and my husband and her husband were all friends and used to come there before any of us were married."

Abrams: "Then her husband might know him, too, huh?"

Nora: "He might."

Abrams turns to Nick: "How come you didn't recognize him before Mrs. Charles told you?"

Nick: "Who notices a gardener unless he squirts a hose on you?"

Abrams: "There's something in that. I remember once when— well, never mind." He addresses the detective who phoned: "Find out anything about Dominges?"

The Detective: "Did a little bootlegging before repeal—bought hisself a apartment house at 346 White Street—lives there and runs it hisself. Not married. No record on him."

Abrams asks the assembled company: "346 White Street mean anything to anybody?" Nobody says it does. He asks his men: "Got all their names and addresses?"

"Yes."

Abrams: "All right. You people can clear out. We'll let you know when we want to see you again."

The guests start to leave as if glad to go, especially a little group of men who have been herded into a corner by a couple of policemen, but this group is halted by one of the policemen, who says: "Take it easy, boys. We've got a special wagon outside for you. We been hunting for some of you for months." They are led out between policemen.

Abrams, alone in the room with Nick and Nora, looks at Nick and says: "Well?"

Nick says: "Oh, sure," and begins to mix drinks.

Abrams: "I didn't mean that exactly. I mean what do you make all this add up to? He's killed coming to see you. He knows you two, and Mrs. Charles's relations, and that's all we know he does know. What do you make of it?"

Nick, handing him a drink: "Maybe he was a fellow who didn't get around much."

At the Landis home:

Aunt Katherine, in the doorway of the drawing room, is surveying the occupants of the room grimly.

Aunt Katherine: "Good evening all."

The men of the family all rise to their feet, some of them with difficulty, to greet Aunt Katherine. The next to Katherine in point of age is Aunt Lucy, Katherine's cousin, a tottering old lady whose only interest is her accumulating years. Next, there is the General, Katherine's brother. He is a tall, solidly fat man of eighty, with a bald head, bushy white brows and whiskers, and the shiny appearance of just having been scrubbed. Although Katherine calls him Thomas, the rest speak of him as the General.

The others, in order of their ages, are:

Burton Forrest, a gaunt man of seventy-two, who has a tic, which makes him crinkle his nose as if he had suddenly smelled a bad smell.

Charlotte, Burton's wife, a short, roly-poly woman of seventy, who is more interested in her dinner than anything else.

Hattie, a spinster of sixty-something. She is very deaf, and wears an audio phone, with its sounding box conspicuously pinned on the front of her chest, and cords going from it to her ears.

William, a few years younger than Hattie. A plump man whose clothes are too tight. He has a great deal of difficulty in understanding things, and, even in this family, is considered not quite bright.

Lucius, a tired man in his late fifties.

Helen and Emily, colorless women of fifty-three or fifty-four . . . married to William and Lucius. They stick together as if not sure of their places in this family that they have married into.

As Katherine makes her entrance, they all greet her with deferential murmurs, addressing her as "Katherine" or "Cousin Katherine" or "Aunt Katherine," according to their ages.

The women sit stiffly erect; the men stand stiffly erect. The men wear white ties and tails. The women's gowns range in style from the Victorianism of Katherine's to the comparatively modern, but none of them is gay. Aunt Lucy, the very old lady, comes tottering up to Katherine.

Aunt Lucy: "I had a birthday last week, Katherine. I'm eighty-three years old. Eighty-three years old. What do you think of that?"

Aunt Katherine: "That's fine, Lucy."

Aunt Lucy: "Eighty-three! Next year I'll be eighty-four."

Aunt Katherine dismisses Aunt Lucy with a brief word: "That's splendid."

She turns to the rest. "While we're alone, I have something important to tell all of you."

Aunt Hattie leans forward in her chair, holding her audio phone toward Katherine.

Aunt Hattie: "What'd she say?"

Lucius: "Shush!"

Aunt Katherine, looking at Hattie, irritated: "Isn't that thing working, Hattie?"

Aunt Hattie: "This works perfectly. It's you! You mumble!"

Lucius, stepping into the breach: "What is it, Katherine?"

Aunt Katherine: "Nora and her husband are coming tonight."

They all look at Katherine, appalled.

Family: "Her husband!"

"After the last time . . ."

"But Katherine . . ."

"Really, Katherine . . ."

This news has brought on Burton's tic worse than ever. The General is regarding Katherine with offended dignity.

The General: "But you said yourself that you wouldn't have him again."

Aunt Katherine: "I know I did. And my opinion of him and what he represents hasn't changed a particle."

Burton: "Then I can't understand why you asked him."

His face twitches violently.

Aunt Katherine: "I have a very good reason for asking him, which you will know in time." There is a muffled sound of a bell. "That's probably they now."

She turns to include the others: "Understand now, I want you all to be pleasant to him."

She walks toward Hattie and Lucius, near the door. The rest of the family look after her. There are murmurs from them.

The Family: "Of course, if you say so.... It's going to be difficult.... Poor Nora. My heart bleeds for that child."

Hattie is still looking from face to face bewildered. Katherine passes the old butler as he goes slowly through the hall: "If that is Mr. and Mrs. Charles, show them right in."

Butler: "Yes, madam."

Aunt Hattie: "What is it? What's happened?"

Lucius, bending down and talking right into her audio phone: "You're to be pleasant to Nora's husband."

Aunt Hattie: "Who said so?"

Aunt Katherine: "I did!"

Aunt Hattie: "I'll be just as pleasant as you are ... no more!"

Nick and Nora, in evening clothes, are waiting for the butler to open the door. Nick is muttering to himself. Nora looks at him, puzzled.

Nora: "What are you muttering to yourself?"

Nick: "I'm getting all the bad words out of my system."

Nora: "You'd better pull yourself together."

Nick: "Don't worry. One squint at Aunt Katherine would sober anyone!"

The door is opened by Henry, the butler.

Nora: "Good evening, Henry."

There is a chill in the massive hallway, with its dim lights. Nick and Nora come in as Henry holds the door open.

Henry, in a hushed whisper: "Good evening, madam—sir."

Nick: "Is this the wax-works?"

Henry: "I beg pardon, sir?"

Nora, smiling at Henry: "Nothing, Henry. Nothing."

She gives Nick a warning look. Starting for the library: "I'll just leave my things down here."

She goes down the hall, taking off her evening coat as she goes. The butler turns to Nick and helps him off with his coat. He touches Nick's things as if the mere contact with them might contaminate him.

Nick: "It's all right—it's not catching."

The butler puts them down and starts toward the drawing-room door.

Butler: "Will you walk this way, sir."

The butler hobbles away ahead of Nick, hardly able to move on his rheumatic legs. Nick looks after him.

Nick: "I'll *try*."

He starts to follow the butler, giving a grotesque imitation of his walk. As he passes the library door, Nora comes out, catches up with him, and grabs his arm, laughing at him.

Butler, announcing them at the door of the drawing room: "Mr. and Mrs. Charles."

As they hear the announcement, they straighten up.

Nick: "Here goes!"

They start to walk in, sedately.

As Nick and Nora come in the door, Aunt Katherine comes forward to greet them.

Aunt Katherine, to Nora: "How do you do, my dear?"

Nora kisses Aunt Katherine and then turns to include Nick.

Nora: "You remember Nick?"

Although she is doing her best to be gracious, Aunt Katherine finds it impossible to look at him.

Aunt Katherine: "How are you, Nicholas?"

As Nick hears his name, he starts. Katherine turns back toward the roomful of people: "Come right in."

Helen comes up to Nora, who turns to greet her.

Nora: "Hello, Cousin Helen."

Helen, giving her a peck: "How are you, you poor child?"

Nick gives Cousin Helen a swift look as he hears the commiserating tone of her voice. But Aunt Katherine has him in tow, and he follows her.

Aunt Katherine, speaking to the whole family: "This is Nora's husband."

Nick looks from one to the other of the people. They are doing their best to appear pleasant, but the result is not very cordial. Aunt Katherine turns back to him: "I think you know everyone."

Nick: "I seem to remember the old faces."

Nora quickly takes Nick's arm and pilots him toward another group.

Nick, under his breath to her as they go: "What's up? They're all so polite."

Nora smiles and takes him to Charlotte and William.

Nora: "This is Aunt Charlotte, and Uncle Willie."

Nick acknowledges the introduction with the same sickly sweet smile that they give him.

Nora: "And now for Aunt Hattie."

From behind them, Charlotte's voice is heard: "Poor Nora is so brave."

Again Nick hears the commiserating "poor" Nora. He whispers to Nora: "What's this 'poor Nora' business?"

Nora: "That's because I'm married to you."

Then, as they reach Aunt Hattie: "Aunt Hattie, you remember my husband?"

Nick: "How are you?"

Aunt Hattie: "Don't mumble, young man. Don't mumble."

Nick, a little louder: "How are you?"

Still Aunt Hattie doesn't hear.

Nora: "She's deaf as a post."

Nick: "You're telling me!"

Aunt Hattie, holding out her receiving box of the audio phone: "What did he say?"

Nick, taking the box, and speaking into it as if it were a microphone: "When you hear the chime, it will be exactly . . ."

But Nora gives him a slight boot from behind. Nick turns sharply toward her. Nora catches sight of Selma in the doorway.

Nora, with a note of relief at seeing a friend: "Selma!"

Selma has managed to regain some of her composure. Nora comes quickly to her, kissing her warmly.

Selma, on the point of breaking again: "Oh Nora . . . Nora. It's so good to see you."

Nora, affectionately: "How are you, Selma?"

Nick approaches, and Selma turns to him.

Selma: "Hello, Nick."

Nick: "Hello."

Selma: "It's sweet of you to come."

Nick, who's really enjoying himself by now: "I wouldn't have missed it for a million dollars."

Nora: "What's the trouble, Selma? Tell me."

But Aunt Katherine comes up quickly, putting a firm hand on Selma's arm: "We'll postpone any discussion until after dinner."

She turns to speak to the rest: "Shall we go in now?"

She holds out her hand to the General: "Thomas?"

The General comes quickly to her side, and gives her his arm.

Nick, to Selma: "Where's Robert?"

Selma is about to speak, but Aunt Katherine hastily intervenes.

Aunt Katherine: "Robert telephoned that he was unavoidably detained. So we'll start without him."

Selma gives her a bitter look and turns away. Nick notices the look between the two.

"We haven't quite enough men to go around, so, Lucius, will you take Hattie and Charlotte? Willie, you take Helen and Ethel? Burton, will you take Nora? And Nicholas, will you take Aunt Lucy?"

Aunt Katherine walks toward the hallway, on the General's arm. Nick goes toward Aunt Lucy, as Burton comes up to Nora. He offers his arm to her.

Nora: "How are you, Cousin Burton?"

Burton: "I'm very well, thank you."

He makes a sudden violent face, as his tic starts in.

Nora: "That's fine."

Unconsciously, she imitates his tic. She realizes with horror what she has done, and turns and starts off quickly without him.

Nick offers his arm to Aunt Lucy. She looks up at him as she takes it, resenting having him as a partner.

Aunt Lucy: "Maybe you didn't know it, but I'm eighty-three years old."

Nick: "Eighty-three?"

Aunt Lucy: "Yes."

Nick: "Well, well. You don't look a *day* over a hundred."

Aunt Lucy: "That's what they all say."

In the drawing room after dinner, Hattie, Charlotte, Helen, and Emily are sitting back in their comfortable chairs, surfeited with food and very drowsy. Aunt Lucy is frankly asleep. Aunt Katherine has the coffee table in front of her and is sipping her coffee, her eyes on Selma, who is at the piano, playing mechanically. Nora wanders over to the piano, her coffee cup in hand, leans over, and speaks softly to Selma: "What was it you wanted to tell me?"

Selma stops her playing and is about to answer, when Aunt Katherine calls sharply: "Nora, will you come here?"

Nora: "In a minute, Aunt Katherine." Then turning quickly back to Selma: "What was it?"

Selma: "Robert has disappeared."

Nora: "Disappeared!"

Aunt Katherine: "Selma, go on playing!"

Selma, looking over at her aunt desperately: "I can't play anymore, Aunt Katherine."

Aunt Katherine: "Nonsense. Go on."

Selma tries to control herself for a second and then she suddenly smashes down on the keyboard with both hands: "I can't! I can't!"

Selma puts her hands to her face and runs from the room to the library beyond, while Aunt Katherine rises to her feet and the other women look wide-eyed and alarmed. Nora says: "Let me talk to her," and goes out after Selma.

In the library, Selma is sobbing on a sofa. Nora sits down beside her, puts her arms around her, says: "Don't, dear. Nick'll find Robert for you. I'm sure he's just—"

Selma sits up, pushing Nora's arms away, crying hysterically: "Sometimes I hate you and Nick. You're so happy together, and here Robert and I haven't been married half as long and I'm so miserable. I wish he'd never come back. I wish he were dead. I don't really love him. I never did, really. I was a fool to have married him instead of David." She puts her head on Nora's shoulder and begins to sob again.

Nora strokes Selma's hair, says: "Well, then, dear, divorce him. Don't let Aunt Katherine keep you from that. If you—"

Selma raises her head again, says: "But I'm such a fool. This is the first time he's gone off like this without a word—without even telling me lies about where he's going—but there have always been other women and I've always known it. But I've let him twist me around his little finger and made myself believe his lies even when I knew they were lies and—he doesn't love me. He married me for my money. Yet he does horrible things to me and then when I see him I let him smooth everything over and I want to think we love each other and everything will turn out all right. And it won't, it won't. It's all lies and I'm a fool. Oh, why didn't I marry David?" She bursts into tears again.

Meanwhile Aunt Katherine has come into the library and shut the door. Now she says coldly: "You *are* a fool, Selma, but you might have the decency not to scream so the servants will find out exactly what *kind* of fool you are."

"Aunt Katherine!" Nora protests. "Selma's not well. She—"

Aunt Katherine interrupts her, nodding her head grimly: "I know she's not well. I know better than anyone else—except Dr. Kammer— how far from being well she really is." Selma flinches. Aunt Katherine says to Nora: "Will you ask Nicholas to come in?" Nora hesitates as if about to say something, then goes out. Aunt Katherine says to Selma: "Fix yourself up. You look like Ophelia." Selma flinches again and begins to fix her hair, dress, etc.

The men of the Forrest family stretched out in their chairs, sound asleep. Their waistcoats are open to allow the tremendous meal they have just consumed to settle. There are two good snorers, William and the General, one on either side of Nick. The snoring, like conversation, appears to be going back and forth.

Nick is seated at the dinner table, leaning forward with animated attention. There are empty places on either side of him where the women had been sitting.

Nick: "No, really! Well, you amaze me! Could you explain that further?"

William lets out a sonorous snore.

Nick: "I wouldn't go so far as to say that."

The General, on the other side, is vying with William in his snorts. Nick turns toward his unconscious figure.

Nick: "What is it?"

As William snores again, Nick turns to him with a restraining gesture: "Just a minute."

He turns back to the General, who snorts again. Nick speaks to him, as if amazed at his statement: "Really!"

He turns to Burton, who is also sound asleep across the table: "Are you going to let that pass unchallenged? You must have something to say to that!"

Burton's snore tops all of the others, as he turns uneasily in his chair.

Nick: "That's the boy. I knew you had it in you."

Nora: "Nick! Nick!"

Nick looks around at her, rising as he hears her.

Nora: "Come here—come here!"

Nick turns and addresses the four unconscious figures with great courtesy.

Nick: "If you gentlemen will forgive me?"

He starts to turn to go to Nora, and then stops to pick up a stiff bunch of flowers from the center of the table and sticks it on the chest of the General, next to him. He turns and joins Nora.

Nick: "I don't know when I've had a more stimulating evening!"

Nick and Nora walk through the hallway. She is holding his arm and seems worried. She says: "Aunt Katherine wants to see you."

Nick: "What have I done now?"

Nora: "Do you know why Robert wasn't here tonight?"

Nick: "Because he's smart."

Nora: "I'm not fooling. He's disappeared."

Nick: "That's swell. Now if we can get rid of—"

Nora: "Be nice to Selma, Nickie. She's having such a tough time of it." Nick stops and turns Nora around to face him, looking at her with suspicion. He says:

"Now come on, tell the old man—what are you getting him into?"

Nora, paying no attention to this: "And do try to be polite to Aunt Katherine. It'll make it easier for Selma."

Nick sighs deeply and they go into the library.

Aunt Katherine comes forward to meet them. She is putting up a great show . . . being very charming to Nick, and speaking as if the whole affair were trifling. Selma is standing in the background, looking out of the window, her hands playing restlessly with the curtain.

Aunt Katherine: "Oh, Nicholas. I'm sorry to take you away from the boys."

Nick, remembering the boys: "That's all right."

Aunt Katherine: "But there's a little something that you can do for us."

Nick: "How long has Robert been gone?"

Aunt Katherine, as if she couldn't quite remember, it was so unimportant: "Let me see . . . about three days."

Selma turns from the window, and comes toward them, speaking violently: "Something's happened. I know it has. I can't sleep. I can't eat. Every time anyone comes to the door . . . every time the phone rings, I know it's someone to say they've found his body."

Nora crosses quickly to Selma, and puts her arms comfortingly around her: "Don't, Selma. Nothing terrible can have happened, or you'd be bound to know."

Aunt Katherine, still keeping up her pretense of treating the matter lightly, in spite of Selma's outburst: "Selma's exaggerating the whole affair. However, I thought you might like the opportunity to do something for the family. I know that you must have come across situations like this in your previous work as a . . . er . . . er . . ."

She cannot bring herself to say the word "detective." Nick realizes, amused, why she hesitates.

Nora, coming out with it: "As a flatfoot?"

Aunt Katherine, turning to Nora: "I didn't mean to be as blunt as all that."

Nick, rubbing it in: "Why not? It's all in the family."

Aunt Katherine winces, but goes on bravely: "Of course, I don't know how to go about such things . . . I don't know what your methods are. But I thought you might . . . er . . . 'snoop' around a little and find out what you can . . . just to put Selma's mind at ease."

Nick: "You haven't notified the police?"

Aunt Katherine is about to answer, when Selma interrupts her, with bitter sarcasm: "Oh no!"

Selma: "Our names might get in the papers. People might find out that I'm married to a drunken wastrel, a thief, a man who's already cost me a small fortune getting him out of scrapes with women, a man who has never done a decent thing in—"

Aunt Katherine raps with her cane on the floor and says: "Selma, stop that nonsense!"

Selma puts her hands over her face and cries: "I don't care what anybody knows, I don't care what gets in the papers, if I can only be happy again once."

Nora goes to her to soothe her.

Aunt Katherine, quietly: "We've kept our private affairs out of the public print up until now, and I hope we shall continue to do so." She smiles at Nick as if conferring a favor on him. "I shall leave it in your hands, Nicholas. I know you'll welcome a chance to help us, and I needn't tell you how grateful we'll be if you see that Robert returns home without any scandal." She smiles at Nora, says: "If you'll forgive me, I'll go back to my guests. When you've quieted Selma, I think she'd better go off to bed." She goes out calmly and majestically.

Nick, looking after her half-admiringly, half-disgustedly, says: "Katherine the Great!"

Selma comes over to Nick, holding out her hands, saying: "I don't know how to thank you, Nick."

Nick takes her hands, says: "You mean you don't know what to thank me for. What is all this fiddle-de-dee?"

Selma: "Robert hasn't been home—I haven't seen or heard from him for three days."

Nick: "Where do you think he might be?"

Selma: "I don't know. It's some woman, of course. It gets worse and worse. Only last week some Chinese restaurant—Li-Chee or something—sent me a cigarette case they thought I'd left there and I know it was some woman that was there with him, though he swore it wasn't."

Nick: "Well, you're at least a cigarette case ahead—or wasn't it worth keeping?"

Nora says: "Nick," reprovingly, while Selma, not knowing he is kidding her, says:

"I sent it back, of course, with a note saying it wasn't mine, but I don't—" She breaks off to look at the butler, who is standing in the doorway. The butler says:

"A—ah—gentleman from the police to see you, Mrs. Landis."

Selma screams, and seems about to faint.

Selma's scream brings in Aunt Katherine, followed by the rest of the family. During the ensuing hubbub, while they are bringing her to, asking one another what happened, Lieutenant Abrams comes in. He nods at Nick, says: "I thought maybe you'd be here," looks at Selma and asks: "Is the lady in trouble Mrs. Selma Landis?"

Nick says: "Yes."

Abrams: "I thought maybe it was." Then, to Nora, who is now looking at him: "Evening, Mrs. Charles."

By this time the others have noticed him. Aunt Katherine looks inquiringly at him. Nick introduces them elaborately.

"Miss Forrest, may I present Lieutenant Abrams of the Police Department Homicide Detail?"

Aunt Katherine asks sharply: "Homicide?"

Selma pushes past her to put her hands on Abrams's arms, demanding: "What has happened to him?"

Abrams (as always, in a manner that may come from stupidity or may come from a shrewd pretense of stupidity): "He was killed this afternoon. Didn't Mr. Charles tell you?"

Selma stares at him in dumb horror.

Nora says: "He doesn't mean Robert, dear. He means Pedro, the gardener we used to have. You remember him." She helps Selma to a chair, then asks Abrams indignantly: "Did you do that on purpose?"

Aunt Hattie says: "I can't understand a thing that's going on." She points at Abrams: "Is this man a burglar? Why doesn't someone call the police?"

Abrams addresses Nick: "You didn't tell 'em about Pedro being killed?"

Nick: "This is my wife's family. They'd think I did it."

Abrams: "I see what you mean. My wife's got relations, too."

The butler appears in the doorway and says: "Mr. David Graham to see Mrs. Landis." Selma starts up from her chair.

Aunt Katherine says: "I think it better that we be home to no one but members of the family this evening."

Selma protests: "I want to see David. Ask him to come in, Henry."

The butler remains in the doorway, looking at Aunt Katherine, who says: "Selma, I don't want to have to—"

Before she has finished this threat, David comes in hurriedly, going straight to Selma and asking: "What is it? What's the matter?"

Aunt Katherine replies coldly: "That is exactly what we'd like to know. Something is said about a gardener being killed and Selma becomes hysterical."

David: "A gardener? What's that got to do with Selma?"

Lieutenant Abrams: "Excuse me, but that's what we're trying to find out. This man is killed coming to see Mr. and Mrs. Charles and a little while later Mrs. Landis phones all excited and talking about killing herself and—"

David, angrily: "And on the strength of that you come here to annoy her?"

Abrams, patiently: "Not only that. Mrs. Charles said she"—indicating Selma—"knew him, and how are we going to get anywhere if we don't talk to the people that knew him?"

Nora says: "I didn't say she knew him. I said she might remember him." She turns to David: "It was Pedro who used to work for Papa when we had the place in Ross."

David: "Oh, yes. I remember him, a tall man with a long gray mustache. But what—"

Abrams: "So you knew him, too. Well, what do you know about him?"

David: "Nothing. I merely saw him when I was a visitor there, and I've never seen him since."

Abrams: "And you, Mrs. Landis?"

Selma: "I may have seen him, but I don't remember him at all."

Abrams: "And how about the rest of you?"

None of the Forrests admits knowing Pedro.

Abrams: "Mrs. Charles says Mrs. Landis's husband might know him. Is he here?"

Selma: "No—he—he'll be in later, but I don't think he'll remember the man any better than I do."

Abrams: "Did you ever go by the name of Selma Young?"

Selma: "Certainly not!"

Abrams: "Anybody here know Selma Young?"

Nobody does.

Abrams: "Now I got to ask you again about that telephone talk of yours with Mrs. Charles."

Selma says: "Please, it had nothing to do with this. It was—was a purely personal thing."

Abrams: "You mean something to do with your husband?"

Aunt Katherine says: "Mr.—ah—Abraham, you are being impertinent. Furthermore, my niece is under a doctor's care, and—"

Abrams, stolidly: "What doctor?"

Aunt Katherine: "Dr. Frederic Kammer."

Abrams nods: "I know of him." Preparing to leave, he says resignedly: "I can't help it if people don't like me. I got my work to do. Good night." He goes out.

David leaves the house with Nick and Nora, parting from them in the foggy street.

When Nick and Nora leave, he asks Harold, the chauffeur: "Where's a good place to get the stink of respectability out of our noses?"

Harold, grinning and chewing his gum, says: "I get it. Well, there's Tim McCrumb's and there's the Li-Chee and there's the Tin Dipper. None of them three ain't apt to be cluttered up with schoolteachers."

Nick: "Suppose we try the Li-Chee."

Harold says: "That's a good pick," while Nora looks at Nick from the corners of her eyes. As they get into the car she says: "You are going to find Robert?"

Nick: "*I* didn't lose him."

Nora: "It would put you in right with the family."

Nick: "And *that's* what I'm afraid of."

In Dancer's apartment at the Li-Chee Club, Robert—drunk and looking as if he has been drunk for several days—is lying back in a chair, holding a drink. Polly is sitting on the arm of his chair, running her fingers through his hair. He is saying: "Comes tomorrow and we'll be out of this town for good—no more wife squawking at me, no more of her family egging her on, no more of this"—waving his glass around the place—"just you and me off someplace together." He pulls her down into his lap and asks: "Good, baby?"

She says: "Swell." Then: "You're sure this—what's his name?— Graham—will come through all right?"

Robert: "Sure. He's nuts about Selma. He fell all over himself when I put it to him. The only thing is, maybe I was a sucker not to ask him for twice as much for clearing out. Don't worry about the money; he'll have it ready in the morning just as he promised."

Polly, reassured, asks thoughtfully: "Does she know about it?"

Robert, scornfully: "Of course not. He couldn't tell her. She's batty as a pet cuckoo. She'd blow up and make him call off the whole thing."

Polly: "Then suppose she finds out about it afterwards and won't marry him."

Robert: "Listen. This guy's a sap and he's in love with her. He wants to marry her all right, but even if he knew there was no chance of that, he'd still pay me to clear out. He thinks I'm bad for her and he lo-o-ves her and wants her to be ha-a-ppy."

Polly laughs and kisses him, says: "If you want to hear me sing, you'd better come on out and find a table. I go on in a few minutes."

Outside the door, Phil has been listening. He turns away from the door not quite quickly enough, as Dancer comes up behind him. Dancer says casually: "Catch a good earful?"

Phil says: "I wanted to see Polly, but I didn't want to butt in if she was busy."

Dancer links an arm through Phil's and starts leading him away from the door toward the stairs, saying: "She's busy. She'll be busy all evening."

Phil hangs back, saying: "I got to see her for a minute."

Dancer jerks him along, says, still casually: "Not this evening. You shake her down for too much dough, Phil, even if she is your sister. Lay off her a while."

Phil pulls his arm free, says: "That's no skin off your face. If she wants to help me out a little, that's her business. Why shouldn't she? I know things that are going on around here that—"

Dancer reaches out, grabs him by the necktie, and pulls him close, saying softly: "Smart boy. You know things. When are you going to start shaking *me* down?"

Phil says: "When I want to shake you down, I'll—"

Dancer stops him this time by slapping his face once, not especially hard. Dancer: "I don't like you, but I've put up with having you around because you're Polly's brother, and she's a nice kid, but don't think you can ride too far on that ticket." He puts his open hand over Phil's face, and pushes him backwards down the stairs, saying: "Now stay away for a couple of days."

Phil tumbles backwards into the arms of Nick, who, with Nora, is coming up the stairs. Nick says: "Mmmm! Big confetti they throw here."

Dancer exclaims: "Ah, Mr. Charles! I'm sorry!" and starts down the stairs.

Phil snarls at Nick: "Why don't you look where you're going, you big clown?"—twists himself out of Nick's arms and goes downstairs out of the place.

Dancer is apologizing again.

Nick says: "Hello, Dancer. This your place? A neat way you have of getting rid of the customers."

Dancer smiles professionally: "Just a kid that hangs around because his sister works here. I get tired of him sponging on Polly sometimes."

Nick: "I felt a gun under his left arm when I caught him."

Dancer, contemptuously: "Just breaking it in for a friend, I guess." He ushers them upstairs.

Outside the Li-Chee, Phil finds a dark doorway from which the Club can be watched, and plants himself there. Nick's car is parked near the doorway. Both Harold and a taxi-driver, who is talking to him, see Phil, but neither pays much attention to the boy. Harold is chewing gum and listening with a bored air to the taxi-driver.

"And I said to him, 'You ain't going to give me a ticket, you big flatfoot, and you know it,' I said. I said, 'I got a right to turn there, and you know it,' I said, 'and I ain't got all night to be sitting here gassing, so go polish your buttons and leave me be on my way, you fat palooka,' I said."

Harold, wearily: "I know, and then you busted out crying."

Upstairs in the Li-Chee, Nick is checking his hat and coat while Nora looks interestedly around the place. Suddenly she grabs Nick's arm, says: "There's Robert!"

Robert and Polly are going into the restaurant.

Nick says: "The night's bulging with your family."

Nora starts to pull him toward Robert, saying: "Come on."

Dancer to Nick: "Is Mr. Landis a friend of yours?"

Nick, as Nora drags him off: "On the contrary, a relation."

Dancer stares thoughtfully after them.

By the time Nick and Nora reach Robert, he and Polly are sitting at a small table near the orchestra. Nora holds out a hand to Robert, saying: "Hello, Robert," with a great show of cordiality. He rises drunkenly, mumbling: "Hello, Nora; hello, Nick," and shaking their hands. Then he introduces Polly: "Miss Byrnes, Mr. and Mrs. Charles." Nick immediately sits down and begins to talk to Polly, giving Nora a chance to speak aside to Robert.

Nora, in a low voice to Robert: "You oughtn't to stay away like this."

Robert: "I know, but Selma's not easy to get along with, and sometimes I simply have to break loose."

Nora: "But you should let her know that you're all right."

Robert: "You're right, of course. But sit down. You can talk in front of Polly. She knows about Selma."

Polly, aside to Nick: "Tell Mrs. Charles not to worry about him— I'll see that he gets home tonight." She puts her foot under the table and touches Robert's. He starts to laugh, then covers his mouth with his hand, and asks:

"Is—is Selma all right?"

Nora, indignantly: "You know she's not, and now with the police bothering her—"

Robert: "The police?" He and Polly both look alarmed.

Nora: "Yes, the idiots. A gardener we used to have was killed. Remember Pedro Dominges?"

Before Robert can reply, Polly exclaims: "Killed? Why, he's—" She breaks off with a hand to her mouth.

Nick prompts her: "He's what?"

Polly, to Nora: "What was his name?"

Nora: "Pedro Dominges."

Polly: "Oh! I thought you said Peter Dominger—a fellow I used to know."

Nick looks at her skeptically. Robert asks:

"What's that got to do with Selma?"

Nick: "Ask the police—they don't know. I wonder if our table's ready." He stands up.

Polly whispers: "I'll see he gets home all right."

Nick: "Thanks. Pleased to have metten up with you." He and Nora move off to where Dancer is beckoning them.

Polly leans over to Robert, speaking swiftly: "Honey, could you get hold of that guy Graham and see if you can get the money right away?"

Robert: "Maybe. Why?"

Polly: "I was thinking there's no sense in waiting until tomorrow. I'll tell Dancer I don't feel well and get the night off and we'll blow town right away. Would you like that?"

A waiter comes up with fresh drinks as Robert says: "I'll try him on the phone now."

Nick and Nora come up to the table. Dancer stands, holding Nora's chair for her.

Nick: "Thanks." He sits down. A Chinese waiter comes to his side, hovering over him.

Dancer: "This all right?"

Nick: "Fine." Then to the waiter, who is handing him his napkin: "Never mind about that. Bring me two Scotch highballs quick." The waiter starts away, but Nick stops him. "No. Better make it three. One for the wife."

Waiter: "Yes, sir."

Dancer leans over toward Nick, adjusting the forks and utensils on the table as he speaks: "You once sent a friend of mine up . . . Lum Ying."

Nick: "Oh, I remember him. He spread a tong war out to include sticking up a bank."

Dancer: "His brother's here now . . . one of my partners."

Nick, with a smile: "Is he a gunman, too?"

Dancer: "No. But you can't tell how close brothers are. Thought you might like to know."

Nick: "Maybe you'd better point him out."

Dancer: "I'll call him over. Lum Kee!"

Lum Kee is a plump, middle-aged Chinese man with a round merry face. He is dressed in American clothes.

Dancer: "Come here."

Lum Kee: "You bet you!"

Nick is looking interestedly at Lum Kee, as he comes up to the table.

Dancer, introducing him to Nick: "I want you to meet a friend of mine . . . Lum Kee."

Lum Kee grins, ducking his head.

Lum Kee: "I'm your friend, you bet you."

Dancer to Lum Kee: "This is Nick Charles."

Lum Kee: "I hear about you, Mr. Charles. Number one detective."

Nick: "Thanks. So you're Lum Ying's brother."

Lum Kee, still grinning: "You bet you—you catch 'em my brother seven years ago. You play trick on him. You bet you."

Nick, nodding solemnly: "No play trick on 'em, no catch 'em. You bet you." Lum Kee laughs merrily. "He still in?"

Lum Kee: "You bet you. Four . . . five years more." He ducks his head politely at Dancer, Nick, and Nora and goes off. Dancer looks meditatively after him.

Dancer, as if casually, to Nick: "That's a good guy to have liking you." He turns and walks away. As the implication of Dancer's casual words dawns on him, Nick looks after Dancer with humorous dismay.

Dancer goes to the table where Polly is now sitting alone and asks: "What's the setup?"

Polly: "They're Bobbie's cousins by marriage and think he ought to go home to his wife."

Dancer purses his lips thoughtfully for a moment, then says: "It's all to the good, them seeing him here plastered, but I guess we can't take a chance on them tipping off the wife and having her bang in. Give the customers one song and knock off for the night. Take him up to your place."

Polly: "I'm getting kind of tired of him."

Dancer: "It's only till tomorrow night. You can turn him loose then. Put a pill in his drink when you get him home, so he'll be sure to stay safe asleep while you run out to do that little errand in the morning." He pats her shoulder.

Polly, without enthusiasm: "All right." She gets up to sing.

Robert at the telephone talking to David. Robert: "That money you promised me tomorrow—give it to me tonight and I'll be half across the country by daylight."

David: "I told you I couldn't raise it till tomorrow."

Robert, snarling: "How'd you like it if I changed my mind between now and tomorrow?"

David: "But, Robert, I—" He breaks off as he thinks of something, then says: "I've got the bonds I was going to raise the money on—if you'll take them."

Robert: "They're negotiable? There's no foolishness about them?"

David: "Certainly they're negotiable! Do you think I'd—?"

Robert: "I don't think anything about you. How soon can you turn them over?"

David: "As soon as you can get here."

Robert: "I won't come there for them."

David: "All right. Where are you?"

Robert: "At the Li-Chee."

David: "Then I can meet you at the corner of . . . and . . . in ten minutes."

Robert: "Okay, but don't keep me waiting, or I might change my mind."

David: "And you'll give me your word you'll—"

Robert: "I've got to go home and pack a bag, but I won't bother your sainted Selma. I won't even see her if I can get out of it." He slams the receiver on the hook, says: "Boy Scout!" at it, and returns to his table.

(Throughout this scene, waiters, etc. have been passing and re-passing Robert at the phone, but none seems to have paid any attention to his conversation.)

Nick and Nora at their table listening to Polly singing. Dancer, in-tent now on keeping them comfortable until Polly and Robert are safely away, comes to the table and asks: "Everything all right, Mr. Charles?"

Nick, shuddering at the first taste of his drink and frowning at the glass: "It's all something."

Dancer laughs with professional heartiness and addresses the waiter: "Ling, no check for this table. Anything they want is on the house."

Nick: "I can't let you do that."

Dancer: "But I insist. You must be my guest—"

Nick, at this point seeing the approach of a group of thugs he knows, and realizing that somebody's going to be stuck for a lot of drinks, says quickly: "We accept with thanks. That's mighty white of you, Dancer." He shakes Dancer's hand as the thugs arrive, and says: "Meet the rest of my party."

Eddie: "We don't want to meet him. He's a crumb."

Nick: "But he's giving the party. It's all on the house."

Eddie: "Well, I'll—well—well!" He turns to his companions, saying enthusiastically: "Boys! Champagny!"

Nick: "Certainly champagne."

Dancer tries to smile as if he likes it. The others crowd him back out of the way as they make room for themselves around the table.

Men: "Say, this is all right."

"Hi'yer, Nick."

"Hello, Nick."

Eddie, a bull-like thug, looks gallantly at Nora. "You certainly can pick 'em, Nick."

He turns to Nora: "I never seen such a guy. Every time I meet him, he's got another good-looking gal."

Nick shoots a quick look at Nora.

Nick, to Nora: "We haven't met in years."

Nora, looking back at him amused and skeptical: "No?"

Eddie, to Nora: "When he gives you the sack, let me know, will yer?"

Nora, smiling up at him, delightedly: "I certainly will."

Eddie, turning to another of the men: "She's hot-looking, ain't she?"

The Other Man: "Shut up, you lug. It's his wife."

Eddie winces and sinks down into his chair.

Another Man, stepping into the breach, pushing Willie toward Nick and Nora: "Come on, Willie."

"Here's Willie."

"You remember Willie. He just got out today."

Nick shakes Willie's hand cordially.

Nick: "Indeed I do. Glad to see you."

Willie: "Likewise."

Nick, turning to Nora: "Darling, this is Willie the Weeper."

Nora, smiling cordially at him: "Delighted."

Willie: "Likewise."

Nick (introducing the rest to Nora en masse): "And the boys."

Nora looks at them and smiles. They sit down, dragging their chairs up. The waiter comes up, listening for their orders.

Nick: "I feel honored to be at your coming-out party, Willie. What'll you boys have?"

Another Man: "Champagne!"

Nick: "Willie?"

Willie: "Scotch."

Nora: "Likewise!"

Eddie: "Scotch, with a champagne chaser."

The men all roar with delight.

Polly, nearing the end of her song, looks questioningly at Robert, who nods and points to his watch and the door to indicate that she should hurry. Lum Kee is watching them. He goes over to Dancer, who has left Nick's table.

Lum Kee: "No trouble, Dancer. I ask you, please."

Dancer, putting a hand on his partner's arm: "Stop worrying, Lum. Everything is okay."

Lum Kee: "All the time you say everything okay. All the time trouble-trouble."

Dancer: "We always get out of it, don't we?"

Lum Kee: "You bet you, but too much money. Pretty soon money not fix something. Then no more Li-Chee."

Dancer slaps Lum Kee on the back and says: "If it's Landis you're worrying about, I'll tell him to stay away. I don't like the guy much either. But you'll find something else to squawk about."

Lum Kee, cheerfully: "You bet you."

Polly, having finished her song, tells the orchestra to play a dance number instead of an encore, and goes toward her dressing room. As she passes Nora, she gives her a reassuring nod. Robert is getting his hat and coat. Dancer crosses to meet Polly at the door and says: "Just keep him in your apartment till evening and we'll both be cutting ourselves a nice piece of gravy."

Polly says without enthusiasm: "I hope so. Has Phil been in tonight?"

Dancer: "For a minute. He went off like he had a date. Go ahead, kid." He pats her back, urging her toward the door. She goes out.

At Nick's table, his guests are still applauding Polly deafeningly, pounding the table with bottles, etc. Nora seems to be talking to Nick, but nothing can be heard. He yells back: "Can't hear you." The words are barely audible. She puts her mouth to his ear and screams: "Do you think that girl will really see that he gets home?"

The noise dies suddenly just as she starts, and everybody in the place looks at her—her scream could be heard a block away. Willie, who has been banging on the table with two bottles, nudges the thug beside him and says: "I don't care whose wife she is, I don't like a dame that gets noisy when she's had a few snifters."

Nick is trying to recover his hearing in the ear Nora screamed in. She asks again, but in a lower voice: "Do you?"

Nick: "She'll see that he gets to somebody's home. You can phone if you want, when he's had time to get there."

Outside, the fog is thicker. Polly starts for a taxi, but Robert says: "It's only three blocks." They turn down the street. Phil comes out of his doorway and follows them. Harold is slumped down in the seat of Nick's car asleep, though his jaws still move a little with his gum. The taxi-driver is saying: "And I said to this truck-driver, 'All right, tough guy, if you don't like me cutting in on you, how would you like to climb down off that hearse and get bopped in the nose?' I said."

At a corner three blocks from the Li-Chee, Robert points to David, waiting in his car, and says: "There's our honeymoon money!" Polly holds back as he goes toward the car, but he takes her arm, saying: "Come on. I want him to see how much better I'm doing." They go up to the car.

Robert: "Have you got the bonds?"

David slowly looks from one to the other of them as he takes a thick sheaf of bonds from his pocket. He hands them to Robert, who eagerly examines them, then says: "Thanks, Sir Galahad," as he puts them into his pocket.

David: "You'll keep your promise?"

Robert: "Don't worry about that—and I wish you as much luck with your bargain as I got with mine." He pulls Polly toward him and kisses her on the mouth. David turns his head away in disgust. Robert laughs at him, says: "There's only one thing. I'm going home to pack a bag. Stay away till I've cleared out. Fifteen minutes oughtn't to mean anything to a man who's waited as long as you have. Ta-ta!" He and Polly turn away. David looks after them for a moment, then sighs as if with relief, and slowly starts his car.

At Nick's table in the Li-Chee, Eddie is complaining: "Where's Polly? I want to hear Polly sing. We come up here and spend all this dough"—indicating the champagne bottles—"and what does she do? She sings one song and quits." Joe, earnestly: "You can't say anything against Polly. She's all to the good."

Another thug, very drunk, his eyes almost shut, asks: "She still live in that place on White Street with the ghosts running up and down the halls?"

Nora, very interested: "A haunted house?"

The drunk, opening his eyes: "Did I say ghosts? I'm drunk, lady. I meant goats." He puts fingers up to his head to imitate horns and says: "Ba-a-a!"

Nora: "Well, that's *almost* as good."

Nick, as if not very interested: "What part of White Street?"

The Drunk: "Three forty-six. I can always remember that number because my old man used to have a livery stable there."

At the mention of the number Nora puts her hand quickly on Nick's and looks at him with a frightened face. Nick pats her hand without taking his attention from the drunk, and asks: "In the place with the goats?"

The drunk, who is going back to sleep, shakes his head and says: "No, that was back in Baraboo, Wisconsin."

Nick: "You know the fellow who owns the house?"

The Drunk: "In Baraboo?"

Nick: "The one Polly lives in."

The drunk shakes his head again: "Nope, but he ought to keep the front door shut so the goats can't get in."

Nick: "He was killed today."

The Drunk: "It don't surprise me. Stands to reason no tenants weren't going to put up with those goats forever." The other thugs exchange glances, then begin to regard Nick with suspicion.

Nora: "Nick, I'm going to phone."

Nick: "He's had time enough to get home." He holds out a handful of change.

Dancer, not far away, sees Nora take the nickel (if necessary, he can have overheard some of the conversation), and he goes quickly over to one of the hatcheck girls and says: "Get on the phone and stay there." She goes to the phone, drops in a coin, and when Nora arrives the girl is in the middle of a long description of a dress that can be written much more accurately by Miss Goodrich than by Mr. Hammett. Nora waits impatiently.

At Nick's table his guests are no longer having a good time; his questioning the drunk looks too much as if he is working on a murder job. Eddie clears his throat, says: "Well, boys, I guess we better be trucking along."

Willie: "I guess we better." Only the drunk seems comfortable.

Nick: "What's the matter? It's early. Don't you like the party?"

Eddie: "Sure we like it. It's swell. But—well, we got to get up early in the morning."

Nick: "Surely you haven't become an early riser in your old age, Eddie."

Eddie squirms, says: "Well, no, but—" He gets a bright idea: "You see, we're giving Willie a picnic. He's nuts about picnics and he's been locked up a long time, so we thought we'd take him out in the country early tomorrow morning and throw a picnic for him. Ain't that right, Willie?"

Willie: "I'm sure nuts about picnics!"

The drunk has opened his eyes and is staring at the others in surprise. He says: "What's the matter with you dopes? What can you lift out in the country?" Then more indignantly: "I ain't gonna ride in the backseat with no *cow*!"

Eddie laughs, says to Nick: "Ain't he a card!" and with Willie's help begins to haul the drunk to his feet.

Dancer, going into his apartment, says to a passing waiter: "Bring me a glass of milk." In his apartment, he goes to the telephone and calls

Polly's number. Lum Kee is lying on a sofa reading a book. Dancer waits patiently at the phone until the waiter comes in with his milk; then he puts down the phone and says: "That bum! I told her to take him straight to her place."

Lum Kee, not looking up from his book: "Mr. Landis?"

Dancer: "Uh-huh. I wanted her to get him in shape so he could go home."

Waiter: "Mr. Landis on phone I hearum say go home pack bag."

Dancer's eyes narrow; then he says: "Oh, sure, that's right. I had forgotten."

The waiter goes out. Dancer stands idly spinning an ashtray on a table for a moment, then yawns, and says: "I think I'll go out for a couple of minutes and get a little air in one of my lungs." Lum Kee nods without looking up. Dancer takes his hat and coat from a closet, says: "That last batch of Scotch we got from Monty's pretty bad."

Lum Kee: "I tell him."

Dancer goes out. Lum Kee puts his book down, takes his hat from the closet and goes out.

The girl at the telephone is now talking about hats, while Nora fidgets with increasing impatience.

In his room, Robert is finishing packing a bag, with occasional glances at the bathroom that connects his room with Selma's. He does not make much noise, but is still too drunk to be completely silent. He has changed his clothes.

Selma turns in bed and makes a faint moaning noise, but does not open her eyes.

In another room a bedside light goes on, and Aunt Katherine sits up in bed, listening. Grim-faced, she unhurriedly gets out of bed and reaches for her slippers.

His bag packed, Robert puts it out in the hall, then turns out the lights and tiptoes through the connecting bathroom into Selma's room, going to a dressing table, pulling a drawer open, and taking out a jewel case. He has transferred part of its contents to his pocket when Selma suddenly sits up in bed and screams: "Robert!" He turns, pushing the case back into the drawer as she snaps on the light.

Robert, with taunting mildness: "Hello, Selma, how are you?"

She runs toward him, crying: "Oh, where have you been? Oh, why do you do these things?"

He takes her in his arms, says: "There, there, darling."

For a moment she relaxes in his arms, then she puts her hands on his chest, pushing herself free, and cries: "No, I won't this time. I won't forgive you. I won't let you make a fool of me again."

Robert, as if to an unreasonable child: "All right, all right, darling. As a matter of fact, I only stopped in for a minute, anyhow, to change my clothes."

Selma: "Where are you going?"

Robert: "A trip, a little trip."

Selma: "You're not. I won't have it. I won't."

Robert, smiling: "Oh, won't you?" He takes a step toward the door, then stops to ask: "Want to kiss me goodbye?" She flies at him in insane rage. He catches her wrists, kisses her lightly on the mouth, says: "Thanks, darling," releases her wrists, and goes out. She stands staring after him with wild eyes, scrubbing her lips with the back of one hand, then runs into his room and pulls a table drawer open.

FLASHES: Robert, smiling, bag in hand, going out the front door into the foggy street.

Polly standing in a small store doorway, straining her eyes trying to see through the fog.

Phil, at the entrance of a narrow alley, his collar up, his right hand under his coat near his left armpit.

Dancer at the wheel of a black coupe, his eyes searching the street.

Lum Kee in a car driven by a Chinese chauffeur.

On a street corner a policeman is hunkered down on his heels scratching the back of a gaunt alley cat. He hears a pistol shot—not too loud—straightens up, and starts across the street.

Robert lies on his back on the sidewalk, his head and one shoulder propped up a little by the wall he has fallen against—dead. Selma stands looking down at him. Her face is a blank, dazed mask. In her right hand, hanging down at her side, is a pistol. Brakes scream and a car comes to a jarring halt at the curb. She does not move. David jumps out of the car and runs over to her, exclaiming: "Selma!" She does not move until he turns her to face him and even then her face does not change. He shakes her, cries: "Selma! What—" He sees the pistol and takes it from her, stepping back a little. As he does so, her eyes lose their blankness and she looks at the pistol.

In a monotone she says: "He was going away. I took that from his room—to try to stop him." She begins to tremble and her face works convulsively—she is about to go to pieces.

David has put the pistol in his pocket. He glances quickly up and down the foggy street, then takes her by the shoulders and shakes her again, putting his face close to hers, speaking very clearly, as if to one who understood English poorly: "Listen, Selma. You're going back to the house. You never had a pistol. Hear me? You haven't been out of the house. Understand? You know nothing about this. Understand?" She nods woodenly. With an arm around her, he leads her quickly to the corner, only a few steps away. There he says: "Now hurry! Back in the house. Up to your room. You know nothing about this. Run!" Automatically obeying his command, she runs blindly back toward her front door. David dashes back to his car, jumps in, and drives off with reckless speed.

In the Li-Chee, the girl at the telephone is now talking about shoes. Besides Nora, half a dozen other people are waiting to use the phone. Nora goes up to the girl and says: "Please, it's awfully important that I—"

The girl, dropping another nickel into the slot: "I can't help it if there's only one phone here. Why don't you carry around one of them portable shortwave sets if you got so many important things to call people about." She goes on with her phone conversation.

Nora goes back to Nick, who is engaged in rearing on his table one of those old-fashioned towers of bottles, salt shakers, oranges, forks, etc., all carefully balanced atop one another. Waiters and customers stand around with bated breath watching him admiringly. He is getting along fine until Nora comes up and says: "Nick!" Then the whole pile comes crashing down on the table. The audience applauds.

Nick bows, then turns to Nora and says: "The divorce is Wednesday." She doesn't laugh.

She says: "Nick, I can't get to the phone. One of the hatcheck girls has been talking for hours."

Nick: "You've come to the right place. Old Find-a-Phone Nick, the boys around the drugstore used to call me." He offers her his arm and they go across the floor and out of the restaurant. As they pass the pay phone—where the hatcheck girl is now talking about underwear and a dozen customers are angrily waiting—Nick says loftily: "Mere amateur phone-finding!" He opens a door, shakes his head, and shuts it. He starts to open the next door, but stops when he sees it is labeled LADIES. The third door opens into Dancer's apartment. He bows Nora in, ushers her to the sofa, hands her the book Lum Kee had been reading, goes to the phone, and calls Selma's number.

The door opens and Dancer, in hat and coat, comes in.

Nick: "Hello, Dancer. Nice men's room you have." He waves a hand to indicate the room and the rather elaborate bath that can be seen through an open door, then suddenly frowns at Nora and asks: "What are *you* doing in here?"

Dancer stands inside the open door looking at Nick with cold eyes, and when he speaks his voice is cold and level: "Once a gum-heel always a gum-heel, huh? I don't like gum-heels, but I thought you'd quit it when you married a pot of money and—"

Nora, indignantly: "Did he call me a pot?"

Nick pays no attention to either of them; Aunt Katherine is on the other end of the wire. She says: "You'd better come over, Nicholas. Robert has been killed."

Nick's expression does not change as he says: "I will," and slowly hangs up.

Dancer, jerking a thumb at the open door behind him: "Well, now, if you're through in here."

Nick, leaning back comfortably in his chair: "Still foggy out?"

Dancer, very deliberately: "Have you ever been thrown out of a place, Mr. Charles?"

Nick, to Nora: "How many places was it up to yesterday, Mrs. Charles?"

Nora: "How many places have you been in, Mr. Charles?"

Dancer: "Look here!"

Nick, raising a hand: "Wait, wait! As I was about to say, it's not for me to tell any man how to run his business—though I *could* give you a few hints—but just the same it doesn't look right for you and your partner and your chief entertainer and one of your best customers all to go out at about the same time. It gives the place a—a—a quite vacant look. Did you notice it, Mrs. Charles?"

Nora: "Oh, decidedly, Mr. Charles. Quite barnlike."

Nick: "Thank you, Mrs. Charles. Now there's another thing. If Mr. Robert Landis came here with a lady who left a cigarette case, you shouldn't have sent it to his *wife*. You know what a fellow Mr. Landis was."

Dancer: "That wasn't me. Lum didn't know."

Nora leans toward Nick, her face strained: "Did you say 'was'?" Nick nods slowly, his face serious now. Nora, softly: "Poor Selma."

Dancer, angrily: "I've had enough of this. I—" He breaks off as through the open door comes the sound of Polly's singing.

Nick: "Ah! Another of our travelers has returned. Now if only—no sooner said than done," he says as Lum Kee comes in. Nick looks from one to the other of them and says thoughtfully: "I wonder which of you would be most frightened if Robert Landis walked in now." Neither man says anything. Nick: "But *you* know there's no chance of that, don't you, Dancer?"

Dancer: I don't know what you're talking about, and I don't care." He advances threateningly. "Get out!"

Nick smiles, shakes his head, says: "You said that before and it's foolish. We're not going to get out—we're going to have more people come in."

He picks up the phone. Dancer, grabbing at the phone: "Give me that phone!"

Nick: "Certainly."

He raps Dancer on the jaw with it. Dancer staggers back, holding his jaw.

Nora, proud of Nick, says to Dancer: "See?"

Nick dials a number, says: "Nick Charles speaking. I want to get hold of Lieutenant Abrams of the Homicide Detail. If he's not on duty, will you give me his residence number?"

Lum Kee crosses to the closet and carefully puts his hat away.

On a dark and seemingly deserted part of the waterfront, David gets out of his car, walks to the edge of a small pier, and throws Selma's pistol as far out into the water as he can.

Through the fog comes a man's voice shouting: "Hey, what are you doing there?" followed by the sound of feet running toward David. David races back to his car and drives off.

In Dancer's apartment, Nick is saying into the phone: "Sure, I'll wait for you, Abrams. . . . Well, I'll *ask* them to wait, but sometimes I think they don't like me well enough to do me favors. . . . Yes. I'll tell them." He puts down the phone and tells Lum Kee and Dancer: "The Lieutenant said something about boiling you in oil if you budged before he gets here. The fellow probably exaggerates."

Polly has finished her song: the sound of applause comes through the door. Dancer turns on his heel and goes out.

A still larger and angrier group of customers is waiting to use the phone. The hatcheck girl is talking about pajamas. Dancer takes the receiver roughly from her and slams it on the hook, snarling: "Get back to work. What are you going to do? Spend the whole night here?" He goes on toward the restaurant.

In Dancer's apartment, Lum Kee says: "Dancer not mean anything, please, Mr. Charles. Good man—only excited. Sometime make a little trouble—not mean anything." He smiles cheerfully at Nick and Nora, as if he had explained everything, and says: "Now we have little drink, you bet you."

Nora rises, saying to Nick: "I ought to go to Selma's. She'll need somebody."

Nick: "Right. I'll put you in the car." To Lum Kee: "Hold everything." Nick and Nora go downstairs.

Harold is sound asleep now. The taxi-driver is saying: "So I said to these two gobs, I said, 'Maybe you boys are tough stuff back on Uncle Sam's battle-wagon, but you ain't there now,' I said, 'you're on land,' I said, 'and you're either gonna pay that fare or I'm going to take it out of your—'" He breaks off as Nick and Nora come to the car, and opens the door for them. Harold wakes up.

As Nora gets in, Nick asks Harold: "Did you see Robert Landis leave?"

Harold: "No, I would've only—" He breaks off, leans past Nick to push the taxi-driver violently with one hand, saying angrily to him: "Putting me to sleep with them yarns about where you told everybody to get off at! I ought to—" He jerks his cap off and turns to Nora, saying earnestly: "Aw, gee, I'm sorry, Mrs. Charles!"

Nick: "Did you see anybody you knew?"

Harold: "Nope, I didn't notice nobody coming out particular—except there was a kid come out right after you went in, and I only noticed him because he was kind of hanging around"—he indicates the doorway Phil stood in—"for a little while. Why? Something up?"

Nick: "What did the kid look like?"

Harold gives a rough description of Phil, adding: "Why?"

Nick: "What happened to him?"

Harold: "I don't know." He calls to the taxi-driver, who is standing back against a wall, looking resentfully at them: "Hey, Screwy! What happened to the kid that was hanging around here?"

The Taxi-Driver: "I don't know. I guess he went down the street half hour ago."

Harold warns Nick: "Maybe he never even seen him. What's up, Nick?"

Nick: "Plenty. Drive Mrs. Charles back to her aunt's," then to Nora: "Going to stay all night?"

Nora: "I think I ought to."

He nods, says: "I'll stop over in the morning." He stands at the curb staring thoughtfully after the car as it drives away.

Upstairs in the Li-Chee, Dancer meets Polly as she leaves the floor and asks her: "What are you doing back here?"

Polly: "It wasn't my fault, Dancer. You know how drunks are. We got outside and he insisted on going home—his home—and I couldn't talk him out of it. I couldn't strong-arm him, could I? So I thought I'd better come back and tell you. I couldn't stop him."

Dancer: "Okay, sister, dress your dolls the way you want to."

Polly: "I don't understand what you mean, Dancer."

Dancer: "A cluck, huh? All right. I'll tell you so you can understand. Somebody cooled off Landis tonight, and the heat's on plenty—right here. You're in it with me, and you're going to be in it with me, because the first time you step out of line—get the idea?"

Polly: "You don't have to try to scare me." (But she is scared.) "I'm shooting square with you."

Dancer, sneering: "You mean starting now? That'll help some. Where's the paper?"

Polly: "In my bag. Shall I tear it up?"

Dancer: "Maybe you *are* as dumb as you act sometimes. Listen. Try to understand what I'm telling you. Landis is killed—dead. Maybe we're going to need that paper bad. So you don't let anything happen to it—be sure you don't."

Polly: "All right, but I still don't get it. I don't know what you—"

Dancer: "Shut up and do what you're told."

At this point, as they move toward Dancer's apartment, they pass the head of the stairs and are joined by Nick, returning from the street.

Nick: "Now let's have that little drink Lum Kee was talking about."

Dancer: "Swell! And, Mr. Charles, I want to apologize for losing my temper like that."

Nick, linking arms with them: "Don't give it a second thought. Some people lose one thing, some lose another, but they all like a drink afterwards."

To Polly, sympathetically: "Tough you couldn't do a better job of seeing Landis got home all right."

Polly, sullenly: "It wasn't my fault. I did the best I could."

Nick says: "I'm sure you did," as they go into Dancer's apartment.

Lum Kee is at the telephone saying: "Better you come right away . . . You bet you." He hangs up, explaining blandly to Nick: "Mr. Caspar. He our lawyer. Sometimes good thing when you have trouble."

Nick: "You bet you."

Dancer: "Maybe, but I think you're going to a lot of trouble over nothing. It's a cinch none of us shot Landis—so what do we need a lawyer for?"

Nick: "Maybe to help you explain how you know he was *shot*."

Dancer: "Well, whatever way he was killed, it's still a cinch we didn't have anything to do with it."

Nick yawns, says: "A cinch is no defense in the eyes of the law," and makes himself comfortable on the sofa.

Dancer smiles ingratiatingly at Nick and says: "I don't blame you for thinking maybe we're tied up in this somehow. It's our own fault for starting off with you on the wrong foot, but—let's have that drink first and talk things over. We can show you we're in the clear." He pushes a button for a waiter.

Nick, indifferently, lying back and looking at the ceiling: "Don't worry about me. Talk it over with the police."

Dancer catches Polly's eye and jerks his head a little toward Nick. She nods and moves as if aimlessly over to the sofa. Lum Kee looks from Dancer to Polly, then goes over and sits on a chair not far from the sofa, but behind Nick.

Dancer calls: "Come in," as the waiter knocks, and moves over so that he is between Nick and the door. (None of these movements should be definitely threatening, though it should seem to the audience that Nick is being surrounded.)

Dancer, to Nick: "What'll you have?"

Nick: "Scotch."

Polly and Lum Kee say: "Same."

Dancer: "And a glass of milk."

The waiter goes out. Polly sits down on the sofa beside Nick and says: "Do you suppose that David Graham could have killed Robert?"

Nick blinks in surprise, then says: "I'm no good at supposing. What do *you* know about David Graham?"

Dancer is regarding the girl with a puzzled look.

Polly: Only what Robert told me—that he was in love with his wife."

Nick: "Oh."

Polly, putting a hand on one of Nick's as if unconsciously: "Wasn't he?"

Nick: "Everybody's in love with *somebody's* wife—I guess."

Polly, moving a little closer to him on the sofa: "Are you?"

Nick, still looking at the ceiling, takes his hand out of Polly's and puts his arm around her, making himself more comfortable. He says: "Everybody doesn't *admit* it."

Polly, bending over him a little, smiles and says admiringly: "I bet you could admit a lot—if you wanted to."

The waiter comes in with drinks, but halts in the doorway at a signal from Dancer. Nick pats Polly's shoulder and says lightly: "My dear, for a girl who's had so much practice giving men the works for Dancer, your technique is remarkably—ah—unpolished."

She jerks away from him angrily.

Nick: "There's the fellow with the drinks. That's what we're wait-ing for, isn't it?" None of the others moves.

Harold begins to apologize again as Nora gets out of the car in front of Selma's: "I feel like busting myself in the nose for that—"

Nora: "That's all right, Harold. Go back for Mr. Charles."

Harold stands looking after her, scratching his head and putting three fresh pieces of gum into his mouth, as she goes to the front door.

The door is opened immediately by one of the detectives who was with Abrams earlier that day. He touches the brim of his hat with one finger; she smiles at him without saying anything and goes down the hall to the open drawing-room door. Aunt Katherine, Abrams, and Dr. Kammer are standing in the drawing room. Dr. Kammer is a powerfully built middle-aged man with very pale skin, thick, short-cut black hair, and large, dark, staring eyes. He speaks very precisely, with a barely noticeable accent, and, though he does not use a cane, one of his legs is stiff at both ankle and knee. His dress is dandified, more European than American, and—except for the dragging of his lame leg when he walks—he has a decidedly military carriage.

As Nora reaches the door, Abrams is saying gloomily to Dr. Kam-mer: "Okay, Doc—if you still want to take the responsibility for not letting me talk to her."

Kammer: "My dear sir, it is not a case of responsibility. Mrs. Landis has suffered a great shock. It was necessary to give her some-thing to quiet her. Can she talk to you in her sleep? She will not be awake for hours."

Abrams: "And then?"

Kammer: "And then we shall see."

Abrams sighs, says: "This is making it pretty tough for me. Well, let me ask you—"

Nora, coming into the room, interrupts him impatiently: "What are you wasting time here for? Nick's waiting for you at the Li-Chee. Robert was there tonight and left with a girl who lives in that apartment house Pedro owns. Pedro Dominges, the man who was killed at our place. She's back there now, and Dancer and the Chinaman, and Nick's with them waiting for you."

Abrams, stolidly: "Good evening, Mrs. Charles—or I guess it's good morning. Did you see him there? I mean Robert Landis."

Nora: "Yes."

Abrams: "What happened?"

Nora: "Nick knows. Go down there. He can tell you everything."

Abrams, not very hopefully: "I hope somebody can tell me something. These people!" He looks gloomily at Aunt Katherine and Kammer, and shakes his head, then continues: "Anyhow, I got to ask a couple more questions. Dr. Kammer, do you often have to give Mrs. Landis things to quiet her?" Kammer stares at him. Abrams turns to Nora for sympathy, saying: "You see—that's the way it's been going."

Nora: "But surely you don't think Mrs. Landis—" She breaks off, looking from one to the other in amazement.

Abrams, patiently: "How do I know what to think if nobody'll tell me anything. Well, Dr. Kammer, let's put it plain: does she take dope?"

Aunt Katherine: "Mr. Abraham, you're insulting."

Kammer: "Certainly not."

Abrams, paying no attention to Aunt Katherine: "Okay. Check that off. Then is she crazy?"

Kammer: "My dear sir, why should you think that?"

Abrams: "Easiest thing in the world. I've seen you three times in my life before this, and all three times you were on the witness stand testifying that somebody was nuts." He begins to count on his fingers. "First it was that guy Walter Dabney that killed a guy in a fight; then it was that Harrigan woman"—he opens his eyes a little wider—"by golly, she shot her husband, too; and then it was—"

Nora goes up to Abrams as if she were about to smack him, and says angrily: "Too! What right have you to say a thing like that?"

Dr. Kammer bows to Aunt Katherine and says: "Miss Forrest, in view of this definite accusation of the gentleman's"—he bows to Abrams—"I think you would be justified in insisting that your attorney be present at any further interviews members of your family may have with the police."

Aunt Katherine continues to regard Abrams in stony silence, as she has throughout this scene except for her one speech.

Abrams groans wearily and says, though not apologetically: "Anybody's tongue's liable to slip." Nobody says anything. He addresses Nora as if he were disappointed in her: "It's what you'd expect out of them—but you ought to know better." When she does not reply, he shrugs his shoulders and goes out.

Nora wheels to face Aunt Katherine and Kammer, asking: "Where's Selma?"

Aunt Katherine: "She's sleeping, my dear," adding quickly as Nora starts toward the door: "Don't disturb her. Dr. Kammer says she must not be disturbed."

Nora looks at them for a moment, then says very deliberately: "I won't disturb her, but I am going to be with her until she wakes up," brushes past them, and goes out of the room.

Aunt Katherine puts a hand on Kammer's arm and in almost a whisper asks: "Well?"

Kammer says: "I think there is as yet no reason for alarm."

Nora goes into Selma's bedroom, where a dim night-light is burning, and stands for a moment by the bed, looking down at Selma. When she turns away to take off her coat, one of Selma's eyes opens cautiously; then she sits up in bed and whispers: "Nora!"

Nora runs to her, exclaiming: "But they told me you were—"

Selma: "I know." She unwads a handkerchief while she speaks, showing Nora two white tablets. "They gave me these to put me to sleep, but I didn't take them. I wanted to see you. I knew you'd come." Selma and Nora go into a clinch. Then Selma asks: "Has David come back yet?"

Nora: "I don't think so. He's not here now."

Selma: "Will you phone him for me—see if he's home?"

Nora: "Of course." She puts out a hand toward the bedside phone.

Selma, catching her arm: "No, not here. That's why I was afraid to phone. The police might be listening in. Go to a drugstore or something. Or—better—go to his apartment—it's a only a few blocks."

Nora, puzzled: "But I don't understand."

Selma: "He took the pistol and told me to come back and not say anything and I want to know if he's all right."

Nora: "The pistol!"

Selma, explaining rapidly, unconscious of the effect her words have had on Nora: "Yes. I took it and ran out after Robert when he said he was going away—you know, to scare him into not going—and he'd insulted me so terribly. And he turned the corner before I could catch up with him, and then there was a shot, and then when I turned the corner, there he was dead, and after a while David came and took the pistol and told me to come back home and not say anything to anybody. And now I don't know whether he's all right or—"

Nora: "Then you didn't shoot Robert?"

Selma, amazed: "Shoot Robert? Nora!"

Nora puts her arms around Selma, saying: "Of course you didn't, darling. That was stupid of me."

Selma: "And you'll go find out about David? I was in such a daze or I wouldn't have let him do it; and I'm so afraid he may have got into trouble."

Nora: "I'll go right away."

Selma: "And you'll hurry back to tell me?"

Nora: "Yes, but do try to get some sleep."

Selma: "I will."

They kiss and Nora goes out.

Nora goes softly downstairs and out of the house without seeing anybody, but as she hurries up the foggy street a man comes out of a dark doorway and follows her.

Aunt Katherine and Dr. Kammer are sitting in silence, as if waiting for something, when they hear the street door close behind Nora. In

unison, they look at each other, then in the direction of Selma's room.
Neither speaks. They rise together, and slowly—he dragging his lame
leg, she leaning on her cane—they go to Selma's room. Selma lies as
if sleeping. Kammer feels her pulse, then picks up her handkerchief
and finds the tablets. He does not seem surprised. He pours a glass of
water and says, not unkindly: "Come, why must you be so childish?
Take these now." Selma, very sheepishly, sits up in bed and takes the
tablets and water.

In David's apartment, he is distractedly walking up and down. He looks
at his watch, goes to the telephone, but puts it down without calling
a number. He lights a cigarette, puts it out immediately, goes to the
window; then repeats his performance with watch and telephone. He
is wiping his face with a handkerchief when the phone rings. He picks
it up quickly. Nora, on the other end of the wire, says: "David, this is
Nora. I'm downstairs. I want to—"

David: "Come up! Come up!" He goes to the door and waits
impatiently for her.

As soon as Nora appears, David asks: "Have you come from her?"

Nora: "Yes. She—"

David, excitedly: "Where's Nick? What'll I do, Nora? It's my fault.
I'm all to blame. If I hadn't given Robert those bonds, he wouldn't have
been going away, and she wouldn't have"—his voice breaks and he almost
whispers the last words—"shot him."

Nora: "But she didn't, David!"

David: "What? She told me."

Nora: "She told you what?"

David: "That she took the gun and ran out after him to try to keep
him from going away and—"

Nora: "But she didn't shoot him. She hadn't turned the corner
when she heard the shot, and when she got there he was already dead.
She told me herself, and she was perfectly calm when she told me."

David sinks back into a chair, his eyes wide and horrified. He tries to speak twice before the words will come out, and when they do his voice is hoarse with anguish. "I've killed her, Nora! I've sent her to the gallows! I thought she shot him. I took the gun and threw it in the bay. I'm a fool and I've killed her."

Nora, frightened, but trying to soothe him: "Perhaps it's not that bad, David. We'll see what Nick says. He'll know how to—"

David: "But, don't you see? If I hadn't thrown the gun away, the fact that it hadn't been fired—and the police could've fired a bullet from it and seen that it didn't match the one he was killed with—don't you see?—it would have been absolute proof that she didn't do it. But now—" He breaks off and grabs one of Nora's hands, asking: "How is she? Do the police—do they think she—" He seems unable to finish the question.

Nora: "Selma's all right. She's lying down. The police haven't talked to her yet. Dr. Kammer wouldn't let them."

David, a little sharply: "Kammer! Is he there?" Nora nods. David, frowning: "I wish he'd stay away from her." He shrugs off his thoughts about Kammer and asks: "Do the police suspect her?"

Nora: "I'm afraid they suspect everybody."

David: "But her especially—do they?"

Nora, hesitantly: "I'm afraid they do—a little." Then, more cheerfully: "But they didn't know about the Li-Chee Club and those people then. We were there tonight and saw Robert, and Nick found out a lot of things about Robert's running around with a girl who lives in the same house as Pedro Dominges, oh! a lot of things, and I'm sure by this time he knows who killed Robert—so there's nothing to worry about."

David, not sharing her cheerfulness: "I hope so. I'll kill myself if—"

Nora, sharply: "Don't talk like that, David. They'll find out who killed Robert—Nick'll find out."

David: "Tell me the truth, Nora, does Nick think she, Selma, killed him?"

Nora: "Oh, he knows she didn't. He knows—" She breaks off, staring with frightened face past David and pointing at the window. David turns, in time to catch a glimpse of Phil's face outside the window. He rushes to the window, but has some trouble with the fastening, so that by the time he gets it open, the fire-escape is empty. As he turns back to Nora, she says in a surprised voice: "Why, that was—"

There is a sharp, triple knock on the door. David goes to the door and opens it. The man who shadowed Nora from Selma's house is there. He asks: "Mr. Graham?"

The man takes a badge in a leather case from his left pants pocket and shows it to him briefly, saying: "Police—"

Nora says: "There was a man on the fire-escape! The brother of that girl at the Li-Chee."

The policeman says: "Yeah?" as if not believing her. He goes to the window and looks out for a moment, then turns back and says: "He's gone." Then he scowls at Nora and asks: "What girl at the Li-Chee?"

Nora says: "Polly Byrnes—the girl Robert Landis went out with just before he was killed."

The policeman says: "Say, you know a lot, don't you, sister? What does all this make you out to be?"

Nora says, with great dignity: "I'm Mrs. Nick Charles!"

The policeman says, apologetically: "I didn't know. I guess then maybe there was somebody on the fire-escape."

Nora asks, indignantly: "Well, what are you going to do—stand here and wait for them to come back?"

The policeman says: "No, I reckon not." He goes to the phone.

David takes Nora out of the policeman's hearing and asks, in a low voice: "Should I tell him about the gun—about Selma?"

Nora says: "No, don't tell anybody until we see Nick."

Dancer's apartment—at the Li-Chee. Nick is lying on the sofa, as before. Lum Kee is sitting in the corner, reading a book. In another chair, Polly is sitting, manicuring her fingernails. Dancer is sitting astride a chair, chewing a toothpick, and looking angrily at Nick. Nick is in the middle of an apparently long and pointless anecdote.

Dancer spits toothpick out on the floor and says, angrily: "Listen, we're putting up with you, but do we have to put with all this talk?"

Nick sits up and looks at him in surprise, saying: "But I thought I was entertaining you."

A Chinese waiter opens the door and says: "Mr. Caspar here—"

Caspar comes in. He is a little man, almost a dwarf, sloppily dressed, with bushy hair, and is addicted to Napoleonic poses. He comes into the room bowing and smiling to everyone and saying: "Well, well—what is it?"

Dancer, grouchily: "Do I know? So a guy comes in and buys a drink. He goes out and somebody kills him. What are we supposed to do, give the customers insurance policies with the drinks?"

Nick says: "Wouldn't be a bad idea—with the kind of stuff you're serving."

Caspar advances toward Nick with his hand out, saying: "I didn't recognize you for a moment, Mr. Charles. You remember me—Floyd Caspar?"

Nick says: "Oh, yes," and pats his pockets as if to make sure he hasn't lost anything.

Caspar goes on: "A man killed! Surely you don't think these people—" he looks at the three others in the room as if they were saints "—would have anything to do with a thing like that!" He puts a hand on Dancer's shoulder and says: "Why, I've known this boy since he was—"

Dancer pushes the hand off roughly and says: "Save it for the district attorney. What're you wasting your voice on this gum-heel for?"

Through the closed door comes the sound of men arguing. Then the door is swung open by Lieutenant Abrams, pushing a Chinese waiter against it. Two other detectives are with Abrams. He looks very tired and very dissatisfied with all the people in the room. When he sees Caspar, he groans and says: "I knew it would be like this. I knew there would be some shyster around to slow things up."

Caspar draws himself up to his full five feet and begins, pompously: "Lieutenant Abrams, I must ask you—"

Abrams pays no attention to him, walks over and sits down on the sofa by Nick, asking, not very hopefully: "Is it right you know something about what's been happening?"

Nick says: "A little."

Abrams says: "It can't be any littler than anybody else seems to know. Do you want to say it in front of them—or do we go off in a corner?"

Nick says: "This suits me."

Abrams asks: "Is this the dame Mrs. Charles was telling me about— that lives in Dominges's apartment and was with Landis tonight?"

Nick says: "Yes. She sings here, but she took time off to see that he got home all right."

Abrams says, gloomily: "She certainly did a swell job." Then asks Polly: "And what did you do after he got home?"

Polly says: "I came back here. I work here."

Abrams says: "When did you find out he was killed?"

Polly says: "After I came back—maybe half an hour. Dancer told me. I guess Mr. Charles told him."

Abrams says: "Never mind guessing. . . . I guess you know your landlord was killed this afternoon?"

Polly exclaims: "What!"

Nick says: "I told her earlier tonight, but she seemed to think it had to do with some fellow named Peter Dufinger, or Duflicker, or something."

Polly says, earnestly, to Nick: "I honestly didn't know, Mr. Charles. I never knew what his name was, except Pedro."

Abrams asks: "What did you know about him besides that?"

Polly says: "Nothing. I've only lived there a couple of months and I never even seen him more than half a dozen times—"

Abrams asks Nick: "You believe her?"

Nick says: "I believe everybody. I'm a sucker."

Abrams asks Polly: "Who do you think would kill Landis?"

She says: "I haven't the faintest idea. Honest I haven't."

Nick says: "Miss Byrnes has a brother who carries a gun. Dancer was chucking him out when I came in. I hear he hung around for a while outside . . . perhaps until just about the time that Polly and Landis left."

When Nick says, "Dancer was chucking him out," Polly looks sharply at Dancer, but when Nick finishes his speech, Polly jumps up and comes over to him, saying earnestly: "Phil didn't have anything to do with it, Mr. Charles. He wouldn't have any reason."

Nick says: "I'm not accusing anybody. I'm just talking." Then he tells Abrams: "Dancer says he threw him out because he was bothering Polly for money."

Polly turns to Dancer, angrily, exclaiming: "That's a lie! You had no right to—"

Little Caspar interrupts her, saying: "Take it easy—take it easy. That's the idea of this police clowning—to get you all at each other's throats. Just answer any of their questions that you want to and don't let 'em get under your skin."

Abrams complains to Nick: "That's the way it goes. I leave that little shyster stay in here because I got nothin' to hide and he keeps buttin' in. If he don't stop it, I'm going to put them where he'll need a court order to get to them."

Caspar smiles and says: "Well, that's never been much trouble so far."

Abrams turns to Polly again, asking: "Where is this brother of yours that didn't kill anybody?"

Polly says: "I don't know. I haven't seen him today."

Abrams asks: "Does he live with you?"

Polly says: "No. He lives in a hotel on Turk Street. I don't know just where."

Abrams says: "You don't know much about anybody, do you?"

Polly says: "I honestly don't know what hotel. Phil's always moving."

Abrams says: "What's the matter—does he have to move every time he don't kill somebody? What does he do for a living—besides not killing anybody?"

Polly says: "He's a chauffeur, but he hasn't been able to get much work lately."

Abrams asks if anybody knows Selma Young. Nobody does.

Abrams asks Nick: "What do you think of it now?"

Nick says: "My dear lieutenant, you wouldn't expect me to question a lady's word."

Abrams says: "It's all right for you to kid. Nobody jumps on your neck if you don't turn up a murderer every twenty minutes." He sighs and, indicating Dancer and Lum Kee, asks: "Well, what about them?"

Nick says: "They seem to have disappeared not long after Polly and Landis went out. Then showed up again with their hats on around the time I heard about the murder."

Abrams asks Dancer: "Well?"

Dancer says: "I went out to get some air. What city ordinance does that break?"

Lum Kee, who has continued to read all through the scene so far, puts down his book and says: "I went with him."

Dancer tries not to show surprise.

Abrams says: "Yeah? Where'd you go for all this air?"

Lum Kee says, blandly: "Air pretty much same everywhere. We go in my car—ride around. Ask chauffeur."

Nick says: "There was another little point: I told Dancer Landis had been killed but he seemed to know that he'd been shot."

Abrams asks Dancer: "How about that?"

Dancer says, disagreeably: "This is the twentieth century—in a big city. How do most people get killed—battle-axes? I just took it for granted, like you would when you don't know you're on the witness stand."

Abrams asks: "Have you got a gun?"

Dancer takes an automatic out of his pocket and gives it to Abrams. From a card case he takes a slip of paper and gives it to Abrams, saying: "Here's my permit."

Abrams asks Lum Kee: "You?"

Lum Kee brings Abrams an automatic and a permit.

Caspar says: "If you're going to take those, Lieutenant, we should like a receipt."

Abrams complains to Nick: "I can't stand that shyster."

Nick: "I was beginning to suspect that."

Abrams asks Polly: "Have you got a gun?"

Polly shakes her head no.

Abrams: "What'd you do with it?"

Polly: "I never had one."

Abrams, wearily: "Nobody has anything, nobody knows anything. I don't see why I don't give up this racket and go farming."

Dancer, to Caspar: "Everybody thought he did a long time ago."

Abrams: "I'm laughing. Did you know this Pedro Dominges?"

Dancer: "No."

Abrams looks at Lum Kee, who says: "No."

Abrams stands up wearily, saying: "Come on, we're going down to the Hall of Justice."

Caspar: "On what charge?"

Abrams, disgustedly: "Charge, me eye! Witnesses. You ask 'em questions—where were you when you were over there?—and you have a stenographer take it down. You ought to know. Your clients spend nine-tenths of their time doing it." He looks at his watch, nods at the door through which the sound of music comes, says: "Or maybe for staying open after hours. Didn't you ever tell 'em about the two o'clock closing law?"

Caspar: "I'm going with 'em."

Abrams: "And you can bring the wife and kiddies for all I care."

The door opens and Nora and David come in accompanied by their detective. David and Polly look at each other with startled recognition, but neither says anything. Nora goes quickly over to Nick, who asks: "What are you up to now?"

Nora: "Have they found out who did it? Who did it, Nick?"

Nick: "Sh-h-h, I'm making Abrams guess."

Abrams looks from David to the detective and asks: "Where'd you find him?"

Detective: "You told me to shadow anybody that left the Landis house. Well, Mrs. Charles did, and went over to his apartment, and I knew you wanted to talk to him, so as soon as I found out who it was I went on up and got him. There's something about a fellow on the fire-escape, but they can tell you better than I can."

Abrams looks questioningly at Nora, who says: "Yes, it was—" She looks at Polly, hesitates, says: "It was her brother," then to Dancer: "The one you threw down the stairs when we came in."

Everybody looks expectantly at Polly, who seems dumbfounded. After a long moment she exclaims: "I don't believe it!"

Nick says: "That's certainly a swell answer."

Abrams asks Nora: "What was he doing on the fire-escape?"

Nora: "I don't know. He went away as soon as we saw him and by the time we could get the window open there was no sign of him. You know how foggy it is. And then this man came"—indicating the detective—"and by the time we could persuade him to do anything it was too late."

The detective, apologetically: "I reckon maybe I wasn't up on my toes like I ought to've been, Lieutenant, but it sounded kind of screwy to me at first." He addresses Nick: "I didn't know she was *your* wife then."

Nick: "You never can tell where you're going to find one of my wives."

The sound of music suddenly stops. Out in the restaurant, the customers, complaining about this unaccustomed early closing, are being shooed out.

Polly flares up, saying angrily: "What are you picking on Phil for? What's the matter with Robert's wife killing him? He told me himself she was batty as a pet cuckoo and would blow up and gum the whole thing if she found out that this guy—she points at David—was paying him to go away. Maybe she did find out about the bonds. What's the matter with that?"

Abrams looks thoughtfully at David and says: "Hmmm, so that's where the bonds came from?"

Dancer is watching Polly with hard, suspicious eyes. Nick, surprised, asks David: "Bonds?"

David nods slowly.

Abrams says to Polly: "This is no time to stop talking—go on, tell us more about this bond deal."

Caspar comes forward importantly, saying to Polly: "No, no, I think this is a very good time to stop talking at least until you've had some sort of legal advice—"

Polly says: "They know about it. Anyway, he does" (indicating David). "Besides, you're Dancer's and Lum's mouthpiece, not mine. How do I know you won't leave me holding the bag?"

Abrams looks pleased for the first time since he's come into the room. He says to Polly: "Now just a minute—that's fine!" He turns to Caspar and says: "So you aren't her lawyer? Well, that'll give us a little rest from your poppin' off. You and your two clients are going outside and wait until we get through talking to the little lady—"

Caspar starts to protest, but Abrams nods to his detectives and two of them take Caspar, Lum Kee, and Dancer out. At the door, Dancer turns to warn Polly: "Don't get yourself in any deeper than you have to."

When the door is closed behind him, Abrams sits down with a sigh of relief and says: "It's a lot better in here without them—especially that little shyster. Now maybe we can get somewhere!" He turns and sees that Nick, Nora, and David are huddled together whispering in a far corner of the room. David is telling Nick about Selma and the gun. Abrams says, gloomily: "There it is again. If people got anything to say, why don't they say it to me?"

The huddle breaks up, Nick saying: "Just a little family gossip."

Abrams says: "I'd even like to hear that." He asks Polly: "Did you ever see Mr. Graham before?"

Polly says: "I saw him tonight, when we went to get the bonds."

Abrams asks: "You and Robert Landis went to get them?"

Polly says: "Yes. He was waiting for us on the corner of _____ Street—and he gave them to Robert."

Abrams asks: "And then what?"

Polly says: "And then nothing. We left him and Robert went home."

Abrams asks: "And what did you do?"

Polly, after a moment's hesitation, says: "I went with him."

Abrams asks: "He took you home with him?"

Polly says: "Well, not in the house. I waited for him a block away—around the corner."

Abrams asks: "And then what?"

Polly says: "I waited a long time and then I heard a shot—only I thought it might be an automobile backfire—it was foggy and I was too far away to see anything—and I didn't know what to do—then after a while a policeman went past the doorway where I was standing—and a police car came—then I honestly didn't know what had happened, but I thought I'd better get out of the neighborhood if I didn't want to get in trouble—so I came back here—"

Abrams says: "Phooey!" and looks at Nick.

Nick says: "I think somebody ought to ask her where she was too far away from—"

Polly stammers: "From wherever it was it happened. If I hadn't been too far away, I'd have known where it was, wouldn't I?"

Nick says: "I give up."

Abrams: "All right—we'll come back to that later. So you were waiting for him? What were you going to do if he hadn't been killed?"

Polly glances uneasily at the door through which Dancer went, then shrugs and says: "We were going away."

Abrams: "Where to?"

Polly: "New York first, I suppose—then Europe, he said."

Abrams (looking at her evening gown): "Dressed like that?"

Polly: "We were going to stop at my place for me to change."

Abrams: "Dancer know you were going?"

Polly: "No."

Abrams: "Think he found it out, and knocked Landis off?"

Polly, shaking her head quickly from side to side: "No!"

Abrams: "You're supposed to be Dancer's gal, aren't you?"

Polly: "I work for him."

Abrams: "That's not what I asked you."

Polly: "You've got it wrong—honest. He knew I was running around with Robert—ask anybody."

Abrams: "How long?"

Polly: "A month—three weeks anyhow."

Abrams: "Get much money out of Landis?"

Polly, hesitantly: "He gave me some."

Abrams: "How much?"

Polly: "I don't know exactly. I—I can tell you tomorrow, I guess."

Abrams: "Did you split it with Dancer?"

Polly: "Why, no!"

Abrams: "Maybe you're lying. Maybe Dancer found out you were going away where you could keep all the sugar to yourself—and he put a stopper to it."

Polly: "That's silly!"

Abrams: "Sure. And hanging up in the air with a hunk of rope around your neck is silly, too."

After a little pause to let that sink in, he says: "Landis hadn't been home for a couple of days. Was he with you?"

Polly: "Most of the time."

Abrams: "Drunk?"

Polly: "Yes."

Abrams: "In your apartment?"

Polly: "There and here."

Abrams: "Anybody else with you in your apartment?"

Polly: "No."

Abrams: "Let's get back to the money. How much did you get out of him—roughly?"

Polly stares at the floor in silence.

Abrams: "As much as a grand or two? Or more?"

Polly, not looking up: "More."

Abrams: "More than five grand?" (Polly nods.) "All right, kick through—about how much?"

Polly shrugs wearily, opens her bag, takes out a check, and gives it to Abrams, saying: "A couple hundred dollars besides that, I guess."

Abrams looks at the check, then up at the girl and asks: "What'd he give you this for?"

Polly: "Well, I was chucking up a job and everything to go away with him, and I didn't want to take chances on being stranded somewhere off in Europe."

Abrams: "Looks like you didn't all right." He beckons to the others, who come to look over his shoulders at the check. It is to the order of Polly Byrnes for $10,000 and is signed by Robert Landis. They look at one another in amazement.

Nick says: "Where do you suppose he got hold of that much?"

Abrams: "Why? Aren't they rich?"

Nick: "The money is his wife's, and she found out some time ago that she had to stop giving him too much at a time—just on account of things like this."

Abrams: "Yeah? How about the signature?"

Nick: "Looks all right to me."

David: "And to me."

Abrams (as if thinking aloud): "But he don't usually have this much money, huh?" He asks Polly: "Sure you didn't take this to the bank today and find out it was no good?"

Polly: "I did not."

Abrams: "That's something we can check up. You know you're not going to have any easy time collecting this—unless his wife's as big a sap as he was."

Polly: "Why? He gave it to me."

Abrams: "Maybe. But his bank account's automatically tied up now till the estate's settled, and then I got an idea you're going to have to do a fancy piece of suing—taking a drunk for his roll!"

Polly: "I'll take my chances. Just the same, if his dying makes all that trouble, that shows we didn't have anything to do with killing him, doesn't it? Why wouldn't we wait till after we'd cashed it?"

Abrams: "We, we, we! So Dancer *was* in on it! How about the Chinaman?"

Polly: "Nobody was in on it. There was nothing to be in on."

Abrams: "Phooey!" He addresses the remaining detective: "Okay, Butch. Take her and her two playmates down to the hall and let the district attorney's office know you've got 'em there. We'll be along in a little while." He turns to Nick: "Or do you want to ask her something?"

Nick: "Yes. Did Robert Landis know Pedro Dominges?"

Polly shakes her head and says: "Not that I—" She remembers something. "Once when Robert and I were going out together we passed him and he said good evening to both of us by name and we couldn't figure out how he knew Robert's, and Robert made some joke about nobody being able to hide anything from a landlord."

Nick: "Thanks."

Polly and the detective go out.

Abrams: "That mean anything to you?"

Nick: "Not too much."

Abrams: "Now, Mr. Graham, I've got to—" He breaks off to look at Nora and Nick, saying thoughtfully: "I don't know whether you two ought to be in here while I'm doing this or not."

Nick, yawning, says: "I know where we ought to be. Come on, darling."

Abrams: "Maybe you *ought* to stay. Now, Mr. Graham, I got to ask a lot of questions that you're not going to like, but I got to ask 'em."

David: "I understand."

Abrams: "First off, you're in love with Mrs. Landis. Right?" David starts to protest, then simply nods. "She in love with you?"

David, trying to speak calmly in spite of the painfulness of this inquiry: "You'll have to ask her."

Abrams: "I will. Did she ever say she was?"

David: "Not—not since she was married."

Abrams: "Before?"

David: "We were once engaged."

Abrams: "Until Landis came along?"

David, in a very low voice: "Yes."

Abrams: "Ever ask her to divorce him and marry you?"

David: "She knew how I felt—it wasn't necessary to—"

Abrams: "But did you ever ask her?"

David: "I may have."

Abrams: "And what did she say?"

David: "She never said she would."

Abrams: "But you hoped she would. And you thought with him out of the way she would."

David looks Abrams in the eye and says: "I didn't kill Robert."

Abrams: "I said you did? But you did pay him to go away."

David: "Yes."

Abrams: "Did she know about it?"

David: "No, not unless he told her."

Abrams: "Were you and Landis on good terms?"

David: "Decidedly not."

Abrams: "On very bad terms?"

David: "Very bad."

The lights go out. In complete darkness Abrams's voice is heard saying: "Stay where you are—everybody!"

From the distance come the sounds of doors crashing, of glass breaking, of feet running, of men shouting; then close at hand furniture is knocked over, a door is slammed open, feet pound on the floor, two shots are fired, bodies thud and thrash around on the floor. Presently a cigarette lighter snaps on, held in Nick's hand. Behind him, in the dim light, Nora's and David's faces can be seen. The three of them are looking down at their feet. Abrams lies on the floor on his back. On top of him, mechanically chewing gum, his face serene, is Harold. One of his feet is on Abrams's throat; both his hands are clamped around one of Abrams's feet, twisting it inward and upward in the old Gotch toehold.

Nick says gently: "Harold, Harold, get up from there. Lieutenant Abrams isn't going to like this."

Harold, cheerfully: "You're the boss." He jumps up.

As Abrams gets up, a hand to his throat, Nick says: "My chauffeur. Stout fellow, eh?"

Abrams goes toward Harold saying: "What do you think you—"

Harold sticks his face into the Lieutenant's and says: "What am I supposed to do? I'm sitting out there and I see the lights go off. Nick and Mrs. Charles are up here and I know what kind of dump it is. Think I'm going to sit out there like a sissy till they throw the bodies out? How do I know you're a copper?" Then, more argumentatively, as he goes on: "Suppose I did know it? How can I tell Nick ain't got hisself in a jam with the police?"

Nick: "All right—but don't you boys think you'd better stop wrangling long enough to find out who turned out the lights and did the shooting?" He asks Harold: "Did you run into anybody else on your way up?"

Harold: "Only the copper, here."

The lights go on.

They are standing in the passageway outside of Dancer's apartment. As they start toward the front of the building, out of the restaurant comes one of Abrams's men with Polly, Lum Kee, and Caspar, and behind them another detective, dragging a Chinese waiter.

Abrams asks in a complaining voice: "Well, now what have you been letting them do?"

One of the detectives, indicating the waiter, says: "Dancer had this monkey pull the switch and beat it out a window. Butch is hunting for him now."

Abrams asks: "And what was that shooting?"

The other detective says sheepishly: "I guess it was me, I thought there was somebody running at me but I guess it was only me in the mirror."

Abrams says wearily: "All right—but this time take them down to the Hall like I told you."

David has taken Nick a little aside and is asking: "Should I tell him about Selma and the gun?"

Nick: "It depends on whether you think she did it."

David: "Of course not—do you?"

Nick: "No. Then the only thing to do is to tell him everything."

At this point, Abrams, returning from seeing his men off, says: "I asked you people not to go off whispering in corners all the time."

David: "Lieutenant Abrams, I've something to tell you. I happened—"

Abrams interrupts him: "All right—but we're all going down to the Hall where we can talk in peace. I don't like the high jinks that come off here."

Nora yawns.

Abrams: "Sorry, Mrs. Charles. I won't keep you any longer than I have to but we've got to do things regular."

*   *   *

A CHEAP HOTEL ROOM

Phil is sitting at a table playing solitaire with a gun on the table. He is smoking nervously and there is a pile of cigarette butts on a saucer near him. Presently there is a knock on the door. He picks up the gun and stares at the door with frightened eyes but doesn't answer. The knock is repeated, louder. After a little pause, Dancer's voice comes through, saying: "This is Dancer—will you open the door or will I kick it in?"

Slowly, as if afraid to open the door and afraid not to, Phil gets up and, holding the gun behind him, goes to the door and unlocks it. Dancer pushes the door open violently, knocking Phil back against the wall, then kicks the door shut; and standing close to Phil, says with threatening mildness: "What did I tell you about trying to cut yourself in on somebody else's game?"

OUTSIDE THE HALL OF JUSTICE—BROAD DAYLIGHT

Harold is asleep in Nick's car. Nick, Nora, and Abrams come out of the building surrounded by a flock of reporters.

Abrams is saying to the reporters: "Lay off us. I told you anything you get, you'll have to get from the D.A." He then says to Nick and Nora: "I could use a lot of breakfast. How about you folks?"

Nick looks at his watch and says: "I could use a lot of sleep."

Nora is too sleepy to say anything.

Abrams insists: "Yeh, but you got to eat anyhow, don't you, and there's a pretty good place not far from here."

Nick asks: "You mean you want to ask some more questions?"

Abrams: "No, not exactly, but there are a couple of points."

Nick: "We'll drop you wherever you're going and you can ask them on the way—but if you get wrong answers it's because I'm talking in my sleep."

As they are about to get into Nick's car, a taxi-cab drives up and Dancer gets out. Abrams goes over and grabs him by the shoulder, asking: "Where have you been?"

Dancer: "Hiding—where'd you think I've been? The lights go out and somebody starts shooting—I haven't even got a gun—I don't know whether somebody's trying to get me or if I'm being framed by you people, or what—so I did the only smart thing I could think of and played the duck and waited for daylight so I can at least see who's shooting at me."

Abrams turns to Nick and Nora and says: "Phooey! I won't be more than a minute. I'm going to turn him over to the boys. I'm afraid to trust myself with him this morning—I'm liable to slap him around too much." He and Dancer go back into the Hall of Justice.

Abrams returns almost immediately, gets into the car with Nick and Nora complaining: "What stories these guys think up." They drive off.

INTERIOR NICK'S CAR

Nick, Nora, and Abrams are sitting together. Nora is nodding sleepily, her head keeps bobbing in front of Nick, interfering with his vision. Whenever Nick turns to speak to Abrams, her head falls back, concealing him.

Abrams: "Sure I believe David Graham—I guess, but how do I know he ought to have believed Mrs. Landis? Well, I'm going to talk to her today if I have to lock up that lame 'nut' doctor while I do it. On the level, Mr. Charles, what's she doing with him around if she isn't at least a little bit punchy?"

Nick: "I don't think she is—just very nervous. You know how idle wives get—look at Mrs. Charles, for instance."

Abrams looks at Nora, who by this time is sound asleep, her chin resting on her chest.

Nick goes on: "And then, living with Robert wasn't doing her any good."

Abrams: "You honestly don't think she did it?"
Nick: "No."
Abrams: "She had the best reason. Graham had paid him to go away and he was going away, so *he* didn't have much reason—Dancer and the Chinaman and the Byrnes gal were taking him all right, but killing him

made it tough for them on the check. Besides, why didn't they grab the bonds and that jewelry of his wife's that he had on him? And that goes for the Byrnes gal even if she was double-crossing the others."

Nick asks: "How about Phil—her brother?"

Abrams: "There's no telling exactly until we get hold of him, but he figures to be out for the dough, too—so why don't he grab the bonds? He don't sound to me like a lad who would kill somebody just because he was running off with his sister."

Nick: "Lots of stickups go wrong—perhaps he had to leave before he could get the stuff."

Abrams: "You mean on account of Mrs. Landis running around the corner with a gun in her hand like she said she did? If he saw her, why didn't she see him, and she didn't say anything about that, did she?"

Nick: "Back in the office, you said Landis and Pedro were killed with bullets from the same gun. She doesn't fit in very well with Pedro's killing; but Polly lived in his house, which ties his killing up at least a little with her and the others."

Abrams: "That's right enough and I guess there's not much doubt that he was killed because he was on his way to tell you something. It's a fair bet that that something he was going to tell you had to do with Robert Landis, but there's something funny about that house that I want to show you. Maybe, if you've got a few minutes—"

Nick: "You don't mean the goats in the hallway?"

Abrams, surprised: "What goats?"

Nick: "Never mind—but Mr. and Mrs. Charles aren't going anywhere but home—to sleep. Think you'll be able to fish Mrs. Landis's gun up from where David threw it?"

Abrams: "I guess so. Anyway, the boys are down there working now." He pauses. "And when we get that, then we'll know. It will only take a few minutes to go over to that apartment house."

Nick: "Call me later. We've been on a train for three days and look what kind of a night we've had."

Abrams: "All right—I could use a little sleep myself but I've got to talk to Mrs. Landis and got to stop at the bank and see about that check."

Harold pulls over to the curb and Abrams gets out. Nora almost falls out after him as he withdraws his support. Abrams helps Nick put her back on the seat and, placing her head on his shoulder, Nick nods goodbye to Abrams, who waves to him as they drive off.

NICK AND NORA IN THEIR CAR GOING HOME

She is sleeping on his shoulder. With his free hand he unties his necktie and takes off his collar. When he twists around a little to unbutton his shirt in back, Nora wakes up and asks:

Nora: "What are you doing?"

Nick: "I'm getting as few clothes as possible between me and bed."

Nora: "That's cheating." She begins to loosen her clothes. They arrive at the house. As they go up the front steps, Nora: "Last one in bed is a sissy!" They run into the house pulling off clothes.

From the living room to meet them come Asta and the reporters that they left at the Hall of Justice, the reporters asking questions: "Do the police suspect Mrs. Landis?" "What connections did Pedro Dominges have with the Landis killing?" etc., etc.

Nick insists he knows nothing about it and has nothing to say as they go back into the living room, winding up with:

"I'm going to give you boys one drink apiece and then put you out."

One of the reporters asks: "Well, answer another question for us and we won't print it if you don't want us to. Is it true that you actually didn't retire as a detective but are working undercover?"

Nick, starting to pour drinks: "No, it's not true, but don't print it, because I don't want my wife's relatives to know I'm living on her money."

A stone with a piece of paper wrapped around it crashes through the glass of the window and knocks the bottle out of his hand. Asta joyfully grabs the stone and runs under a sofa with it, and starts to chew the paper off while Nick and the reporters scramble after him. By the time Nick recovers the stone with the paper, the note has been pretty well chewed up. He spreads it out, glances at it, and puts it in his pocket before the reporters, who are crowding around him, can read it.

Nick: "Silly little woman. I told her to stop writing me."

The reporters, failing to get anything else out of Nick, rush out to see if they can find out who threw the stone. Nick smoothes the note out and he and Nora, patching it as well as they can where Asta's teeth have torn it, read it. It is crudely printed:

> MR. CHARLS PHIL BYRNES ALIAS RALPH WEST
>
> IS A EX CON AND WAS MARRIED TO POLLY IN
>
> TOPEKER THREE YERS AGO. HE LIVES AT THE MIL

The rest of the note has been chewed off by Asta.

Nick, indifferently: "Well, what are we supposed to do, send them an anniversary present?"

Nora: "Nick, phone Lieutenant Abrams!"

Nick: "And have him up here to keep us awake some more?"

Nora insists: "Phone him, Nick. Don't you see, if Phil was her husband . . ."

Nick grumbles: "I guess you're right," and goes out of the room.

Nora plays with Asta for a minute or two and then goes to the door of the next room, where the phone is. Not seeing Nick, she calls him. There is no answer. After a little hesitancy, she goes up to the bedroom. Nick, in pajamas, is asleep. On her pillow is a sign: SISSY.

AUNT KATHERINE AT TELEPHONE AT HER HOME

Dr. Kammer is sitting in a chair nearby. She calls a number and asks: "Mr. Moody. This is Miss Forrest calling."

STRING OF SHORT SHOTS

Printing press running off extras with enormous headlines about "MEMBER OF PROMINENT FAMILY KILLED."

Editorial Room of newspaper office—men being assigned to cover this story.

Then up to Publisher's Office, where Peter Moody, a very dignified old man with a grave and courteous manner, is picking up the phone, saying: "Yes, Katherine, how are you? I'm awfully sorry to hear about Robert's death."

Aunt Katherine: "Thank you, Peter. It's terrible and that's what I called you about. The police, it seems, are trying to make a great deal of mystery out of what must have been—it couldn't have been anything else—simply an attempted holdup. I hope I can count on you to do your best to give the whole terrible affair no more publicity than is absolutely necessary."

Peter Moody: "Of course, of course, Katherine. But you must understand that if the police make it news we must print it."

Aunt Katherine: "I understand, but you will handle it as quietly as possible?"

Moody: "Certainly, I can promise you that. And will you please convey my sympathy to poor Selma."

Aunt Katherine: "Thank you, Peter."

As Peter Moody puts down the phone, a man comes into the office bringing an early copy of the extra that had been run off with the enormous headlines seen in the previous shot.

Moody looks at it and nods with approval, saying: "Very good."

Aunt Katherine phones her brother, the General, who is having his whiskers trimmed by a valet almost as old as he is. The valet hands him the phone, saying: "Miss Forrest, sir."

The General hems and haws between his words a good deal: "It's terrible, Katherine—I just heard—I'm on my way over."

Aunt Katherine: "Yes, terrible, Thomas, and I want to see you—but first will you see if you can get in touch with the mayor?"

General: "The mayor?" He clears his throat some more.

Aunt Katherine: "Yes. I'm sure poor Robert was killed by a robber but the police seem determined to make as big a mystery out of it with as much resultant notoriety for all of us as possible. I wish you would ask him to do what he can."

General: "Certainly, my dear," clearing his throat again, "I shall look after it immediately."

As Katherine hangs up, he gives the valet the phone, saying: "Get me the mayor" in the tone one says: "Get me the newspaper."

As Aunt Katherine turns from the phone toward Dr. Kammer, the butler appears at the door to announce Lieutenant Abrams.

Several hours later the General arrives at Nick's house. He hands his hat to the Butler, who opens the door and says: "Take me to Mr. Charles immediately."

Butler: "But he's still asleep, sir."

The General snorts, saying: "Yes, yes, so you said when Miss Forrest phoned. Devilish inconsiderate of all of you."

The Butler says apologetically: "But we never disturb him when he's asleep, sir."

The General snorts some more: "You said that over the phone, too. Now stop this silly nonsense and take me to him."

The butler, overawed by the General, takes him up to Nick and Nora's room. They are sleeping soundly. The General prods one of Nora's shoulders with his fingers and says: "Here, here, wake up."

Nora stirs a little and mumbles something but doesn't open her eyes.

The General prods her again, saying: "Come—this is no time to be sleeping. Devilish inconsiderate of all of you."

This time Nora opens her eyes and stares up at him in amazement.

General: "Wake up your young man, my dear. Why doesn't the fellow sleep at night?"

Nora asks: "But what's the matter, Uncle Thomas?"

General: "Matter? We've been trying to get you for hours. Wake him up."

Nora shakes Nick, who says without opening his eyes: "Go away, Porter, I told you not to call me till Sacramento."

Nora: "Wake up, Nick, Uncle Thomas wants to talk to you."

Nick: "Tell the white-whiskered old fossil to do his snoring in somebody else's ear—I'm busy."

Nora: "But Nick, he's here, standing beside you."

Nick sits up blinking and says: "Why, Uncle Thomas, how nice of you to drop in on us like this."

General: "Come—enough of this nonsense. Selma has been arrested and you lie here snoring."

Nora looks horrified.

The General snorts some more: "The mayor did nothing to stop it—the bounder."

Nick: "Maybe he didn't know."

The General asks: "Didn't know what?"

Nick: "That I was snoring."

General: "Come, get up. You know about these things—Katherine is counting on you."

Nick, putting on his robe and slippers, says: "You don't need me now, you need a lawyer."

The General says contemptuously: "A lawyer—old Witherington is running around in circles, completely at sea; no ability at all—that fellow."

Nick: "Then why don't you get another lawyer?"

The General draws himself up: "Witherington has been our family attorney for years."

Nick: "Well, what do you expect me to do?"

General: "To make the police stop being so silly—to get Selma out of there right away—to put an end to all this beastly notoriety."

Nick asks: "Is that all?"

General: "Come—we're wasting time—get into your clothes."

In a barely furnished office in the Hall of Justice, Nick is talking to Abrams.

Abrams: "I know how you feel about it, Mr. Charles. I guess I'd feel the same way if it were one of my family; but what can we do? Everything points to her."

Nick asks: "You mean you found out some things I don't know about?"

Abrams: "Well, not much maybe, but there's that check thing."

Nick asks: "What check thing?"

Abrams: "Maybe the district attorney isn't going to like this much, but I'll tell you: I went down to Landis's bank and that $10,000 check he gave the girl is perfectly okay. It was okay because his wife had put $10,000 in there for him just the day before."

Nick looks surprised. He asks: "Are you sure?"

Abrams: "Sure, I'm sure. I saw it myself."

Nick: "Did you ask her about it?"

Abrams replies wearily: "Yes, and there's some kind of hanky-panky there, too, but I can't figure out just what it is. She started to say she didn't and then the old lady, Miss Katherine"—he breaks off to add—"that one's a holy terror—"

Nick: "Make two copies of that."

Abrams: "—she spoke up and said: 'You did, Selma, you told me so yourself,' and then Mrs. Landis said yes, she did."

Nick asks: "So where does that fit in?"

Abrams: "So maybe she gave it to him and found out he was passing it on to the girl—how do I know? Every time I tried to pin her down she gets hysterical."

Nick asks: "Find out anything else at the bank?"

Abrams: "No. He had given the Byrnes gal a check for $100 and one for $75 like she told us." He takes the checks out of a desk drawer saying: "Here, if you want to see them."

Nick looks at them and asks: "Have you got the $10,000 check he gave her?"

Abrams: "Yes." He gives it to him.

Nick stands up, tilting back a light-shade, holds one of the small checks with the $10,000 check over it up against the light and tries the big check with the other small one. Abrams stands up to look over his shoulder. Nick fiddles with the checks until the signature of the top one is exactly over the bottom one.

Abrams exclaims: "A forgery!"

Nick nods, saying: "Yes, a tracing. Nobody ever writes *that* much the same twice."

Abrams picks up the telephone and says: "Give me Joe," then says: "Joe, go out and pick up that Polly Byrnes for me." When he puts down the phone, Nick asks: "You aren't holding any of them?"

Abrams shakes his head and says: "No. The guns we got from the Chinaman and Dancer are .38s all right like he was killed with, but the experts say they are not the guns that did it. I'm still not sure this forgery is going to help Mrs. Landis much. I already told you I knew there was some hanky-panky about those checks."

Nick asks: "You haven't found her gun yet?"

Abrams: "I got a couple of men in diving suits working over the bottom down around where David Graham threw it. But it was night, you know, and we can't be too sure of the exact spot."

Nick: "And you think you are going to convict her if you don't find the gun?"

Abrams: "Maybe I do and maybe I don't. It's what the district attorney thinks."

Nick: "Does he think she killed Pedro Dominges?"

Abrams: "That's not funny, Mr. Charles. Her alibi covering that time is just no good at all. She claims a cigarette case had been mailed to her from the Li-Chee and she sent it back saying it wasn't hers; but she thinks it belongs to some woman who was there with Robert, so that afternoon when she's kind of nuts over him not being home for a couple of days, she goes down there to see if she can find out about him. Of course that joint don't open till evening and so she didn't see anybody that could tell us she was there. She says she went back home again and that just about covers the time that Dominges was being killed. On the level, Mr. Charles, we had nobody else but her that we could hold."

Nick: "Found your Selma Young yet?"

Abrams: "No."

Nick: "How about Phil?"

Abrams: "Sure, maybe, if we can find him."

Nick takes out the note that was thrown through the window, gives it to Abrams.

Abrams reads it carefully, then asks: "And where did this come from?"

Nick: "Somebody wrapped it around a dornick and heaved it through my window."

Abrams asks: "Where's the rest of it?"

Nick: "Somewhere in my dog's intestines."

Abrams reads slowly: "—lives at the Mil—"

Nick pushes the telephone book over to him and says: "Maybe that won't be so tough. Polly said he lived in a hotel on Turk Street."

Abrams: "That's right," and opens the telephone book to the hotel classification and runs his finger down the Mi's, finally coming to the Miltern Hotel, _____ Turk Street.

Abrams: "That could be it—want to give it a try with me?"

Nick: "Right!" They get up. As they go toward the door, Nick says: "You noticed that whoever wrote the note misspelled easy words like my name and years, but did all right with 'alias' and 'married'?"

Abrams: "Yeah, I noticed."

EXTERIOR OF MILTERN HOTEL

A small, shabby, dirty joint with a door between two stores, and stairs leading up to an office on the second floor. Abrams, Nick, and two other detectives get out of a car, which draws up with no sound of sirens. One of the men remains at the outer door. Nick, Abrams, and the other detective start up the stairs. They go up to a small and dark office. Nobody is there. Abrams knocks on the battered counter. After a little while, a man in dirty shirt sleeves appears.

Abrams: "Is Mr. Phil Byrnes in?"

The Man says: "We ain't got no Mr. Byrnes—not even a Mrs. Byrnes."

Abrams: "Have you got a Ralph West?"

The Man: "Yep."

Abrams: "Is he in?"

The Man: "I don't know—room 212—next floor."

Abrams says to the detective with him: "Get on the back stairs."

Abrams and Nick walk up the front stairs and down a dark hall until they find 212. Abrams knocks on the door—there is no answer. He knocks again, saying in what he tries to make a youthful voice: "Telegram for Mr. West." There is still no answer. He looks at Nick. Nick reaches past him and turns the knob, pushing the door open.

Nick: "After you, my dear lieutenant."

Sprawled on his back across the bed, very obviously dead, is Phil, fully dressed as when we last saw him.

Nick points to something on the floor between them and the bed. It is a pair of spectacles, the frame bent, the glass ground almost to a powder. Abrams nods and comes into the room, stepping over the glasses, and leans over Phil.

Abrams: "Dead, all right—strangled and he was beaten up some before the strangling set in." He looks down at one of Phil's hands, then picks it up and takes half a dozen hairs from it. Turning to show them to Nick, he says: "Somebody's hair in his hand."

Nick looks at the hairs, then at the broken glasses on the floor. He says nothing. It is obvious he is trying to figure something out.

Abrams goes out saying: "Wait a minute—I'll have one of the boys phone and then we'll give the room a good casing."

Nick moves around the room looking at things, opening and shutting drawers and looking into a closet, but apparently not finding anything of interest until he sees an automatic on the floor under one corner of the bed. He bends down to look at it but doesn't touch it.

While Nick is looking at the gun, Abrams returns to the room.

Nick: "Here's another .38 for your experts to match up."

Abrams: "Hmm, what do you think?"

Nick: "I don't think—I used to be a detective myself."

Abrams: "Nobody downstairs seems to know about any visitors, but I guess the kind he had wouldn't have gone to the trouble of knocking on the counter like we did."

He leans over Phil and begins to go through his pockets.

Abrams straightens up and says: "I guess the heater's his. He's wearing an empty shoulder holster." He holds up a flat key and adds: "And I guess this is the key to the Byrnes gal's apartment. It's got her number stamped on it."

Nick: "Another good guess would be that Selma Landis didn't do this."

Abrams: "Fair enough, but he wasn't killed the way the other ones were, either."

Policemen enter, some in plain clothes, some in uniform, and Abrams starts to give them instructions about searching the room, looking for fingerprints, questioning the occupants of adjoining rooms, etc., etc.

Nick: "And I think you ought to have your laboratory look at that hair and the cheaters," indicating the broken glasses.

Abrams: "Okay." He looks curiously at Nick.

Nick: "And the sooner the better."

Abrams, again: "Okay." He addresses one of the men standing and listening to them. "Do it." He hands him the hair. Then turning back to Nick, says: "Anything particular on your mind?"

Nick: "Ought to be on yours, with three murders tied together in just about twenty-four hours. Now that we've been told he's her husband and he's dead, don't you think we ought to see Polly as soon as possible?"

Abrams says: "There's something in that," and tells one of his men, "Don't let these lugs dog it while I'm gone." He and Nick go downstairs. In the office he uses the telephone. When he's through, he grumbles: "They haven't picked her up yet." He scratches his chin, then says: "I've got a man waiting up in her apartment. Want to take a run up there? I told you there's something funny about the place that I'd like you to see."

Nick: "All right. Don't you think now we've got something more to talk about to Dancer?"

Abrams says in a hurt tone: "I think of things sometimes. I told them to pick up him and the Chinaman both."

They go downstairs to the street.

*　*　*

At Aunt Katherine's, all the Forrests except Selma are assembled. They are very excited and keep moving around so that Asta, who obviously doesn't like any of them, has a great deal of difficulty keeping out of their way. Nora and Dr. Kammer are also there.

The General is standing, glaring down at Nora, and asking indignantly: "Do you mean to say that this—ah—husband of yours actually advised David to tell the police about Selma and the pistol?"

Nora says defiantly: "Yes."

The General starts to walk up and down the floor, sending Asta into hiding again, and rumpling his whiskers and growling: "Why, the fellow's a scoundrel—an out and out scoundrel."

Nora: "Nick's not—he knows what he's doing."

The General snorts and says angrily: "Nonsense—nobody knows what they're doing. The whole country is full of incompetents and scoundrels nowadays."

Aunt Hattie nudges Aunt Lucy and asks: "What is Thomas saying now—he mutters so."

Aunt Lucy, who has been sniffling into her handkerchief, sobs: "Poor Selma. This is a terrible thing to happen to me—only a week after my eighty-third birthday."

Nora jumps up and says: "Nick's not incompetent and he's not a scoundrel. You're all acting as if you thought Selma really killed Robert."

Aunt Katherine and Dr. Kammer exchange significant glances. The General clears his throat and says: "It's not a case of anybody killing anybody—it's a case of his being so devilish inconsiderate of the family. Has the fellow no feelings?"

William, who is considered not too bright by the family, runs his finger inside his too-tight collar and asks: "Does anyone know if the police have considered the theory that Robert might have committed suicide?"

Aunt Katherine snaps at him: "That will do, William," while the rest of them glare at him.

Burton, his tic working overtime, asks: "Well, where is this Nicholas? Why isn't he here to explain himself?"

Nora: "Because he's out trying to clear Selma while you all sit around here and criticize him."

The General says: "I'd never have asked him if I'd known what the fellow'd been up to."

Nora rises with great dignity and calls Asta. She faces the family and says: "I'm sure he doesn't care what any of you think. He's not doing it for you—he's doing it for Selma. Goodbye."

What would otherwise have been a dignified exit is spoiled by her bumping into the antique butler as she goes through the door. After the butler has gotten his breath, he says: "Mr. Graham on the phone for you, Mrs. Charles."

She goes to the phone and says: "Hello, David."

David, at the other end of wire, asks excitedly: "Where is Nick? I tried your house and the detective bureau but he wasn't there. Lieutenant Abrams wasn't in either."

Nora: "They're probably out together. Oh, Lieutenant Abrams said something about wanting Nick to go over to that apartment house with him. Maybe they're there. What is it, David?"

David: "Something's happened—I've got to see Nick. What apartment house?"

Nora: "I'm leaving here now. I'll meet you and take you there. Where are you?"

David: "I'm in a drugstore at Mason and Bush Streets."

Nora: "Wait for me—I'll be right over."

They hang up and she, after making a face at the direction of the room where she left the family, goes out and gets into her car.

Abrams and Nick arrive at the building where Polly has an apartment. It is a large, shabby building, set at the foot of Telegraph Hill. Across the street from it the hill rises steep and unpaved, with winding, wooden steps leading up between scattered frame houses. The end of the street, even with the house's left-hand wall, is closed by a high board fence. From the fence, as from the house wall, the ground falls perpendicularly fifty or sixty feet to a rock-strewn vacant lot covering several blocks. In the street and on the hill above, goats are roaming. As they approach the door a goat runs out and dodges past them and goes to join the others. The front door is open. Abrams and Nick go in. Abrams knocks on a door on the left side of the corridor. The door is opened by a plain-clothesman, who says: "Nary hide or hair of her yet."

A policeman in uniform and another in plain clothes are bent over a table doing a crossword puzzle together. They rise hastily as Abrams comes in but he pays no attention to them.

Abrams, as they go in: "This is Polly's apartment. There's nothing much here except you'll notice the rug's new."

Nick looks at the rug and says: "Oh, I saw a new one once in a store window."

Abrams, patiently: "All right, but wait—maybe it don't mean anything, maybe it does."

Nick asks: "What do you think it means?"

Abrams sighs and says: "If I knew, do you think I'd be wasting your time dragging you up here? We'll go back here, now." He leads the way out of Polly's apartment down the hall to an apartment on the same floor in the rear, unlocking it with a key from his pocket, saying as he opens the door: "This is the fellow's that was killed—that Pedro Dominges."

Nick says quickly: "Another new rug—I said it first."

Abrams, pointing to the other end of the living room where there is a rug rolled up and lying against the wall: "There's another one."

Nick asks: "What is this rug racket? Are we hunting for an Armenian?"

Abrams: "Maybe you're right in kidding me—maybe none of this means anything, but just the same, he brought twelve rugs only a couple of days ago and that's just how many apartments he's got in the place." He walks over to the table and says: "Here's the bill. And the one apartment that didn't get a rug was rented only last week to somebody named Anderson. No front name—no Mr. or Miss or Mrs. according to his books here. I want to show you that next."

Nick asks: "What have you found out about him?"

Abrams: "Nothing. This guy Dominges ran this place by himself. We haven't found anybody who ever saw this Anderson."

There is a terrific uproar from the corridor. They go to the door to see Asta, a goat, and Nora (at the other end of Asta's leash) all tangled up together, while David is trying to untangle them. When the goat has finally been chased out, they all return to Pedro's apartment.

As Nick helps Nora brush off her clothes, she says: "Why, that drunken man was right—there *are* goats in the hall."

Nick: "You can always trust my friends, drunk or sober. Is that what you came down here to find out?"

Nora: "No. David has something to show you."

David takes from his pocket a sheet of paper, on which in the same crude printing as on Nick's note is:

> IF YOU WANT TO SAFE THAT DISSY
> DAME OF YOURN YOU BETER MAKE
> DANCER TELL HOW HE FOWND OUT
> LAST NIGHT PHIL BYRNES WAS
> POLLY'S HUSBIND
> A FRIEND

After they read it, Abrams asks: "How'd it come to you?"

David: "It was under my door when I woke up today."

Nick: "The same half-smart attempt at illiteracy as the one I got."

Abrams: "Yeah—but that don't have to mean that what it says is wrong. Running out yours got us something, so why don't we run out this?"

Nick: "We'll have to wait until you pick up your people. Now how about this Anderson?"

Abrams: "To tell you the truth, Mr. Charles, I don't believe there ever was any Anderson, but you can—"

Nick: "Tut-tut—don't be so skeptical; you read his fairy tales when you were a child."

Abrams, patiently: "Okay, kid me—but what I mean is—I don't believe *this* Anderson ever was and I'll show you why when we get upstairs. As a matter of fact I don't believe anybody took that apartment."

Nora: "I took that."

They look at her in surprise. She has gotten up from the chair and has gone over to an enlarged snapshot hanging on the wall.

Abrams: "You did what, Mrs. Charles?"

Nora: "I took that picture. They're the servants we had at Ross." She points them out: "There's Pedro, Elle, Ann, etc."

Pedro looks much as he did before except that he is six years younger, and his mustache, while not small, is not definitely long nor is it as white as it was when we saw him.

They all get up to look.

Nick asks: "You're sure that place you had wasn't on Coney Island?" He turns to Abrams and says: "I apologize for the domestic comedy. Let's go up and look at the apartment that you say wasn't rented by a fellow whose name wasn't Anderson."

Abrams leads the way up to the next floor, unlocks the door, leading them into the apartment over Polly's, saying to Nick: "See the rug—" The rug is stained and very worn.

Nick: "I get it—it's *not* a new rug."

Abrams: "Yeah, that's one of the things I meant. I've got something else to show you—" He points to a corner of the room where there is a pile of old and battered iron pipe. "But the chief things that we found was that Pedro had the lock changed on the door only yesterday and all the fingerprints we found in here are his."

Nick walks to a window, raises it, and looks down the side of the cliff. He says: "A nice drop from here. Would I be guessing wrong if I said that this apartment was right over Polly's?"

Abrams: "No, I guess not."

Nick asks: "Well?"

Abrams: "I don't know, Mr. Charles, for a fact, but not putting a new rug in and only his fingerprints here makes it look to me like he was kind of using the place and not figuring on renting it."

Nick asks: "And you think he changed the lock so he couldn't get in again to keep tenants out?"

Abrams, patiently, as usual, says: "I told you there was something funny here. I told you I didn't know what it was all about."

Nick: "Pedro was killed first. What are you picking on him for?"

Abrams: "Do I know from nothing? If you can think of anything, play your string out."

Nick: "No hard feelings. Don't take me too seriously. Suppose you were going to put a rug down, what would you do first?"

Abrams: "I don't know—I guess I'd get somebody to lug it upstairs."

Nick: "Swell. And then what?"

Abrams: "Then you start at one end of the room and roll it across the floor."

Nick asks: "On top of this one?"

Abrams scratches his head and says: "No, I guess not."

Nick: "All right—let's take this one up first, then."

Abrams: "Okay. You take that corner and I'll take this one."

Nick: "Who, me? Haven't you got hired men downstairs?"

Abrams. "Sure." He goes outside the door and yells: "Hey, Francis —you and that other cutie who was trying to find a three-letter word for ape, come up here."

Nora in a hoarse whisper asks: "What is it, Nick?"

Nick: "Do I know?" Men are dying all around and you ask me riddles."

There is a clumping on the stairs and the plainclothesman and the uniformed policeman who were working on the crossword puzzle come in.

Abrams says to them: "You boys roll this three-letter word meaning rug down to the other end of a four-letter word meaning room."

They say "sure" very eagerly, push furniture out of the way, and start to roll the rug up. They roll it halfway when Nick says:

"Maybe that'll do for the time." He walks over to a spot they have uncovered where six floor boards have been cut across in two places to make about a square foot. "Let's look at this."

Abrams, followed by his two men, goes to the spot Nick has indicated. Abrams opens a pocketknife, puts the blade in, and the sawed boards come up in a section, leaving a foot-square hole. He looks down, then puts his hand in and brings up a pair of flat ear pieces on a steel band such as telephone operators wear, attached to a wire running down into the hole.

Nick: "I suppose we know what this is. Send one of the boys downstairs to recite the alphabet in Polly's place."

Abrams jerks a thumb at the plainclothesman and says: "Go ahead, Francis."

Francis goes out. Presently, from down below through the ear pieces comes Francis's voice: "A,B,C,D,E—" A moment of hesitation, then: "A,B,C,D—"

Nick: "Okay for sound. It was for listening in, all right."

Abrams: "Yeh, that's that. What do you guess this Pedro was up to?"

[Note: all thru this scene, Asta shows that he is very fond of David, ignoring both Nick and Nora in favor of him.]

Nick: "Well, there's still this junk to figure—" He turns toward the pile of iron pipe in the corner. Asta is busy chewing it. "Get away from the evidence, Asta."

Abrams: "He won't be hurting it much—there was only Pedro's fingerprints on it. What do you guess it was for? I couldn't be thinking anybody would pipe gas through it."

Nick: "Why not? With a layout like this you can pipe gas in several directions at once." He sits down on the floor and begins to screw sections of the pipe together.

[This is actually a ladder, but he keeps the rungs sticking out in all directions and keeps it from being recognizable until suddenly when he puts the last piece on and turns it around.]

Nick, holding the finished ladder up, says: "Fifty will get you two-fifty that it will just about reach to Polly's window below, with this piece left over—" he picks up an extra part from the floor "for good measure when he got there."

He takes the ladder to window, lowers it, and hangs it on the sill. It reaches exactly to the sill of Polly's apartment below.

Abrams: "What do you guess he wanted to do that for?"

Francis sticks his head in the door and says: "We got Byrnes. Do you want her up? And we got Dancer and Lum Kee, too."

Abrams looks at Nick and asks: "Will they clutter it up for you? Do you think you got as much out of this place as you want?"

Nick: "The more the merrier. Perhaps not as much as I want, but as much as I think I'm going to get."

Nick asks Abrams: "What kind of clothes did you find in the place?"

Abrams: "None—not a stitch. Nothing to show anybody ever lived here. That's why I told you I don't believe anybody ever did."

Nick asks: "Where does that fit in? Do you think Pedro was using the place himself—spying on the people downstairs? He's killed first and, half a day later, Robert Landis, who visits downstairs, is killed and the next day, the brother or husband or something of the gal he visits is killed. How are you going to blame all that on Pedro?"

Abrams, wearily: "Mr. Charles, how many times have I told you there was something funny here I don't understand; and some hanky-pank about the checks I don't understand? Did I ever pretend I knew what all this led to?"

Nick: "Oh, yes—about the checks. We've got to ask these people about them when they come upstairs and maybe they won't want to say right out. What would be wrong with getting Mrs. Landis over so we'd have her here to chuck at them if they think we're fooling?"

Abrams: "I don't know, the D.A.'s kind of—"

Nick: "What—with a police escort?"

Abrams: "Okay—I'll send for her."

Nick: "God will reward you."

Three policemen, one in uniform, bring in Polly, Dancer, and Lum Kee.

Abrams: "Francis, phone the Hall and tell them to bring up Mrs. Landis."

Francis goes to the phone.

Nick, aside to Abrams: "Maybe they don't know. Throw it hard enough to bounce."

Abrams says to Nick: "Okay." Turns to Polly: "Your husband was killed this afternoon. What do you know about it?"

Polly: "I—what?"

Abrams, to Dancer: "Her husband was killed this afternoon."

Dancer: "Her what?"

Abrams: "Cut it out! We're not playing charades."

They look at him blankly.

Abrams, counting out syllables on his fingers, says: "Pol-ly had a hus-band named Phil e-ven if he was sup-posed to be her bro-ther and he was found dead on Turk Street this af-ter-noon."

Polly and Dancer turn to face each other at the same moment, exclaiming simultaneously: "You—!!!" and then breaking off as they realize each is saying the same thing.

Abrams: "*You—you*—you what?"

Neither of them says anything.

Nick says to Abrams: "Simple enough—she started to accuse *him* of killing Phil because he found out he was her husband and he started to accuse *her* of double-crossing him by not telling him Phil was her husband."

Abrams says to Polly: "He was your husband, wasn't he? Married three years ago in Topeka?"

She nods, glancing sidewise at Dancer. "But I didn't want to have any more to do with him and so when he showed up last week I didn't say anything about it."

Abrams: "What did he go to the pen for?"

Polly: "Blackmail."

Abrams: "And what did he have on you that he was hanging around shaking you down for?"

Polly, hesitantly: "Well, he knew about me and Robert and I didn't want Robert to find out I was married and then I was kind of sorry for Phil. He was broke and had come out of the pen with bad lungs."

Abrams: "And why did you keep it from Dancer?"

Polly: "It was nobody else's business and a girl in this racket gets along better without people knowing about things like that."

Abrams: "You didn't know Dancer found out about it, did you?"

Polly: "Not until—" and breaks off with a frightened look at Dancer.

Abrams: "Go ahead—not until what?"

Dancer: "I never found out about it up to now." Then to Polly: "I wish I had, baby."

Abrams says to Dancer: "Stick your mouth out of this until you get your invitation. You'll get it." Then to Polly: "And now you think he killed Phil because he found out?"

Polly stammers: "No—I don't—I—"

Abrams breaks in very sharply: "Isn't it the truth, sister, that you and this husband of yours were working together on Robert Landis and something went wrong and you had to kill him?"

Polly shakes her head and says: "No."

Abrams, paying no attention to her answer: "And then isn't it just as true that Dancer found out about it and killed Phil?"

Dancer interrupts again: "Listen, I never found out about it till I come to this room."

Abrams: "Whenever you found out about it, what do you think now—don't you think they were double-crossing you?"

Dancer shrugs and says: "Maybe I do, now, but I didn't know anything about it till you told me."

Abrams asks him: "Do you think Phil tried to stick Landis up and had to kill him?"

Dancer replies contemptuously: "I don't know what a punk like that would do."

Abrams's manner has become increasingly irritable through this scene so that when, as he starts to ask Dancer: "Now do you—" and Nick interrupts him by saying: "Let's go into the check business—" Abrams turns around and says, sharply for him: "Who's doing this?"

Nick says very mildly: "It's hardly ever been my party. Come on, Nora."

Abrams says very earnestly: "Aw listen, Mr. Charles, I'm not getting any rest out of this at all and I'm kind of jumpy. What were you going to say?"

Nick: "I thought I said it—about those forgeries?"

Dancer says to Nick: "I've put up with your gum-heeling for a day or two, but I got a business to run. I better be down there running it than barbering here with you. Why don't the two of us just go out in the hall and see who smacks who in the nose and call it square?"

Nick: "No, let's do it the hard way. The ten-grand check Landis is supposed to have given Polly is a forgery."

Dancer: "So what's it to me?"

Nick: "The signature was traced from one of the other checks he gave her."

Dancer: "I'm still asking you—what's that to me?"

Nick: "Maybe Polly can answer that." He asks her: "Did you do the tracing or did he?"

While Polly is hesitating, Dancer says very distinctly: "I told you before, I don't know anything about that check. Whatever was between Landis and Polly was between them."

Nick says to Polly: "You were right—they *are* letting you hold the bag." Before Polly can answer, Dancer, addressing Nick, but talking for Polly's benefit, asks: "What bag? This check you're talking about—has anybody tried to pass it yet? What kind of charge have you got against her until she does?"

Nick and Abrams look at each other and Abrams says: "Wise guy." Then to Polly: "Come on, answer that question now."

Polly says hesitantly: "Well, I don't know—I—" and breaks off, looking all the time at Dancer, hoping for a cue.

Dancer says nothing and gives Polly no sign.

Polly: "Honestly, Lieutenant Abrams, I don't think that check is a forgery."

Abrams asks: "Where did you get it?"

Polly: "Well, I—" and breaks off again.

Abrams: "What are you covering this lug up for, sister?" He takes the note David had given him out of his pocket and shows it to her, saying: "See, he had already found out Phil was your husband."

Polly reads the note and her eyes widen. She looks at Dancer.

Dancer: "If you're helping to frame me, Polly, okay; I'll have to figure out what I do about that. But if you haven't made a dicker for yourself with the police, I don't see where you'll be getting anywhere just running off at the head for the fun of it."

Abrams starts toward Dancer, saying angrily: "Listen, you—"

The door opens and Caspar comes in. He bows very formally to everybody in the room, then says to Dancer: "I just heard a moment ago." Then very pompously, to Abrams: "Lieutenant, I cannot permit you to—"

Abrams turns to Nick and groans: "Now look—we got this five-and-ten-cent-store Darrow with us again."

Caspar says to Nick: "Good evening, Mr. Charles."

Nick bows, buttoning up his coat and patting his pockets to see if he's lost anything.

Caspar goes over to Dancer, puts a hand on his shoulder, and says: "My dear boy—I'm entirely at your service."

Dancer shakes the hand off his shoulder and snarls: "You ought to be—for the dough you charge me."

Caspar tries to smile as if he thought Dancer were joking. He asks Lum Kee: "What are these policemen doing now?"

Lum Kee, bland as usual, says: "Trouble, trouble—they want to see us—we go—why not? They police, we innocent, you betcha."

Abrams growls: "Aw, cut it out. Hold your conferences on your own time. We've got work to do. Has anybody here ever been in this apartment before?"

Some of those there say "No," some shake their heads.

Abrams looks questioningly at Nick. Nick says: "Perhaps Polly could help us if we told her what it's all about."

Polly: "What?"

Nick: "You know this place is right over yours?"

Polly: "Yes."

Nick, indicating the ear pieces: "With that dingus you can hear a pin drop in your place." She stares at the ear pieces in surprise. Nick goes on. "And if you'll go to the window, you'll see a ladder running down to your window." She goes to the window, looks at the ladder, then turns back to Nick, still more bewildered. Nick picks up the extra piece of pipe and says: "And nobody's head would be helped much by being patted with this."

Polly: "But I don't understand—"

Nick, looking at Dancer and Lum Kee, says: "Is there anybody here that *does* understand?"

Dancer looks sullenly at him but doesn't say anything.

Lum Kee says cheerfully: "We run restaurant—you detective."

Nick, to Polly: "Even if you don't understand, who can you think of that would have this much interest in you?" hefting the pipe in his hand.

Polly: "Nobody."

Nick: "Phil had a key to your apartment. Has Dancer?"

Before she can reply, Dancer takes a key out of his pocket and tosses it on the floor, saying: "Yes. So what would I need that trick ladder for?"

Nick asks: "Has Lum Kee?"

Polly: "No. of course not."

Nick: "Who else?"

Polly: "Nobody."

Nick: "Did Robert have one?"

Polly: "No. What do you think I did, put them around under doors?"

A policeman opens the door and Selma comes in. She and Nora immediately run to each other, uttering exclamations of affection.

David exclaims: "Selma," and goes over to them asking, "are you all right, dear?"

She exclaims: "David!" and holding out her hands to him, she starts to ask him a question. "Did you—" and then breaks off, glancing nervously at Lieutenant Abrams. "Oh, it's been terrible," she tells Nora and David.

Nora: "I know, dear, but it'll soon be over. Nick will have everything cleared up in no time. He's wonderful."

Nick: "Nice of you to say so, darling." He goes over to greet Selma.

Selma: "Oh Nick, I'm so grateful to you. Have you really—?"

Nick: "Now don't start asking us questions. The game is for us to ask you. Have you ever seen any of these people before?" indicating in turn, Polly, Dancer, and Lum Kee.

To each Selma replies "No."

Nick asks: "Have you ever been in this building before?"

Selma: "No."

Nick: "Did you know that Robert and Miss Byrnes were friends?"

Selma: "No."

Nick: "All right. Now this next question you've answered before, but the police weren't altogether satisfied with the way you answered it. I want you to remember that Robert's dead, so whatever you say isn't going to hurt him though it may help us find his murderer and get you out of this mess."

Selma: "What is it, Nick?"

Nick: "That $10,000 check of yours that was deposited in Robert's account. Did you or didn't you write it?"

Selma hesitates, looks from Nick to Abrams then down to the floor, and in a very low voice, says: "I didn't."

Abrams, who has been a very interested listener up to this point, now takes his hat off and throws it angrily on the floor. But when he crosses to confront Selma, his voice and manner are more hurt than angry. He asks: "Why couldn't you have told us that before? Whatever got into you to—" He breaks off as her lips begin to tremble, and grabs a chair, saying: "Now, now, sit down, Mrs. Landis, be comfortable. One of you boys get Mrs. Landis a glass of water." Then again to her: "Now, now, maybe there's not a great deal of harm done anyhow." Then aside to Nick, as she sits down: "If this dame gets hysterical again I'll go nuts."

Selma: "Thank you. I'm quite all right."

Abrams mumbles in Nick's ear: "You ask her the rest. She always blows up on me."

Nick says to Selma: "Since you've gone this far, I think you'd better tell the police why you didn't tell them the truth before."

Selma: "I started to, but Aunt Katherine wouldn't let me."

Abrams growls: "That old battle-axe."

Nick asks: "Why wouldn't she?"

Selma: "She said there was enough scandal with Robert being killed that way, without this."

Nick: "Thanks. That's fine." Pats her on the shoulder, turns away.

Abrams: "Maybe that's fine for you, but it could stand a little more explaining for my part."

Nick: "The explaining room is out there," indicating the kitchen. "Shall we try it now?" He and Abrams go into the kitchen. Nick continues: "The gadget is that Aunt Katherine thought Robert forged the check and she was willing to let the $10,000 go to keep people from knowing there had been a forger in the family as well as a murdered man—" Then as an afterthought, he adds: "Especially since it was Selma's $10,000."

Abrams asks: "Had he ever done anything like that before?"

Nick, earnestly: "That boy had done everything."

Francis comes to the door and says: "Telephone for you," to Abrams.

Abrams goes out.

Nick spies a battered cocktail shaker on the shelf, and begins to look through the closets for something to put in it. The closets are absolutely bare. He disgustedly throws the cocktail shaker in the garbage can as Abrams comes back.

Abrams: "The laboratory says those red hairs were probably from a wig and that the broken specs were only windowglass. Were you kind of expecting something like that?"

Nick: "Kinda."

Abrams: "And the gun's not the one those people were killed with. Expect that?"

Nick: "Kinda."

Abrams: "But what's really good is, the boys picked up some pretty nice fingerprints of Dancer's in the joint. Let's go in and see how he likes that."

Nick: "All right, but mind if I get in a question first?"

Abrams: "Go ahead, help yourself."

They return to the room where the others are.

Nick asks Lum Kee: "Did you ever mail to Mrs. Landis a cigarette case that you thought she left in the restaurant about a week ago?"

Lum Kee: "Maybe yes, maybe no. All the time people leave things."

Nick to Dancer: "I know he didn't. You sent it to her pretending you thought it was hers and when she sent it back with a note saying it wasn't, you traced her signature on the bottom of a $10,000 check payable to Robert, and sent it over for deposit in his account because you knew the bank wouldn't question that and when they eventually found out it was a forgery, he'd be blamed for it because he'd done things like that before. Then you were all set to forge a check on his account for the same $10,000 while Polly kept him busy so that the bank couldn't reach him to ask him about it if they got suspicious. And so then if he's killed, who's going to be able to prove that he didn't forge his wife's name to the check to get money to give to this girl he was in love with?"

Dancer asks scornfully: "And then I suppose I knock him off and stir up all this fuss before I get the dough? What kind of a stumble-bum does that make me out to be?"

Nick: "I'll let you know in a little while. Take the witness, Lieutenant Abrams."

Abrams: "I'll tell you what kind of a stumble-bum you are. You're the kind that left fingerprints all over Phil Byrnes's joint when you killed him."

Caspar comes forward between Dancer and Abrams, saying: "Lieutenant Abrams, I cannot allow—"

Dancer takes him by the back of the neck and pushes him out of the way, snarling: "Shut up! Everything *you* say is used against *me*." Then to Abrams: "Yeah, I was at Phil's place last night and when I left he was on the floor with a split lip and a goog and a couple of dents in him here and there but he was just as alive as you are, if that means anything."

Abrams: "You mean you went up there when you had the switch pulled in your place?"

Dancer: "Yeah."

Abrams: "What for?"

Dancer looks thoughtful for a moment, then says: "Okay, I don't know what I'm letting myself in for, but I'm not going to let you hang any murder rap on me. This Robert was a sucker and Polly and I were taking him. Maybe it was some kind of check razzle-dazzle like he (jerking a thumb at Nick) said, maybe it wasn't. Even if it had been, what would be the sense of killing him? Nobody'd have believed him if he'd said he hadn't forged his wife's name. Maybe we even talked him into doing it; anyways, he's cooled before we get anything. This guy," jerking his thumb again at Nick, "says Phil followed Robert and Polly down the street. Knowing Phil, I figured he tried to stick Robert up that night and had to kill him. I don't like having a punk gum things up for me that way, so why shouldn't I go over and push him around a little to learn him manners. But I didn't kill him."

Abrams asks: "Did you ever wear a wig?"

Dancer seems completely surprised. Then he says: "No, but you ought to see my collection of hoopskirts."

Abrams asks Lum Kee: "Did you?"

Lum Kee says: "No," pulling a lock of his hair. "Good hair—see?"

Abrams groans and says to Nick: "I *hate* comedians." Then he asks Polly: "Did you?"

Polly: "No."

Abrams: "Have you thought of anything that might have something to do with this layout?" indicating the window from which the ladder is hanging and the earphones.

Polly: "No. But maybe this was all just a gag. Nobody came down and hit me on the head with that pipe and Robert wasn't killed in my place."

Nick asks her: "You know why that was, don't you?"

Polly: "No."

Francis says to the detective standing beside him: "What a swell gal she'd be to take out—all she can say is 'No.'"

Nick: "I'll tell you. This mysterious Anderson, probably in a red wig, phony glasses, and gloves to keep from leaving fingerprints, was sitting up here at his listening post waiting for a good chance to come down and polish off Robert, and hearing most of the things that were said down there between you and Phil and you and Dancer and you and Robert until he knew more about all of you than any of *you* did. But for one reason or another, he put off the killing until he learned that you and Robert were going away the next day. It was that night or never with him, but he got a bad break. Pedro came up and wanted to put a new rug down. That would have exposed the listening post and spoiled everything; so when he tries to talk Pedro out of it—"

Asta, who has been playing with David over by the open window, now lifts his leg against the chair.

Nora yells: "Asta!" then complains, "Now I'll have to take you out just when I was so interested. Couldn't you wait until I get back, Nickie?"

David: "I'll take him out for you."

Nick to Abrams: "Murderers get funnier every year, don't they?"

Abrams: "Huh?"

Nick: "Just when you get ready to arrest them they want to take dogs out walking!"

Everybody looks at Nick in surprise.

Nick: "David is Anderson. He didn't recognize Pedro any more than Robert or I did, but in spite of the disguise, Pedro finally recognized him just as Polly told us he'd recognized Robert. I suppose David gave him some hocus-pocus story, but Pedro, knowing Robert was spending a lot of time in the apartment just below this, probably knowing that Robert married Selma and knowing that David had been engaged to her when Pedro was working for Nora, and knowing Nora married a detective, thought he'd better change the lock and keep David out until he could come over and ask Nora's and my advice. He was foolish enough to tell David what he was going to do and David followed him over and shot him in the vestibule."

David turns to Nora, who is standing beside him by the window, and asks: "Nora, is he fooling?"

Nora says nothing. She is too busy listening to Nick, as are the others.

Nick: "Sure. And *you* were fooling when you said you hadn't seen him since he worked for Nora and pretended you remembered him as a man with a long, gray mustache. He's got one now all right, but if you'll look at that picture downstairs, you'll see that it was neither very long nor very gray then. And what was Phil doing on your fire-escape except to try to shake you down because we know he'd followed you and Polly that night? We know the boy liked to shake people down; but you weren't alone that night, so he beat it and made a date with you for the next night and got himself killed."

David protests: "But—"

Nick, paying no attention to him, continues: "And what do you suppose Pedro was trying to say when he died? That he'd been killed by *Miss Selma's young man*, which would be a servant's language for your status back when he worked for Nora."

Selma says: "But Nick, why should David have killed him? He'd given him the bonds and Robert was going away."

Nick: "He didn't want Robert to go away—he wanted to kill him. That's why he had to do it that night; otherwise he'd have had to hunt all over the world for him. Promising to pay him, with Polly knowing it, would make it look as though he had no reason for killing him. He intended killing him that night he met him, but Polly was along, so he couldn't. But he followed him and shot him when he came out of the house."

Selma: "I can't believe—"

David grabs Nora and forces her backwards out of the window so that only her legs are inside and she is held there only by his arms. His face has become insane; his voice, high-pitched and hysterical. He screams: "I'm not going to the gallows! Either you give me your word that I go out of here with a five-minute start, or Nora goes out of the window with me."

The policemen's guns are in their hands, but everyone is afraid to move except Lum Kee, who, standing by the corridor door, softly slips out, and Selma, who starts toward David, crying: "David!"

David snarls: "Keep away, you idiot!"

Nick, talking to gain time, trying not to show how frightened he is, says to Selma: "See, he's not in love with you. He was, but when you turned him down for Robert, he probably came to hate you almost as much as he did Robert. But playing the faithful lover let him hang around until he could get a crack at Robert. That's why when he saw you hop around the corner with a gun in your hand right after he'd shot Robert from the car, he circled the block and came back in time to frame you while he pretended he was covering you up. He had probably meant to frame Phil or Dancer—which he did after he'd had to kill Phil while you were in jail."

David, from the window, says: "You're stalling for time, Nick, and it's no good. Five minutes' start or another of your lovely family goes down on the rocks with me."

Nick: "Don't be a sap, David. The chances are they'd never hang you. You ought to be able to get off with a few years in an asylum. What jury's going to believe a sane man did all this?"

David: "That's a good idea! So I won't have to jump out the window with her. Either I get my five minutes or she goes down alone."

Nick turns to Abrams and says: "Lieutenant, I—"

There is a commotion at the window. Nora goes farther out backwards. David turns and leans out of the window, looking at something below. Outside, Lum Kee, in his stocking feet, is hanging by his toes and one hand to the rungs of the ladder, with his other around Nora's waist, and his head bent down, trying to avoid David's blows. Inside, Nick snatches a pistol from the nearest policeman and shoots David. David somersaults out of the window and crashes to the rocks some sixty feet below. Nick has gone to the window and is pulling Nora in. He shakes her violently by the shoulders and says:

"You numbskull, why didn't you keep away from him after I told you he was a murderer?"

She says just as sharply: "You fool, why didn't you—"

They both break off and go into each other's arms.

Abrams turns from looking out of the window and says: "Some of you boys go down and gather him up. A good enough ending for it. I guess that Doc Kammer would have had no trouble at all getting *him* off."

Lum Kee climbs over the sill. Nick and Nora turn to him together to thank him for saving her, Nora adding that it was especially wonderful of him, inasmuch as Nick had once sent his brother to the pen.

Lum Kee says: "Sure. Mr. Charles send him over—number one detective—I no like my brother—I like his girl—thank you many times—you betcha."

He moves uncomfortably and looks down at his stocking feet. He is standing in a puddle. He smiles blandly and says: "I go down and get my shoes," while Nora exclaims reproachfully, "Asta!"

THE END

AFTER THE THIN MAN

Afterword

In the opening frames of *After the Thin Man*, a billowing locomotive speeds through space and time with turns of night and day, and rushing American landscapes. The two and a half years that passed between the release of the original *Thin Man* film, in May of 1934, and its first sequel, released on Christmas Day 1936, evaporate in twenty seconds. Nick and Nora Charles, who had celebrated Christmas in New York, arrive just in time for New Year's Eve in San Francisco.

At its core, *The Thin Man*'s sequel remains faithful to both Hammett's original story and MGM's original film adaptation. *After the Thin Man*, wrote Norbert Lusk in the *Los Angeles Times*, "succeeds in recapturing and carrying on the charm and originality of Nick and Nora Charles, who set a fashion in characterization all their own." As Hunt Stromberg insisted, "Nick is always the same!—he's a—CHARACTER." And Nora remains his inimitable wife, friend, and foil. Important, the voices of *The Thin Man* also stay true. The Hacketts preserved Hammett's quirky dialogue, with its rare blend of silly and cynical, sloshed and smart. "Have you ever been thrown out of a place, Mr. Charles?" threatens Dancer. "How many places was it up to yesterday, Mrs. Charles?" asks Nick. "How many places have you been in, Mr. Charles?" replies Nora.

As in the first *Thin Man*—and as in John Huston's 1941 adaptation of *The Maltese Falcon*—sizeable blocks of Hammett's conversations are transferred undisturbed. Hollywood's studios hired Hammett because he knew how to write dialogue that rang true, amused, and informed. Shrewd filmmakers didn't muddle it.

Hunt Stromberg stressed another constant in his *Thin Man* project—the inherent tension between Nick and Nora's personal histories. Portrayals of "his" and "her" people "should be of exactly the opposite type and tempo," Stromberg said, so that "contrast between the two backgrounds will become more poignant." Nick was a man of the people, with all their intemperate foibles. Nora was a product of the moneyed upper class, and while she was intrigued by Nick's world, she was not insensible to its offenses. The surprise party at the Charles's home, the dinner party at the Forrests', and encounters with Nick's criminal acquaintances amplify the contrast. Nora's raised eyebrows and the couple's furtive banter make good comedy. Their ability to transform social dissonance into connubial delight also reflects on the economic realities of the Depression Era, when moviegoers welcomed an imaginative world in which class barriers were permeable and wealth was not a precondition of happiness. Nick appropriated Nora's glamorous lifestyle, but his low-life friends had a lot of fun, too.

There are, of course, significant differences between *After the Thin Man*'s screen story and its final production. Fewer changes than might be expected can be attributed to the Production Code Administration's censorship. While Joseph Breen, head of the PCA, had said that "It will be necessary to limit all unnecessary drinking to an absolute minimum," Nick, Nora, and the rest indulge liberally throughout the film. Breen also objected to Nick handling Nora's underwear in the opening train sequence, to Phil striking Polly, and to David's mention of "divorce"— all in scenes that remain largely intact. Asta's "toilet gag[s]" were more troubling. In the wake of PCA complaints, proposed leg-lifting scenes disappeared—although the Hacketts' sequences illustrating Mrs. Asta's infidelity remain. Canine cuckolding, it appears, was less offensive to Mr. Breen than urination.

The most salient difference between the screen story and its film adaptation is Pedro Dominges's death scene. In a late addition to the story that was not well received by Stromberg or the Hacketts, Hammett has Pedro shot at the Charleses' front door during the New Year's Eve surprise party sequence. "We must not forget that your script was written really without any preparations for the Hammett injection of the Pedro incident," Stromberg complained to the Hacketts on August 31, 1936. "And that we felt Saturday that the script was detached and irrelevant as Pedro seemed to be just dragged in and not really dramatized in scenes and premises." Stromberg suggested a reconstruction that might have mitigated the problem, but Hackett and Goodrich settled on a more drastic revision. They cut the initial shooting scene entirely. Instead, Pedro's character is introduced late in the film, found dead in Polly's apartment house. While his white mustache still provides the key to identifying David as the murderer, Pedro is demoted to janitor, rather than the building owner and former bootlegger made good. Had Hammett continued to develop his story alongside Stromberg and the Hacketts, he might have worked through their objections and found a more graceful solution. But Hammett had moved on.

Although their treatment of the Pedro situation is less than ideal, Albert Hackett and Frances Goodrich deserve kudos for the final adaptation of Hammett's screen story to film. When they began work on the original *Thin Man* film, director W. S. Van Dyke had asked them to focus on fleshing out the Charleses' relationship, rather than articulating the murder mystery. In *After the Thin Man*, they take on the same task—drafting train-car, domestic, and nightclub scenes that brighten the film. With Hammett's departure from Hollywood, however, the Hacketts were left to transform a complicated mystery story into a filmable screenplay. They reshuffled the clues and key sequences that Hammett left behind. They compressed his secondary points into simple shots. And they trimmed extraneous or impractical material. Director Van Dyke must have been relieved by their revised version of the final confrontation, which plays out inside Polly's apartment with a pistol and a tossed hat, rather than on both sides of an open window, by way of a makeshift pipe ladder, a dodgy gunshot, and a gruesome fatal plunge.

The Hacketts can also be credited with *After the Thin Man*'s closing scene, in which Nora knits what Nick suddenly realizes is a baby's sock. For movie fans, Nora's pregnancy was a charming turn of events, but the Hacketts had other intentions. They wanted to put an end to the Charleses' adventures and, most important, to the possibility that they might be compelled to write another sequel. Hackett and Goodrich were bored with the Charleses' endless wit and tired of struggling with Hammett's complicated situations. When Stromberg refused to allow them to kill off Nick and Nora, they resorted to parenthood, which they hoped would be enough of an encumbrance to extinguish the *Thin Man* film franchise. Like Hammett, they'd had their fill of Nick and Nora's fabulous fable. Nonetheless, by the fall of 1937, all three would be back at work on the *Thin Man*'s next installment.

                                                              J. M. R.

ANOTHER THIN MAN

Headnote

Dashiell Hammett was never shy about mining his own material. In *The Maltese Falcon* he reworks elements from no fewer than seven earlier stories, often derived from his own experiences as a working detective. In *Another Thin Man* Hammett draws heavily on one source—his penultimate Continental Op story, "The Farewell Murder," published in *Black Mask* magazine in January 1930, one month before *The Maltese Falcon* was released in hardcover by Knopf.

"The Farewell Murder" and *Another Thin Man* share wily plot devices, a partial cast of characters, and Hammett's trademark dialogue. Both tales turn on the disappearance of a knifed body from a dark road, escalate with the death of a pet, and conclude with crooks intent on outsmarting the legal system. Both feature a querulous patriarch, a daughter with unscrupulous associates, and the staff of a country manor. But it's clear that Hammett modified the story to suit the medium. Filmmakers in 1938 labored under notably different demands than did pulp-magazine writers in 1930. The Continental Op was a true hard-boiled character—physically and emotionally toughened. To keep order in his dark and violent world, the Op had to be cagier and in some ways more callous than the crooks. Regular readers of the pulps would barely have blinked when the Op, in "The Farewell Murder," coolly assesses the grisly killing of a young dog and fabricates damning testimony on the body of a dying man. MGM's filmmakers and the *Thin Man*'s fans would have been appalled by such calculated insensitivity in the *Thin Man*'s debonair leading man. Nick Charles had hard-boiled roots but an uptown sensibility, a family, and an affection for the good life. Hammett dialed back his earlier tale's grittier aspects.

Hammett's May 13, 1938, screen story also includes an eighteen-page sequence from a darker partial draft. In that passage, ignored in *Another Thin Man*'s later development, Assistant District Attorney VanSlack attempts to use violence to coerce Nick into admitting complicity in a pair of murders. After reporters arrive and defuse the situation, the section winds to a dead end. The incident is better suited to an Op story than to film works in the late 1930s, especially given the constraints of the Production Code Administration. The PCA frowned on drinking, sexuality, and violence (presenting plenty of opportunity for criticism of the *Thin Man* films), as well as derogatory depictions of figures of authority. Hammett skewered law enforcement officials routinely in his fiction. In film, however, VanSlack's ignoble behavior was guaranteed to rile the censors. The story that follows here adheres to Hammett's more durable story line—which fueled the Hacketts' screenplay and, ultimately, the second of the *Thin Man* sequels.

J. M. R.

ANOTHER THIN MAN

Dashiell Hammett

May 13, 1938

AN ELABORATE SUITE IN A NEW YORK HOTEL

It is late afternoon in September. Hotel maids, valets, etc., pass through, unpacking, bringing flowers, etc. Nora in negligee is at telephone with an open address book before her.

Nora into phone: "No we can't, dear—we've got to go on down to Colonel MacFay's for the weekend as soon as we get unpacked. Colonel MacFay—you remember—used to be my father's partner.... No, I really can't, darling. If it were anything else I could persuade Nick to get out of it, but this is something about our financial affairs and you know how mercenary he is.... Yes, we had a lovely trip; Nick was sober in Kansas City. I'll give you a ring Monday as soon as we get back, darling. I'm dying to have you see the baby.... We kind of like him." She puts the phone down and makes a face at it.

Nick, bringing Nora a drink, says: "You're a bitter woman, Mom."

The phone rings again and Nora answers it, speaking to another friend.

A bellboy, a youngish man with a small, cheerful, wizened face, comes in carrying an enormous bunch of flowers. When he turns from putting them on the table, he and Nick recognize each other.

Nick frowns disapprovingly at the boy's uniform and says: "God help honest folk in a hotel like this. How are you, Face?"

Face grabs Nick's hand saying: "Gee, I'm glad to see you, Nick, even if it does spoil one of the prettiest jobs I ever lined up for myself." He unbuttons his coat, sighs, and says: "Oh well, if I could have thought of this, I'll think up something else."

Nora hangs up the phone again and turns toward them.

Nick says: "You remember Face Peppler? He came to a party of ours the last time we were in New York."

Nora says: "Of course." She holds out her hand.

Face: "Gee, I'm glad to see you, Mrs. Charles."

Nora looks at his unbuttoned uniform coat.

Face: "I was hopping bells here until a minute ago when Nick seen me."

Nora says to Nick: "But, Nick, if he's trying to go straight now, I don't think you ought to—"

Face interrupts her by laughing heartily: "Aw, Mrs. Charles, it was nothing like that. Give me two days more and I'd have had a million dollars. Well, anyway, I'd have had a pretty bank roll."

An assistant manager comes in, bowing primly to Nick and Nora, asking: "Is everything satisfactory? Is there anything we could do to make you more comfortable?" He sees Face and says sharply: "Thirtle!"

Face takes off his coat and hands it to the assistant manager. "I've quit. I'm visiting here." He starts to unbutton his pants. "These are my friends."

Nora says sweetly: "Oh yes, Mr. Peppler—Thirtle is an old friend of ours."

Nick puts his arm on Peppler's back and says: "You must have a drink, old chap. I have some incredible Scotch."

The assistant manager bows himself out in a daze.

Face shakes hands warmly with Nick and Nora, saying: "You people are okay for my money."

A nervous man in chauffeur's livery comes in and says: "Mr. Charles?"

Nick says: "Yes?"

Chauffeur: "Colonel MacFay's car, sir."

Nick says: "Thanks. Be down in a little while."

The chauffeur fidgets with his cap, then says: "Excuse me for saying so, but it's getting a little late."

Nick: "I'll try to hurry."

Chauffeur: "Thank you, sir." He goes out.

From the rear of the suite comes Asta's voice raised in deafening complaint.

Nora says: "Nicky's doing something." She hurries toward the noise, Nick and Face following her.

In the kitchen Nick Jr. is sitting on the floor calmly chewing on a bone that he has taken from Asta. Asta is not trying to snatch the bone back, but is walking around and around the baby complaining noisily.

Nick Jr. is a fat, year-old boy who is interested in very little besides eating and sleeping. He eats anything that comes to hand and can sleep anywhere. His vocabulary is limited, consisting chiefly of two words— "Drunk" for things he does not like and "Gimme" for things he does. He seldom laughs and never cries and does not think his parents are amusing. He ordinarily regards them with the same sort of mild curiosity or tolerant boredom with which he regards the rest of the world. He is calmly chewing his bone, playing no attention to Asta.

Nora picks him up, takes the bone out of his hand, and gives it to Asta, who runs off with it. The baby watches Asta out of sight without any particular expression on his face.

Face says: "Gee, a baby! Yours?"

Nick and Nora say: "Yes," trying not to look proud of themselves.

Face wiggles a finger in front of the baby's nose, saying: "Googoo, googoo!"

The baby looks at him blankly.

Nick and Nora try to stir the baby into some semblance of liveliness, but with no success. After watching their antics for a moment, the baby says, "Drunk," and turns to Face again.

Face, a little abashed by the baby's patient stare, asks: "A boy?"

Nora says: "Certainly!"

Face: "That's great. How old is he?"

Nora says: "Be a year next Tuesday."

Face: "Tuesday? Swell. Say, we'll give him a party . . . Tuesday afternoon! I'll get my brother to let me bring his kids over. He's got two of the cutest little monkeys—leave it all to me. Tuesday afternoon—that's a date."

Nora says confusedly: "Well, I don't—"

Face pats her on the back: "You leave it all to Facie, Mrs. Charles. I'll give you a baby party you never seen the like of."

He goes out, picking up Nora's address book from beside the telephone as he passes without their seeing him.

Nora looks at Nick in consternation.

Nick says: "We can stay down at MacFay's until Tuesday night."

Nick, Nora, the nurse, Nick Jr., and Asta go down to the street, where the nervous chauffeur is standing beside a car into which a bellboy and the doorman have just finished putting their bags.

The chauffeur, looking at the two women and the baby, asks Nick in a somewhat surprised tone: "Are you going to take them?"

Nick says: "I don't know how to get rid of them. Maybe we can ditch them somewhere on the road."

The chauffeur says: "I'm sorry, Mr. Charles, I didn't mean to—" and breaks off to look at his watch and then at the sky. It is now early twilight, although the streetlights have not yet been turned on.

They get into the car. The nurse sits in front with the chauffeur; Nick, Nora, the child, and dog sit in the rear.

Nora, looking at the chauffeur, asks: "What's the matter with him?"

Nick replies: "We had a couple of girls lined up."

DISSOLVE THROUGH THE NEW YORK STREETS, OVER THE TRIBOROUGH BRIDGE, ALONG LONG ISLAND ROADS

As darkness closes down, the chauffeur drives faster and faster until, by the time they have turned off the highway into a dark, tree-lined side road, Nick, Nora, the baby, and Asta are bouncing around on the backseat. The baby bounces peacefully without opening its eyes.

Nick calls to the chauffeur: "You're working too hard. If we don't get there in three minutes, it'll still be all right."

The chauffeur pays no attention to him. Nick leans forward, touches the chauffeur's shoulder. The chauffeur jumps, jerks his head around, and almost sends the car off the road. His face and the back of his neck are covered with sweat.

Nick says: "Not so fast, son, the baby has a hangover."

The chauffeur mumbles: "Yes, sir—I'm sorry," then almost immediately begins to step up the speed again.

Suddenly he emits an ear-piercing scream of terror and sends the car hurtling ahead. Through a window, Nick catches a glimpse of a Negro man lying on his back on the side of the road. The man's body is arched so that its weight rests on heels and head. The five-inch handle of a knife sticks up from the left side of his breast.

Nick yells to the chauffeur to stop. The chauffeur pays no attention, and, when Nick touches him on the shoulder, he screams again but does not slow up.

Nick, standing up in the lurching car, puts his forearm around the chauffeur's throat, his other hand on the wheel, finally chokes the chauffeur into submission, and stops the car. Nick Jr. opens his eyes once to look at this and then goes back to sleep.

Nick says to the nurse: "Come back here."

She jumps out and gets in the rear of the car. Nick pushes the chauffeur over into the nurse's seat and climbs in behind the wheel. The chauffeur jumps out of the car and runs off into the woods.

Nora asks: "What happened?"

Nick says: "You wouldn't believe me if I told you," turns the car around, and drives back to where he saw the Negro.

There is no body there, and, with the help of the car's lights, he can find no signs that one has been there.

Nora asks: "What are you hunting for?"

Nick says: "I thought I knew, but now I'll take anything I can find. Listen, I'm willing to call the whole thing off and drive right back to New York."

The nurse says: "Oh yes, sir, that would be fine."

Nora says: "We can't do that, Nick. Colonel MacFay expects us. What was the matter with the chauffeur, Nick?"

Nick answers: "He was scared and now I am. Let's go somewhere and get a drink and think this over."

Nora says: "The nearest drink would be at the MacFays', but I wish you would tell me what is going on—what we came back here for."

Nick says: "You're a stubborn woman, Mom."

He turns the car around again and drives on. Presently they come to a high grilled gate that blocks the road. When Nick has honked the horn, a gangling youth appears on the other side of the gate holding a double-barreled shotgun partly out of sight behind the gatepost. His manner is half-frightened, half-sullen.

He asks: "What do you want?"

Nick says: "We're bringing back Colonel MacFay's car."

The youth says: "I can see that all right, but how do I know what you want?"

Nick says: "This is the Charles family. We have come down to spend the weekend."

The youth says: "Anybody can say that, but wait—I'll see," and vanishes into a cottage set beside the gate. His voice can be heard talking over the telephone. "He says their name is Charles—I don't know—He looks like a pool parlor dude and he's got a couple of ladies and a baby and a dog. Oh, all right."

He comes back without his shotgun and swings the gate open. They drive on to a large house set in the middle of extensive grounds.

The front door is opened by a neat, elderly woman with a placid face. This is Mrs. Bellam, the MacFay housekeeper.

Nick says to her: "I'm sorry, but we lost your chauffeur somewhere along the road."

She replies serenely: "Oh, bless you, it's quite all right. Thomas," indicating the servant who has appeared behind her, "will bring up your bags. I suppose you'll want to wash up. Colonel MacFay is waiting dinner for you, but you don't have to hurry."

She leads them upstairs into their rooms. One is for Nick and Nora, with a connecting bath leading to the nurse and Junior's room.

MACFAY LIVING ROOM

In the MacFay living room are four people.

Colonel Burr MacFay is a tall, scrawny man of seventy, actually still vigorous, but a hypochondriac and suspicious of those around him, though his bark is worse than his bite.

Lois, his adopted daughter, is a girl of twenty—very pretty, with a sweet and simple manner.

Dudley Horn, her fiancé, is a large man in his thirties. He is an engineer, MacFay's right-hand man, rather good-looking, and affects a candid, open-faced, man's-man manner.

Freddie Coleman is MacFay's secretary, a nice boy of twenty-two or twenty-three, who is very much in love with Lois and is writing a play in his spare time.

Colonel MacFay is complaining over a glass of sherry, his voice a nasal whine: "I won't have it. I won't put up with it. I'm not a child and I won't have it."

Horn, leaning against the mantelpiece, holding a Scotch and soda, says good-naturedly: "What's the good of saying we won't put up with it when we are putting up with it?"

Freddie, leaning forward in his chair, frowning earnestly, says: "But maybe he did kill him."

MacFay, glaring at Freddie, whines impatiently: "Him! Him! *I'm* the one that doesn't want to be killed."

Lois, patting a collie that is standing with its head on her knee, looks anxiously at her foster-father and starts to say: "But, Papa dear, you—" as Nick, Nora, and Asta come in. Asta goes over to investigate the collie.

MacFay greets Nick and Nora: "Come in! Come in! You're late."

Nick: "Had a little trouble. Did your chauffeur tell you about the black man in the road?"

MacFay presses his lips together, says nothing.

Nick: "He wasn't there when we went back."

MacFay, explosively: "I don't care about your black men and your roads. I care about what happens to me. I—" He breaks off, pushes his face into what is meant for a smile. "You know Dudley."

Nick and Nora say: "Yes," and shake hands with Horn.

MacFay: "And this is my adopted daughter, Lois, and my secretary, Mr. Coleman."

When the introductions have been acknowledged and Lois has given Nick and Nora each a drink, MacFay says: "Dinner is waiting. Come on, bring your drinks in."

As they go into the dining room, Lois tells the servant to feed the dogs.

Dinner is served by two badly trained servants who keep looking over their shoulders as if frightened, and jump at every unexpected sound. One of them, turning from putting soup on the table, knocks Nick on the elbow with the butt of a pistol in his pocket.

MacFay, who attacks his soup hungrily, complains after each spoonful. "They know this isn't good for my stomach. I ought to have some kind of light broth, but they don't care—nobody cares what happens to me." He empties his plate before the others are half through and has a second helping. When he has finished that, between complaints that it is so badly cooked that it wouldn't be food for him even if it weren't too heavy, he bangs his spoon down on a plate and says to Nick: "I'm not a child—I won't be frightened."

Nick asks: "What is there to be frightened of?"

MacFay replies: "Nothing, nothing but a lot of idiotic and very pointless trickery and play-acting."

One of the servants grumbles sullenly over the dish he is taking from the table: "You can call it anything you want to call it, but I seen what I seen." Nobody pays any attention to him.

Nick says: "What kind of trickery and play-acting?"

MacFay puts his arms on the table, leans over them toward Nick, and says: "Suppose you had a man working for you and he did something they put him in jail for. He did it, you didn't do it, and you even tried to get him off and to get his sentence cut down, but you couldn't. And now, after he gets out, he comes to you and says it's all your fault and wants you to give him a lot of money. And when you're not fool enough to do that, he says he hopes you're not going to be pig-headed about it because he's dreamed twice about your dying, and the third time he dreams things, they come true. He says he hopes you're not going to die before your conscience makes you do the right thing by him. What would you think?"

Nick says: "I wouldn't think I ought to hurry up my dying on his account."

MacFay stares at Nick blankly for a moment, then says: "You'll excuse me, but that's just about as stupid an answer as I've ever heard."

Nora nods brightly at Nick and assures him: "Yes it is."

One of the servants says to the other: "A fat lot of help this new guy's going to be to us."

MacFay taps his glass with a knife and says angrily to the servants: "Shut up! Where's the roast?" He points to Nora's glass. "Her glass is empty." He holds up the knife and complains: "See how they take care of my silverware. It hasn't been cleaned decently in a month." He puts the knife down, pushes back his plate, and leans over the table. "Listen," he whines to Nick, "this isn't April-foolery, this man means to murder me. He came here to murder me, and he will certainly murder me unless somebody does something to stop him."

Nick asks: "But what has he done so far?"

MacFay shakes his head impatiently. "That isn't it. I don't ask you to undo anything that he's done. I ask you to keep him from killing me. What has he done? He's terrorized the whole place—that's what he's done."

Nick asks: "How long has this been going on?"

MacFay says: "A week, ten days."

Nick asks: "Do you think the black man on the road is part of it?"

MacFay retorts: "I don't think anything about it. You used to be a detective. I asked you down here to help me, not to bring me more wild stories."

Nick asks: "Have you said anything to the local authorities?"

MacFay whines: "I'm not altogether a fool. Of course I have, but what good did it do? Has he threatened me? Well, he told me he has dreams about me dying, and I know him well enough to know that's a threat. But to the sheriff it isn't a threat. Have I any proof that he is responsible for all these things that have happened—that he's turned this place upside down? The sheriff says I haven't. As if I needed proof! So it comes to this: The sheriff promises to keep an eye on him. 'An eye,' mind you. Here I have, with my family and servants and the guards I've hired, twenty people with forty eyes, and he comes and goes when he wants, so what good's the sheriff's 'eye'?"

Nick asks: "Who is this fellow?"

One of the servants mutters: "It's not him, it's that black devil."

MacFay says: "Church is his name—Sam Church. He's an engineer—worked for me ten years ago."

Nick asks: "How long was he in jail?"

MacFay says: "Ten years. He got out a month ago."

Nick: "You think he really means to kill you?"

MacFay bangs on the table and shouts: "No! No! No! I don't *think* he means to kill me, I *know* it!"

Lois tries to soothe MacFay, saying: "Mr. Charles is only trying to get it straight in his mind, Papa."

MacFay: "There's nothing to get straight. This man means to kill me and I am asking Mr. Charles not to let him do it. That's simple enough, isn't it, even for Mr. Charles?"

Nora shakes her head, no.

Mrs. Bellam, the placid housekeeper, puts her head in at the door and says: "The swimming pool is on fire."

Everybody jumps up from the table. The servants disappear.

Nora exclaims: "Nicky!" She starts upstairs to the baby.

Nick tells Freddie: "Better stay here with the Colonel and Miss MacFay."

Nick and Horn go out, Horn picking up a heavy walking-stick in the vestibule. They go out the front door, separating a little as they go around the side of the house toward where a wooden bathhouse is burning fiercely at one end of a large swimming pool.

The muzzle of a double-barreled shotgun is suddenly jabbed into Nick's face from a clump of bushes and a voice roars: "One move out of you and I'll blow your head right off the end of your neck. Hey, Barney! Hey, Slim! I got him!" A big man comes out of the bushes, holding the end of the shotgun within half an inch of Nick's nose.

Two other men with shotguns, yelling: "Hold him! Kill him if he bats a eye!" come running toward Nick and his captor.

Horn comes around the clump of bushes and says to the man with the shotgun: "Take that gun out of Mr. Charles's face and stop bellowing."

Nick: "I'm mighty glad to see you, Mr. Horn."

The man with the shotgun steps back, mumbling: "How was I going to know who he was?" He turns to his mates, who have arrived by then, and says: "It ain't the right one. It beats all how that fellers come and go without nobody seeing hide nor hair of them."

The three men with shotguns move off toward the fire.

Horn says to Nick: "The Colonel's guards. They've never seen anything and never will."

Nick spies Lois's collie lying on its side a short distance from the burning building and goes over to it.

Horn, following him, asks: "Dead?"

Nick: "Yes. Its head almost cut off."

Horn says in a somewhat choked voice: "He was a swell dog. This is going to be tough on Lois."

Nick: "Is this the kind of thing that's been going on?"

Horn, still looking gloomily down at the dog: "More or less. I don't know how seriously you're going to take it. Most of it's pretty silly, but it's nasty, too."

Lois comes running up and kneels beside the dead dog. Horn squats with an arm around her, trying to console her.

Nick goes over to where the three men are standing looking at some faint blurred prints in a damp patch of ground.

Nick: "Find anything?"

One of the guards: "Only them, and they don't look like nothing and don't lead nowhere."

Nick, looking at the prints: "Our man wore rags wrapped around his shoes."

The guard, suspiciously: "You know a lot about them things, mister."

Nick: "Back home I'm a scoutmaster." He suddenly thinks of something and goes back to Lois and Horn, asking them: "Wasn't Asta with this dog?"

Lois: "Yes, they were fed and let out together."

Nick begins to whistle and call to Asta, who after some time is found hiding in a folded beach umbrella with only the tip of his nose showing.

When Nick, Lois, and Horn return to the house, MacFay is still at the table, eating a meringue glacé. Nora has returned to her place, holding Nick Jr. on her lap, and Freddie is awkwardly trying to play with him without any cooperation from the baby.

MacFay looks up as they come in and says: "If it's any more of that foolishness, I don't want to hear a single word about it. It'll only upset my stomach and these frozen desserts are unwholesome enough anyway."

Lois says: "Papa, they killed Sandy," and explains to Nora: "I've had him ever since he was a puppy." Then she sees Nick Jr., and goes over to play with him.

Nick Jr. regards her with his usual complete lack of interest.

Horn says: "They set fire to the bathhouse, too."

MacFay slams his spoon down on the table and stands up whining: "I'm tired of hearing about these things. I'm an old man and I'm sick and you should have some consideration for me. Freddie, bring the Consolidated Transportation correspondence upstairs. Good night! Good night! Good night!" He goes out, followed by Freddie.

Nick says: "He's a cheerful old fellow."

Horn laughs and Nora rises, saying: "I'm going to put Nicky to bed."

Lois says: "Let me help you!" and goes out with her.

In the living room, Nick and Horn are given coffee and brandy by a frightened servant.

Nick asks: "Is this Sam Church staying in the neighborhood?"

Horn answers: "Yes, he's rented the Kennedy cottage at the foot of the Hill Road."

Nick asks: "Have you tried talking to him?"

Horn says: "Yes, but *that* didn't do any good. I used to work under him and he seems to think I had a hand in sending him over. We never got along very well anyhow."

Nick asks: "What's he like?"

Horn replies: "He's all right, I suppose, but don't think you can frighten him off with rain on the roof. He's a tough baby."

Nick says: "Does MacFay really owe him anything?"

Horn says: "Not the way we look at it. His job was to get results without bothering the Colonel with too many details. We were trying to put over a, well, call it a public utilities enterprise—and some details that were pretty illegal were traced as far as Church, but not as far as the Colonel, and so Church went to jail."

Nick says: "In other words, if everything goes okay, the Colonel gets the profits, and if they go wrong, Church gets the blame."

Horn says cheerfully: "That's about it."

Nick continues: "And that's your job with the Colonel now?"

Horn answers: "Something like it."

Nick: "This deal that Church got tripped up on—where did it happen?"

Horn, beginning to smile: "Out West—California."

Nick: "Ten years ago, huh?"

Horn: "Closer to twelve; it took a little while to catch him and convict him." His smile broadens. "I know what's worrying you. Your wife's father was alive then. You'd like to know whether he was in on it with the Colonel or whether the Colonel was playing a lone hand."

Nick: "Well?"

Horn: "I don't know the answer. I don't suppose anybody does but the Colonel. There were no records to show anything—that's why Church took the fall alone."

Nick, after a thoughtful pause: "What do you think is behind all these Halloween tricks? What do you think Church is really up to?"

Horn says: "Trying to scare the Colonel into coming across with money."

Nick asks: "Do you think he'll do it?"

Horn says: "I don't know. The Colonel scares easily, but I've never seen it cost him anything."

Nick asks: "If he doesn't come across, will Church kill him?"

Horn replies: "That's hard to say. He'd kill you—like that—" he snaps his fingers, "for profit, and he might do it for fun, but I can't see him brooding much over revenge."

Nick asks: "Could any of the people on the inside here be working with him?"

Horn says: "I don't think so. The servants aren't much good, but I imagine they're honest."

Nick asks: "How about the secretary?"

Lois, coming into the room behind them, says lightly: "I won't have you suspecting Freddie of things. He's a nice boy."

Horn, rising to give her his chair, says: "All men who are in love with you are nice," and explains to Nick, "He's my rival. He only puts up with the Colonel's nonsense so he can be around Lois." He sits on the arm of her chair and puts his arm around her.

Lois asks Nick: "Do all fiancés have these pet jokes, and does the girl have to keep on laughing at them?"

Nick says: "Only until she gets him to the altar. Did you and Nora get the Charles offspring tucked in?"

Lois says: "Oh yes—isn't he the loveliest baby?"

Nick says modestly: "We'll do better when we've had more practice," and rises adding: "I'd better go up and see him. He never closes an eye until I say good night to him."

Nick goes up to his bedroom, where Nick Jr. is peacefully sleeping beside Nora, who is reading in bed.

Nick asks: "What's he doing in here?"

Nora says: "You don't suppose I'm going to have him out of my sight again in this place? And we're going back to New York tomorrow morning."

Nick says: "That's all right with me. I ought to get hold of some accountants and maybe we should cut the trip short and go back to the Coast."

He begins to undress.

Nora asks: "What are you talking about?"

Nick says: "Money—your property—our property—that Colonel's been managing. A day like this begins to make you lose faith in your fellow man. I'd hate to wake up some morning and find that I'd married you for a fortune that MacFay had either stolen or got messed up so that somebody could take it away from us by due process of law."

Nora: "I love you, but you're an awful silly man sometimes."

Nick: "I'm not silly, I'm just timid. Some men are afraid of airplanes and some are afraid of thunderstorms—I'm afraid of losing money. I'd better go have a talk with this Church fellow in the morning."

Nora: "What for?"

Nick: "He worked for MacFay back when your father was alive. Maybe he can tell me whether your father was mixed up in this—"

Nora, interrupting him indignantly: "Of course he wasn't mixed up in it if it was anything wrong! My father was just as honest as yours!"

Nick laughs. "Some day you'll find out what a hot recommendation that is. But, sweetheart, I'm not trying to write dirty words on your old man's tombstone. I've just got to find out where we stand."

Nora: "All right, but leave my father out of it. You're a fine one to talk, anyway. I still remember when you were working for Father as a private detective, every time you took me out you charged it up to him on your expense account, and he never knew it till after we were married."

Nick: "Ah, I was a *brilliant* young man!"

The next morning Nick takes a walk accompanied by Asta. A country-man they meet on the road tells him how to find the Kennedy house. "You can't miss it," he says, "it's got a terra-cotta roof and sits back from the road to the left on the other side of the hill."

Nick and Asta climb the hill and as they start down the other side, pass an expensive coupe parked a little off the road, partly hidden by foliage. Nick starts to go on, then stops and goes cautiously over to examine the parked car. Finding nothing of interest there, he looks around and discovers that twigs have been broken by someone forcing his way through the bushes. He pushes the bushes aside and sees a man lying facedown on a rock on the hillside, looking through field glasses at a house at the foot of the hill. The house has a terra-cotta roof.

The man is large, tough-looking, middle-aged, wearing very thick rimless spectacles. He takes the field glasses from his eyes and rolls over on one elbow to scowl at Nick, asking in a hoarse voice: "Now what are you sticking your pretty nose in here for, chum?"

Nick says: "Sorry. The door was open."

The hoarse-voiced man says: "All right, you made your joke. Now pull your freight." He takes a police badge in a leather case from his pants pocket, shows it to Nick briefly. "Get going."

Nick salutes, says: "Just as you say, Chief," and backs out through the bushes again, takes a step or two on his way, stops to write down the license number of the automobile, and then continues on to the cottage at the foot of the hill.

When he knocks on the door, it is opened by a good-looking young Negro (the one he saw in the road the previous night), who smiles, and, speaking with a Spanish accent, says: "Good morning, sir. Mr. Church waiting breakfast for you." He bends down to scratch Asta's head.

Nick says: "You're going to catch pneumonia lying in damp roads after dark."

The Negro laughs and says: "No sir—I dress warm in this country."

He ushers Nick into a room where a man and woman put down newspapers and rise to meet him.

The man is perhaps forty years old, big, hard-faced, sunburned.

The woman is twenty-seven, quite six feet tall, muscular, and attractive.

There are a couple of partially packed traveling bags in the room and through a door a trunk can be seen.

The man says: "I'm Sam Church. Sit down. Breakfast will be ready in a few minutes." He indicates the woman. "This is Smitty—you can talk in front of her."

Nick says: "Thanks, I've had breakfast." He looks at the traveling bags. "Going away?"

Church says: "Sure. Back to Cuba. We were just waiting to see you. It would be nice if you would give us the gory details first, though. What'll you drink?" He claps his hands and calls: "Dum-Dum."

Nick asks: "What gory details? You don't mean the dead dog and the burning bathhouse?"

Church says: "No—afterwards."

Nick says: "Nothing happened afterwards."

Church says in a surprised tone: "But I dreamed—" He breaks off and looks suspiciously at Nick, asking: "You're not tricking me, are you?"

Nick says: "No."

Church says: "Will you give me your word that nothing happened afterwards?"

Nick says: "My word."

Church sinks back in his chair, shaking his head in bewilderment. He says to the Negro who has appeared in the doorway: "Give Mr. Charles a drink, and you'd better give me one, too—a big one."

Nick looks from Church to the woman.

She smiles reassuringly at Nick and says: "He's nuts, and, if you listen to him, he'll have you nuts, too."

Nick asks her: "Do you know what this is all about?"

Church says: "It's all simple enough. Some years ago the Colonel and I got in a jam and I took the fall for him on his promise that he'd see I didn't lose by it. But he ran out on me and when I got out of prison last month I went to see him to give him a chance to make good in a financial way, which is the only way that means anything to me. He said no soap, so I went on down to Cuba, knowing sooner or later I'd figure out some way to collect from him. My first night there I had a dream about him being killed. You can laugh if you want, and Smitty will laugh with you, but *I* don't laugh at my dreams. So I came on back, hoping to make the Colonel listen to reason before it was too late. And on the way back I had the dream again. I went to see the old boy and told him about the dreams, hoping to shake him loose from a few dollars, but you know how pig-headed he is, so there was nothing else for me to do but hang around on the off-chance that something would happen to loosen him up before I had the third dream, because the third one's the end on my schedule." He takes a deep breath. "Well, last night I had the third dream."

Nick: "How does he die in those dreams?"

Church: "Oh, he's all battered up, throat cut from ear to ear—it's all very messy—just the kind of death you'd expect the slob to have."

Nick: "It would be funny if it happened that way."

Church: "It's funnier that it didn't, though I'm glad enough to know I don't have to say goodbye yet to my chances of getting money out of him. Listen, are you sure he was all right this morning?"

Nick: "He wasn't up when I left."

Church, somewhat excitedly: "Had anybody else seen him?"

Nick: "Not that I know of."

Church jumps up, exclaiming: "That's it, then!" He puts his hands in his pockets and walks the length of the room, scowling thoughtfully at the floor.

Smitty smiles at Nick, putting a forefinger up to her temple and making little circular movements with it.

Nick: "You've got a lot of faith in your dreams."

Church, absent-mindedly: "Why not?" He sits down again, studying Nick. "Well, that's the end of *him* as a possible gold mine. Now we've got to think about you."

Nick: "Me?"

Church, still thoughtfully: "He was a hard man to do business with and I've got a hunch you're going to be even harder."

Nick: "Then why bother with me? I can introduce you to a lot of rich people."

Church, ignoring this suggestion: "On the other hand, you look like a reasonable chap. Do you think we could talk business?"

Nick: "You'd have to show me why we should first."

Church: "Don't kid me. Your wife's father was MacFay's partner back in the days when my foot slipped."

Nick: "He was MacFay's partner in some deals, not in others. Prove to me that he had anything to do with this deal, and I'll give you a check right now for whatever you think is reasonable pay for your time in the pen."

Church sighs. "Yes, that's always the catch in it—proof. Nobody but me was putting anything on paper, Charles. That's why nobody but me went over. I expected this. I knew you were going to be tough to deal with. And I can't honestly tell you I've ever dreamed about you"—a pause—"or about your wife"—another pause—"or about your baby"—a longer pause—"yet."

Nick, starting his punch before he leaves his chair, jumps up and hits Church in the eye, knocking Church and his chair over backwards. Dum-Dum whips a wooden-handled knife from his waistband (the same one seen sticking from his chest when he lay in the road the previous night) and throws it at Nick. The knife slits Nick's coat in passing and sticks in a wall.

Church, on the floor, says sharply: "Stop it, Dum-Dum!"

Smitty, shaking her head in disapproval, says: "Men are such rowdies," and raises her skirt to return her pistol to its holster on her thigh.

Asta, always a great help, charges across the room after the knife, jumps up, pulls it from the wall, takes it to Dum-Dum, and then backs away from him, barking happily, tail wagging, waiting for him to throw it again.

Church stands up patting his eye. His face is calm.

Nick: "That's to remind you *not* to dream about my family."

Church: "Oh, I'll remember all right." He addresses Dum-Dum: "Finish packing. We'll catch the noon train."

Nick: "Still heading for Cuba?"

Church: "Still Cuba. I need time to think you over, and that's a good place to think. If you get down that way before I come back to see you, look me up. Sometimes I dream about roulette wheels."

Nick: "You're coming back to see me sometime?"

Church: "Yep. I think as time goes on you'll see your way clear to do business with me."

Nick, indicating Church's bruised eye: "You mean *continue* doing business with you." He calls Asta and goes to the door, where he turns and bows to Smitty, saying: "Thanks for not shooting me."

Smitty smiles good-naturedly, says: "It would've only made things worse."

The coupe and the hoarse-voiced man are no longer on the hilltop.

At MacFay's, Nora—with the baby—Lois, Horn, and Freddie are swimming. They come out of the pool as Nick approaches.

Nora, looking at the rip in Nick's coat: "What have you been doing now?"

Nick: "Asta plays too rough."

Nora: "It's not a tear, it's been cut."

Nick: "Uh-huh. A very peculiar thing happened. We were going down the hill to see Church, walking along, minding our own business, not bothering anybody, when who should we meet but three very old women, all bent over like this, walking along—"

Nora: "Minding their own business, not bothering anybody. Did you see Church?"

Nick: "Yes, ma'am."

Nora, after waiting a moment for him to go on: "Well, don't be so coy. Speak up. What did he say and what clever replies did you make?"

Nick: "You're a tough audience, Mrs. Charles."

Horn: "How *did* you make out with him?"

Nick says: "He had his third dream last night and was packing to head for Cuba on the noon train when I left."

Horn laughs.

Lois turns to look up at the house, saying in a frightened voice: "You mean he dreamed Papa was—"

Nick finishes the sentence for her—"Dead."

Horn puts his arm around Lois: "Come, darling, don't be foolish." Then he looks uncertainly at Freddie, who clears his throat nervously.

Lois looks from one to the other and insists: "Has anybody seen Papa this morning?" None of them had. Without another word, she turns and runs toward the house, with the others following.

They go to Colonel MacFay's room. He is huddled on the bed in a grotesque position, with the covers in disarray over him. Horn peers down at MacFay's face while Nick bends over to feel his pulse.

MacFay sits up in bed and says angrily: "The first decent sleep I've had in weeks and you have to come in like a pack of wet Indians and spoil it! What do you want?"

Leaving Lois to pacify him, the others sneak out sheepishly.

Nick and Nora are in their room packing when MacFay comes in and asks: "What is this Lois tells me about your going back to the city today?"

Nora says: "We have to, Colonel MacFay. We—well, this is no place for the baby the way things are."

"The baby?" MacFay glares at Nick Jr.—"He's big enough to—" then breaks off and begins to whine: "Nobody's doing anything to the baby. It's me that's in danger—it's me you're deserting." He turns to Nick. "Besides, I haven't had a chance to talk to you. There are things you ought to know about the business—about your investments."

Nick, interested: "What things?"

Horn appears in the doorway and says: "I phoned the village to check up, and they really did leave on the noon train."

MacFay says irritably: "What are you talking about?"

Horn explains: "Church told Charles this morning that he was leaving for Cuba, and he got off all right, with a trunk and a lot of bags, and the Negro and a tall woman."

MacFay turns to Nora: "See, my dear, they've gone. There'll be no more trouble."

Nora looks undecidedly from MacFay to Nick.

MacFay pats her on the cheek and says: "There, there, my dear, as a favor to an old man—an old friend of your father's."

He goes out.

Nora looks at Nick, asks: "What do we do?"

Nick, staring after MacFay, says: "It's a shame the way I'm beginning to distrust that old duffer."

Nora: "Stop being so silly. He was Father's partner. He wouldn't—"

Nick: "Maybe it wasn't so smart leaving him in control of the businesses our money is invested in all these years. He might've come to look on our money as practically his own."

Nora: "Stop it!"

Nick: "I don't care about myself. I can always make a good living as a detective. But what are you and Nicky going to live on? That's what I worry about at night."

Nora kicks him.

MacFay and Horn go into a room furnished as an office, where Freddie is sitting at a typewriter.

Freddie jumps up on his feet and says: "Good morning, Colonel MacFay."

MacFay walks past Freddie and fishes a discarded piece of carbon paper from the wastebasket. "You could have used this a time or two more."

Freddie says: "I'm sorry, I—"

MacFay cuts him short. "Being sorry doesn't bring back money that's wasted." He sits down at his desk. "Tell Lois I want to see her."

Freddie goes out.

MacFay starts to look at his mail, complaining: "That boy's not worth the room he takes up. Do you know what I found him doing yesterday? Practicing a kind of tap-dance with the typewriter keys."

Horn, standing at the window, says casually: "I think Freddie's mind is more on Lois than it is on his work."

MacFay says: "Lois? Ridiculous! I'll kick him out so fast it'll make his head swim."

Horn, still casually, says: "I've got a young cousin that might suit you if you are going to make a change—a smart boy just out of law school."

MacFay looks suspiciously at Horn and whines: "I've had enough of people's relations. None of them are ever any good." He returns his attention to his mail.

Horn shrugs and looks out of the window at Lois crossing the lawn with Freddie.

She is asking: "Is Papa in a very bad humor this afternoon?"

Freddie answers: "You won't like me to say it, but not much worse than usual."

She pats his arm and says: "Be a little patient, Freddie. He's not well, and he hasn't had an easy life, and now that he's getting old I know that he is difficult sometimes. But if you knew him as well as I do, you'd know he doesn't mean one-tenth of the things he says."

Freddie exclaims: "Be a little patient? Good lord! When I think of the things I've had to put up with. If it hadn't been for you—"

She puts her hand on his arm and says: "I know, I know, and I'm grateful."

They go into the house.

When they come into the room where MacFay and Horn are, MacFay looks up from his correspondence and asks point-blank: "See here, Lois, has this young nitwit been making googoo eyes at you?"

Lois and Freddie look at him dumbfounded.

Horn says good-naturedly: "Come, come, Colonel MacFay, if there was anything like that, it seems to me I ought to be the one to ask questions."

MacFay, ignoring Horn, says to Lois: "Answer me. Has he been making love to you?"

Horn, scowling at MacFay, says bluntly: "This is pretty damned insulting to all three of us."

Lois cries: "Papa—how can you say things like that?"

Freddie, the last to recover his speech, says, half in tears: "This is too much. I'm through—I'm leaving!" He starts out the door, then turns back and yells: "I know Lois is engaged to Dudley, but my feelings for her are my own business!"

MacFay, thus outnumbered, whines: "How am I going to know what's going on if I don't ask? Everybody hides everything from me. You all think I'm just a useless old fool."

Lois goes over to him, runs her hand over his head, and says: "No we don't, but sometimes you are a problem. Won't you ever learn not to say these terrible things to people?"

Horn goes out after Freddie, who has left the room, and catches him at the head of the stairs, saying: "You're not going to be foolish, are you?"

Freddie says: "I'm going away."

Horn says: "Don't do it, kid. Lois is going to feel that it's partly her fault. You ought to know what to expect from the old man by now."

Freddie says: "But I couldn't stay—I feel too ashamed."

Horn says: "So do Lois and I, and so does the old man if he'd admit it. Try it a little longer, kid. We don't want you going like this."

While Freddie hesitates, MacFay's voice comes through the open doorway. "Freddie!"

Freddie looks at Horn, nods, and starts back to the office. Horn puts his arm around Freddie's shoulder. They go into the office.

MacFay says: "Where's that bill from Nichols and Brackett?"

Lois says gaily: "I know what's coming and you needn't bother. A sports dress for $62.50. I haven't worn it yet, so I can send it back tomorrow and there'll be no hard feelings."

MacFay says: "That's not it. I don't begrudge you the dress, but it's for your own good—you're too extravagant."

Lois: "I guess you're right. I guess that's why I didn't wear it before you saw the bill—so I wouldn't have to keep it if you didn't want me to."

MacFay whines: "Oh, you can keep it, but I wish you'd be a little more careful."

Nick and Nora come in.

Nick, briskly: "Shall we have that little business chat now, Colonel?"

MacFay: "Whenever you're ready. There's no particular hurry."

Nick: "But you wired us to come straight down as soon as we got to New York. We thought—"

MacFay: "You'll forgive an old man's inconsiderateness, children. There's really nothing but routine matters."

Horn winks at Nick. (Lois and Freddie have left the room.)

Nick: "I get it. You wanted me down here on account of Church—and used the business angle as bait."

MacFay: "Now that it's over, perhaps I should confess that there may be a little truth in what you say." He pinches Nora's cheek. "You'll forgive the old scoundrel, won't you?"

Nick: "I wouldn't be too sure it's over."

MacFay: "What do you mean?"

Nick: "My guess is that whatever Church meant to do in the first place, he still means to do."

MacFay starts up from his chair, then sinks down with a little laugh and relaxes again. "You're trying to frighten me as punishment for bringing you down here on the run. You can't do it, son. As soon as Church found out you were here, he lit out, and that's all there is to it."

Nick: "I hope you're right, but his talk to me didn't sound like that."

MacFay shakes his head from side to side. "The years it takes young men to learn not to pay any attention to what other young men say!"

Nick: "He wants to include Nora and me in this shakedown on the grounds that her father was your partner. Was he tied up in this mess?"

MacFay: "What difference can all that make now?"

Nora, reproachfully: "Colonel MacFay!"

Nick: "If Church went to jail to shield Nora's father, we want to settle with him."

Nora nods vigorously.

MacFay, angrily: "You want to settle with him! Sure! Neither of you know what it means to have to scrape together your dollars. You don't have to work for money! People die and leave it to you! What's a few thousand here, a few thousand there? It grows on trees!"

Nick: "That's not answering my question. Was Nora's father in with you on this deal?"

MacFay to Horn: "Run along, Dudley."

Horn goes out, shutting the door behind him, and stands there listening.

MacFay, patiently to Nick: "You knew Nora's father, son. Did you think he was a crook?"

Nick: "No."

MacFay: "Do you think I'm a crook?"

Nick, hesitantly: "No-o."

MacFay: "Can you pretend you think I'm a crook?"

Nick: "Yes, I can do that all right."

MacFay: "I thought you could. Well, Nora's father knew mines and he knew timber as well as anybody in the world, but he didn't know the first thing about finance. I did. I built his fortune for him. If it hadn't been for me, he'd never have had a hundred thousand dollars in his life."

Nick, pityingly: "As poor as that!" To Nora: "You'd never have got a first-rate husband that way."

MacFay: "So if I'm a crook, and my partner's an honest man who doesn't know anything about finance, why should I give him a share in the profits from any crooked deal I put over? I have to do all the work myself, don't I? Even if I use his money now and then, why should I let him know it? Isn't it enough to give him his share of the profits from straight deals, where he knows what's going on and where I need his honest knowledge of mining and timber?"

Nick, blinking at MacFay: "There's probably a catch in that somewhere, but you certainly make it sound reasonable."

Nora goes over and kisses MacFay on the cheek. She says: "I don't understand it, but I know you've said something nice."

MacFay pats Nora's hand, says: "So you needn't worry about your father ever having been mixed up in anything like that."

Nora: "And if you hadn't told us this, we'd have paid Church and he'd probably never have bothered you anymore."

MacFay: "You young idiots! Money's not to pass out to the first person that asks for it."

Nora: "But it would have been our money and you—"

MacFay: "*Your* money? Yes, but *I'm* the one that slaved getting it together for you and I feel about it just as I do about my own."

Nick and Nora exchange suspicious glances.

Nick clears his throat, says: "That's swell of you. Now about those routine business matters you mentioned. Don't you think we may as well—uh—you know—kind of go over them now that we're here?"

MacFay: "If you want to." He puts his hand on a desk drawer.

Nick, trying to speak casually: "I sometimes feel ashamed of myself for not knowing more about business than I do. I think a man ought to—well, I'm going to try to take more of an interest in things. For instance, if a man's money is invested in—say in any kind of business—he should know something about it; he should be able to understand—uh—balance sheets and things."

Nora: "Why, Mr. Charles, I'm proud of you!"

MacFay, dryly: "You're not still pretending you think I'm a crook?"

Nick laughs insincerely. "Oh, of course not! But seriously, my conscience hurts me sometimes. Here we are, going along not bothering about anything, just okaying—uh—routine matters when you show them to us. Kind of like butterflies, you might say. And there you are, having to shoulder all the responsibilities, look after all the details for us. It's not right. Is it hard to learn to—uh—you know—make heads or tails of these rows of numbers and things?"

MacFay: "No, all it takes is a little application."

Nick: "Well, suppose instead of just skimming the surface the way we usually do, would it take too long if we—uh—went into things a little more thoroughly this time?"

MacFay: "An excellent idea, and I've all the time in the world. Pull your chairs up." He smiles maliciously. "We'll take our lumber company first. It's a little simpler than the others." He takes a bale of papers from a drawer and puts it on the desk, selecting one sheet of paper from the bale and putting it on the desk in front of them. "To start at the beginning, this graph shows the production of lumber, seasonally adjusted, for our company—that's the solid line—for all other companies in the United States combined—that's the dotted line—for all Canadian companies—the double lines, and for all Canadian and United States companies, exclusive of our company—the chain line—from January 1929, to the present month, both inclusive. Here"—passing them another sheet of paper covered with columns of typewritten figures—"are the figures, if you wish to check them."

Nick: "Not at all."

MacFay: "Study them. Don't fall back into your habit of skimming over things again."

Nick and Nora bend their heads over the figures.

MacFay: "You'll notice that production, seasonally adjusted, has been falling off since June." He fishes out another sheet of paper. "You can see by this that new business in the last couple of months has slowed up and unfilled orders are some 20 percent below last year's figure, while gross stocks are considerably higher than they were a year ago."

Nick, trying to pretend he knows what it is all about, asks: "How large a stock of grosses do we usually have on hand?"

MacFay dives into his bale of papers again.

Nora, who has been counting on her fingers under the desk, nudges Nick and whispers: "The first row of figures in that left-hand column is added up right."

Nick, whispering: "But are they seasonally adjusted?"

Nora nods: "Like a watch!"

Nick: "Good!"

MacFay gives them a still larger sheet of paper with still more figures on it. "Now here are our yearly figures from 1929 to 1936, both inclusive. You'll find them very interesting." He leans over to point out the various columns to them. "Here are the Sales, here Depreciation and Depletion, here Net Income—you'll notice that the figure for 1931 excludes unrealized inventory loss—then Interest, Interest Times Earned, Earned Per Share, Cash Dividends, Surplus For Year—you'll notice there were deficits for the years 1931 to 1934, both inclusive; and here below are Invested Capital—the 1934 figure is after drastic adjustments in the value of land and development—then Percentage Earned on Capital, Properties, Percentage Earned on Properties, Cash and Equivalent, Working Capital, Current Ration, and, last of all, Profit and Loss Surplus. Now here's a statement of . . ."

We leave Nick and Nora nodding determinedly, but groggily, at each item the Colonel shows them.

IN A SHABBY SALOON

Face Peppler is standing at the bar with a big thug.

Face, giving the bartender a dollar bill: "Give me twenty nickels—twenty."

The big thug, plaintively: "I want to go to Nick's party, Face. I love Nick."

Face, as if repeating something he had said before: "It's a *kid's* party, Whacky. Nobody can't go unless they bring a kid."

Whacky: "But Pete and Larry are going."

Face: "Larry's got a kid, and I'm lending Pete one of my brother's brats."

Whacky: "I'll bring a kid." He buttons his coat with an air of determination. "What kind of kid do you want?"

Face grabs his lapel. "Wait a minute, Whacky! No snatch, for God's sake! We don't want to put the big heat on this party!"

Whacky mumbles: "Well, I want to go."

Face: "Okay, but borrow a kid legitimate. Don't show with no hot tot."

Face carefully counts the nickels the bartender gives him, then, with the nickels in one hand, Nora's address book in the other, goes into the telephone booth and dials the first number in the address book.

Face, into the phone: "Is Miss Adams there? . . . This is Nick Charles's society sekkatary. Put her on the wire."

At the other end of the wire, Miss Adams is being handed a telephone by a maid. Miss Adams: "Hello."

Face: "This is Nick Charles's society sekkatary. We're throwing a binge for Nick's kid Tuesday afternoon. Can you make it?"

Miss Adams: "Nick Charles? Are they in town?"

Face: "Are they in town? *You* ought to be in town like they are! But, hey!—wait a minute. Have you got any kids?"

Miss Adams: "Kids? Why, no!"

Face: "Then don't bother. Give it a skip." He hangs up muttering, "That dame wasting my nickels!" dials another number, says into the phone: "Is Mrs. Alliston there? This is Nick Charles's society sekkatary . . ."

MACFAY'S OFFICE

The lights have been turned on.

MacFay, straightening up from the last sheet of paper in his bale, is saying: "And now I think I've given you a pretty good rough picture of the situation."

Nick and Nora rise with deep sighs of relief. Nora seems to be having trouble focusing her eyes. Nick's hair is rumpled, his tie askew, and his face tired.

Nick, pulling himself together and trying to sound hearty: "This has been awfully nice of you, Colonel MacFay, and we've learned a lot. It's—uh—it's opened up—uh—new vistas to us. Hasn't it, Nora?"

Nora: "It's been marvelous!"

MacFay: "But sit down. That's only the lumber company. You'll find the railroad much more interesting. It's more complicated." He takes a larger bale of papers from another drawer. "And after that, we'll take the mining properties."

Nora strikes a pose with a hand to one ear and says: "I hear Nicky crying." She moves toward the door. "Isn't that like him—to make a fuss just when I've found something so fascinating!"

Nick: "I'll go with you."

Nora: "Oh, no! I'll be right back, and you must show me afterwards what Colonel MacFay explained to you while I'm gone, because I don't want to miss a thing."

Nick, glaring at her: "Well, at least send me in a Scotch and soda."

MacFay: "No, son. I want to give you a piece of advice. A lot of men say liquor and business don't mix. I don't say that, but I do say there's one time they don't mix. Drink all you can handle any other time, but don't touch it while you're checking up the figures."

Nora: "That sounds like mighty sound advice to me."

As she goes out, MacFay is beginning: "First, I must tell you that the courts have authorized us to make payments of 20 percent of the principal amount on equipment trust certificates, series D, maturing December 15th."

Nora goes to her room, blows a kiss at Nick Jr., who is sleeping, smiles at the nurse, and begins to change for dinner.

LIVING ROOM OF SMITTY'S APARTMENT IN NEW YORK

It is a typical middle-class furnished apartment, to which Smitty has added feminine touches in the shape of some beribboned cushions, a doll or two, etc.

Dum-Dum is sitting on his heels in one corner of the room eating a dish of ice cream.

Smitty, at the telephone, is saying: "I want to speak to Lieutenant John Guild, Homicide Bureau. This is Mrs. R. Culver Smith speaking." She gets Guild on the phone. "This is Mrs. R. Culver Smith."

He asks: "Who?"

She says disgustedly: "This is Smitty."

He says: "Oh, Smitty—how are you? What do you hear from Tip?"

She says: "He's still kicking about wanting a larger cell—but that ain't what I called you about. I don't know whether it's one of those half-smart tricks that you people think up, or what it is, but some guy phoned me a little while ago, all excited. He won't tell me who he is except he claims he's a friend of Tip's, and he wants to know if I'm going to be home after midnight. He won't tell me what it's all about except that it's something that won't get me in a jam if I give him a square break, but he said he don't want any monkey business, because he's got two murder raps hanging over his head and he's playing for keeps. That wouldn't be some kind of charade you boys thought up, would it?"

Guild says: "It's all news to me. What are you going to do about it?"

Smitty says: "I ain't going to do anything but keep as far away from trouble as I can until Tip gets out of Sing Sing."

Guild says: "That's showing sense. I think the best thing for you to do is to stick around home after midnight and give us a chance to see what this setup is."

Smitty says: "Yeh, but I don't want to get into any trouble with people thinking I'm rattling on them either."

Guild says: "Oh, it's nothing like that. We'll keep your nose clean both ways."

Smitty says hesitantly: "Oh, all right then," and puts up the telephone as Church, in his shirt sleeves, comes in from the adjoining room, holding ice wrapped in a towel to his black eye.

Church asks: "Oke?"

Smitty says: "Oke. But I'm afraid of these fancy rackets. There are too many things can go wrong."

Church laughs at her fears. "It's airtight—we can't miss."

She smiles ruefully. "If that don't sound like Tip. I guess I'm just a sucker for men who are too slick for their own good and mine. Seven years I've been married to *him*, and he's so slick that he ain't been out of the can long enough to finish our honeymoon."

Church says: "You like that guy, don't you?"

Smitty says: "No foolin'."

Church says thoughtfully: "So do I." Then he asks: "Going back to him when he gets out?"

Smitty says: "Yep! I like you a lot, Sam, but Tip's my boy." She laughs reminiscently. "Living with him you never know what kind of a jam you're going to get into from one minute to the next. Did I ever tell you about the time I had my operation and he gave the hospital a rubber check that bounced back before they got me on the table? Was I burned up! Another time in Boston he was fooling around on the side with a little hatcheck girl . . ." She breaks off saying, "But you don't want to listen to all this."

Church kisses her lightly and says: "I like to hear you talk about Tip."

She says: "But on the level, I don't like these schemes where a lot of pieces have to fit in together." She dovetails her fingers. "If I was a man and wanted to steal, I'd rather take my chances just socking somebody with a hunk of pipe."

Church says good-naturedly: "You'd miss a lot of fun."

Smitty says: "Fun? It's no fun to me. Anyway, if we've got to go in for all this razzle-dazzle, why don't you do something about pulling that Nick Charles away from there? I don't trust him. He looks like a guy with insomnia to me"—she smiles at Church's eye—"and a fast punch."

Church: "I don't want him around, but I don't see how he can gum our game. It was airtight without him, and it'll be airtight with him." He touches his black eye. "Don't let this goog bother you. A lot of winners have had them."

Smitty: "All right, if you say so, but maybe I ought to know more about the ins and outs of what you're doing."

Church: "Losing confidence in me since I stopped that punch?"

Smitty: "No, I *still* haven't got that much sense."

The doorbell rings. Smitty looks at Church.

Church wriggles a thumb at Dum-Dum, who gets up swiftly and carries his ice-cream dish into the next room, putting it on a table, and flattening himself against one side of a connecting doorway. Dum-Dum's hand pushes his coat aside a little to rest a handle of the knife in his waistband.

Church nods his head and Smitty goes to the door.

Diamond-Back Vogel, the man Nick saw watching Church's cottage from the hilltop that morning, is there.

Vogel says in his hoarse voice: "Hello, Smitty! Busy?"

She says: "Never too busy to see a friend. Come on in. What do you know?"

Vogel says: "Nothing much." He follows her into the living room. He says: "Hello, Church" without much warmth.

Church says casually: "How are you, Diamond-Back?"

Smitty says: "Sit down."

Vogel sits down, says: "No, I've only got a minute. A guy came in from up the river this morning with a line from Tip."

Smitty asks: "What is it? What does he say?"

Vogel stares at Church.

Smitty says: "Go ahead—Sam's all right. What did Tip say?"

Vogel says: "For you he's all right maybe, but I don't know if he's all right for Tip. Come on out in the kitchen."

Smitty says to Church: "You don't mind, do you?"

Church says: "No."

Smitty and Vogel go into the kitchen.

"What did Tip say?" Smitty asks. "Is he all right?"

Vogel growls: "He's okay, but he's been thinking again. He sent down a lot of forms, orders for material and stuff, with the warden's signature forged on them, and he wants you to get hold of somebody that can pass himself off as the warden's go-between and collect a rake-off for placing these phony orders with business houses. He says make a fifty-fifty deal with whoever you get."

Half-laughing, half-angry, Smitty exclaims: "Nothing can stop that boy!" She holds out her hand. "Have you got the stuff he sent?"

He takes some papers from his pocket and gives them to her. She tears them up.

Vogel nods approvingly, asks: "You spend a lot of time with Church, don't you?"

Smitty says: "Don't start that again. He's just a good friend like I told you."

Vogel growls: "And a guy can get to be too good a friend, too, like I told you. Be seeing you."

He goes out. Smitty returns to the living room.

Church says: "I'm going to skin a knuckle on that four-eyed gent some day."

Smitty laughs and says: "Take big sister's advice and—A, don't try it; and B, if you think you have to, try to catch him without the cheaters on, because I've heard experts say he's plenty good as long as he can see."

Church says: "But he can't see very well without—?" He holds thumbs and forefingers up in circles to indicate glasses.

Smitty says: "So they tell me."

Church says: "Maybe that's something to remember." He looks at his watch and calls: "Dum-Dum."

The Negro comes in.

Church says: "It's time to get going, son." He holds out his hand. "Good luck."

Dum-Dum, smiling broadly, shakes Church's hand and says: "Thank you, sir," pulls a wadded cap from his pocket, says: "Adios" to Church and Smitty, and goes out.

AT MACFAY'S

Lois and Horn are sitting on the shore of a lake, looking out over the water. His arm is around her; she is leaning back against his shoulder.

Horn: "Happy, darling?"

Lois: "M-m-m!"

Horn: "It's not too chilly?"

Lois: "I'd never be chilly this way."

In the living room, Freddie is fooling with the dial of a radio. After a moment, he turns the radio off impatiently and goes to a window, where he stands looking out, biting a fingernail.

In a linen closet, Mrs. Bellam, the housekeeper, is placidly counting sheets.

In Nora's bedroom, she is lying in bed reading, with Nick Jr. sleeping beside her. She turns her head once to smile in the direction of MacFay's office, then goes back to her reading.

In the office, Nick's collar is open and he has taken off his coat. A tray on a table near the desk holds the remains of their dinners. The desk is piled high with papers now.

MacFay is saying: ". . . showing a consolidation net profit of thirty-one thousand, eight hundred sixty-four dollars and twenty-two cents after all charges and normal federal income taxes, but before provision for surtax, equal, after preferred dividend requirements, to fifty-eight cents a share on the combined class A and B common stock."

Nick, trying to prop his eyes open: "I wouldn't've believed it."

MacFay: "*But*, production in August showed a substantial decline, though part of the sharp July increase was retained, and the average for the two months is well above that for the second quarter."

Nick: "Wait till Nora hears that!"

STREET IN HARLEM, NIGHT

Dum-Dum walks briskly up the street, looks around, then goes into the dark entrance of a building. He takes a pint bottle from one of his pockets, drinks from it, and sits down comfortably on the vestibule floor, legs sprawled, back against the wall, chin down on his chest, cap down over his eyes. After a little while, a man comes out of the building, glances timidly at him as he passes, goes on, then returns cautiously to fumble at Dum-Dum's pockets.

Dum-Dum remains motionless except to raise one foot and kick the man in the face. The man tumbles out of the doorway, jumps up, and hurries off. Dum-Dum takes another drink from his bottle, then slumps there as before.

AT MACFAY'S

Nick is lying in bed with his eyes shut, his back to Nora's bed.

Nora: "Aw, stop sulking."

Nick: "You've no loyalty. There isn't another wife in the world who would have left her husband in there to be seasonally adjusted like that."

Nora: "What do you suppose 'seasonally adjusted' means?"

Nick: "I wouldn't tell you. But if you'd stuck around a little longer you would have met 'adverse long-run consequences' and 'major cyclical downswing.' There's a sweetheart!" He repeats, softly and fondly: "Major Cyclical Downswing. Can't you see him? A little threadbare and shiny at the elbows, but still hale and hearty, with a booming, if somewhat whiskey-roughened, voice, and a contemptuous snort for those bounders who want to know what army he was ever in. Dear old fellow!"

He tries to go to sleep again.

Nora: "It's too early to go to sleep, Nick."

Nick: "What time is it?"

Nora, looking at the clock beside the bed: "One o'clock."

Nick: "Sh-h-h! Colonel Both-Inclusive MacFay will hear you. No numbers are that simple. It must be one point three one six two at least."

Fingers tap lightly on the door.

Nora: "Come in."

Lois enters. She is wearing nightgown, robe, and slippers.

Lois: "I saw your light and wondered if you couldn't sleep, too."

Nick: "Some of us could and some of us couldn't." He gets out of bed saying: "Old Major Cyclical Downswing Charles has just the thing for you." He pours her a drink.

Nora says: "I don't think there's anything to worry about now, dear. They—"

Lois says: "Oh, it's not that. I'm not worried. I—" She laughs. "I guess I'm too happy to sleep." She goes to the window and looks out. "It's lovely out. Dudley and I took a long walk over by the lake, and then I couldn't get to sleep for thinking about—" She goes over to Nora's bed, sits down, and hugs her. "I guess you think it's silly to be this happy about getting married, but Dudley really, really is so marvelous."

Nick, starting to offer Lois her drink, quickly gulps it down himself.

Nora pats the girl's shoulder and asks: "When are you getting married?"

Lois says: "The first of the month."

There is the sound of a shot and the lights go out. There are distant sounds of doors slamming, of a man's voice calling out in alarm, of a piece of furniture being upset, and of a body falling.

Nick strikes a match and lights candles on a dressing table. Nora is sitting up in bed clutching Nick Jr., who does not wake.

Lois gasps: "Papa! See if he's all right."

Nick says: "Stay here."

He goes out into the hallway carrying one candle. From the other end of the hall, Horn, barefooted, in pajamas, is approaching with a flashlight. Freddie, dressed, comes out of his room with a candle. There are sounds of people moving in other parts of the house. The three men come together at MacFay's bedroom door.

The door is ajar. Horn pushes it open and throws the beam of his flashlight on the bed. MacFay's bare legs protrude from a wadded pile of blankets that cover the rest of him, except his right arm, which, grotesquely bent, dangles down to the floor.

Nick goes to the bed, lifts enough of the covers to look at MacFay's face. Freddie and Horn look over his shoulder. They stare at the dead man in horror for a moment; then Nick puts the covers back gently over his face. He touches the dangling hand to feel its temperature and straightens up as the housekeeper comes into the room.

Mrs. Bellam is fully dressed and carries a small Bible with one finger marking her place in it. Her face and manner are placid as ever.

Freddie says: "I'm going to be sick," and goes out of the room hurriedly.

The housekeeper says with no sign of excitement: "I heard the noise."

Horn says hoarsely: "MacFay's been murdered."

Mrs. Bellam says quietly, as if to herself: "'The Lord giveth and the Lord taketh away.' Do you want me to phone the sheriff?"

Nick says: "Yes."

She goes out as Lois comes in.

Just inside of the doorway, Lois halts and stands trembling with fear and grief. She says: "Dudley, is he—" She breaks off and tries again: "Is he—" but still cannot finish the sentence.

He goes to her, puts his arm around her, keeping his body between Lois and the bed. He says gently: "Yes, he's dead."

She tries to go past him to the bed, but he holds her, saying: "Not now, darling. You can't look at him now."

Horn leads Lois out.

Nick, left alone in the room, tries the light-switch beside the door, and the wall-lights go on as Freddie returns.

Both windows are open. The bedside lamp is lying on the floor with the wire torn out of it. Neither of its light bulbs is broken. On the bedside table a glass has been upset, spilling water on the table and on the crumpled newspaper, telephone, cigarette box, matches, etc. on the floor below. In one corner of the room an old-style Frontier model .44-caliber revolver lies on the floor. There is a bullet hole high in one wall.

Nick asks: "Ever see the gun before?"

Freddie says: "Yes, it's Colonel MacFay's." He points to an open drawer at the bedside table. "He kept it there."

By this time there are three or four partially dressed servants crowded in the doorway, looking into the room with excited faces.

One of the servants says: "He went out the front door."

Nick asks: "Who?"

The servant says: "I didn't see nobody. I just seen the front door was open when I went down to fix the fuse."

Nick: "What fuse?"

The servant: "The one that was blowed out."

Nick: "How did you know it was blowed out?"

Servant: "I didn't know nothing. I was just doing what Mrs. Bellam told me. When she come out of here she told me to see if any fuses was blowed out and I went down and there was and I put in a new one and that's when I seen the front door was open."

Freddie: "Here's Mrs. Bellam now."

The housekeeper comes in carrying a tray with two cups of coffee and some toast on it. She says: "I don't suppose you'll be getting back to sleep again tonight, so maybe you'll feel better for this." She puts the tray down, looks at the bed, shakes her head, and says mildly: "Poor soul—seems he always expected to be murdered like this."

She goes out, driving the servants away from the door as she goes.

Horn comes in.

Freddie asks: "How's Lois?"

Horn says: "She'll be all right. I left her with Mrs. Charles." He looks at the bed. "That's a mean way to die."

Nick asks: "Know any good ways?"

The sound of cars and motorcycles arriving comes through the open windows.

The arriving party consists of the assistant district attorney, the examining physician, three deputy sheriffs, a photographer, a fingerprint expert, and three state troopers on motorcycles. From time to time more troopers, deputies, etc., come until there are altogether some fifteen or twenty of them. These are well-trained men who go to work immediately with a minimum of noises and confusion. Floodlights are turned on the grounds around the house and men afoot and on motorcycles set off to examine every part of the estate. Servants and outer guards are rounded up for questioning.

The assistant district attorney, followed by a deputy sheriff, photographer, medical examiner, and fingerprint man go up to MacFay's room.

VanSlack, the assistant district attorney, is a tall, stooped, colorless young man with a vague face; the same vagueness characterizes his words and manner.

He looks uncertainly around the room and says: "I am Assistant District Attorney VanSlack."

Horn says: "How do you do. This is Nick Charles, Freddie Coleman, and I'm Dudley Horn, and here is—" He finishes the sentence by motioning with his hand toward the bed.

The photographer, setting up his camera, says to the medical examiner: "You can have it in a minute, Doc." He asks Horn: "Anything been moved?"

Horn looks at Nick, who says: "Only this doesn't belong here." He takes up the tray with the cups of coffee and toast on it.

VanSlack says: "If you gentlemen will, eh—" and steps back out of the room.

The others follow him out into the corridor. Nick puts the tray on the floor.

VanSlack asks: "Do you know who found him?"

Nick says: "The three of us. We met at the door."

VanSlack, clearing his throat again, says: "I don't suppose you saw anything."

Nick says: "Just what you see in there now."

VanSlack asks: "Was there any special reason for you three meeting here? I mean had you heard anything—perhaps—"

Nick answers: "A shot."

VanSlack says: "Oh—there was a shot? Did it—do you mind telling me where you were when you heard it?"

Nick says: "I was in my bedroom at the other end of the hall with my wife and MacFay's daughter."

VanSlack says: "That is MacFay in there, isn't it?"

Nick says: "I'd hate to think anybody was playing that kind of joke on us."

Horn says: "I was asleep."

VanSlack looks at Freddie, who says: "I was in my room. I was—" he hesitates "—writing."

This dialogue is punctuated from time to time by the flare of the photographer's flashlights through the open bedroom door.

VanSlack says: "I don't suppose any of you know who saw him last?"

After a moment of hesitancy, Freddie says: "I guess I did. I was in there a little after midnight, to have him sign some mail."

VanSlack asks: "Did you happen to notice what he was doing when you left?"

Freddie says: "Yes, he was reading the afternoon paper. That is—he picked it up as I went out."

VanSlack asks: "Was he in bed?"

Freddie says: "Yes. I turned off all except the bedside light when I left."

The photographer looks out to say: "It's all yourn, Doc."

The doctor goes in to the bed and starts to examine the body.

VanSlack says: "If any of you gentlemen happen to think of anything that might help us, just tell one of the boys, will you? I oughtn't to be very long in here."

He, the deputy sheriff, and the fingerprint man go into the bedroom and shut the door behind them.

Horn says: "He's not exactly my idea of a human bloodhound."

Nick says: "Maybe that's nothing against him."

VanSlack opens the door and says: "Mr. Charles, eh—could you—that is, have you a minute?"

Nick says: "Sure."

He goes into MacFay's room and VanSlack shuts the door.

VanSlack says: "I thought perhaps—of course everybody knows your reputation—perhaps you wouldn't mind sort of looking at things with us. It's pretty confusing, isn't it?"

Nick says: "I'll be glad to do anything I can, but the way you people are going at it, it doesn't look as if you need much of anybody's help."

He looks around the room. The deputy sheriff and photographer are measuring the height of the bullet hole from the floor, the distance of the gun from the bed, etc.; the fingerprint man is at work on the window sills, and the examining physician is busy with the body.

VanSlack says modestly: "Well, we try to keep up to date. You see, not having very much of this sort of thing ourselves we have plenty of time to keep in touch with what progress crime detecting agencies are making in other places. Of course that doesn't take the place of practical experience." He points to the gun. "You don't happen to know who that belongs to?"

Nick says: "The secretary said it was MacFay's. He kept it in the drawer there."

VanSlack says: "I thought maybe it would be."

The medical examiner turns from the bed and says: "Throat cut from ear to ear with a fairly large, heavy blade. Death instantaneous.

Bruise on left temple, blunt instrument. Right wrist broken. That ought to be enough to go on. If there is anything else, I'll give it to you after I go over him more thoroughly tomorrow. Been dead half an hour." He looks at Nick. "Does that check with the time you found him?"

Nick says: "Check."

VanSlack says: "Thank you, Doctor."

The medical examiner goes out.

VanSlack looks worriedly at the bullet hole, at the gun, at the bedside lamp, glass, etc., at the dead man, and then at Nick, and says uncertainly: "We'll say, for instance, that MacFay heard the murderer—he could have come in through either the door or the window—we ought to be able to find out which—and grabbed the gun." He turns to the deputy sheriff and says: "From the looks of that hole, Les, where would you say the bullet was fired from?"

Les says: "I figure it had to come from pretty close to the floor there alongside the bed."

VanSlack: "Then the murderer was already bearing down on his arm when MacFay got the shot away; or it could be, with one of those old guns, that it went off when it hit the floor after the murderer had broken his arm and made him drop it." He says to Nick: "I hope this sounds reasonable to you."

Nick says: "It does—and a paraffin test would tell you whether MacFay pulled the trigger or the gun went off after it hit the floor, if that point's worth bothering about."

VanSlack says: "Well, we always try to be as thorough as we can. So next, our murderer would have knocked MacFay back on the pillow with that blow on the temple, perhaps stunning him, and then cut his throat, pulling the bed-clothes over him to keep the blood from spurting around. Now we've got to try and figure out how he entered and left. What do you think on that point, Mr. Charles?"

Nick says: "One of the servants said the front door was open."

VanSlack says: "But if you and the other gentlemen came as soon as you heard the shot, wouldn't you have seen or heard, or—you know what I mean?"

Nick says: "This room's right at the head of the stairs. I didn't get here that quick. The lights were out, you know, and I had to stop to find a candle."

VanSlack says vaguely: "Oh, the lights went out."

Nick says: "Yes, the servant says a fuse blew out. An electrician ought to be able to tell you whether it could have happened when the wires were torn out of that upset lamp."

VanSlack says: "Oh yes—an electrician. Certainly."

Nick says: "You know about Sam Church?"

VanSlack says: "Yes—and the Negro. We're doing everything we can to catch them, of course. But sometimes it's so hard to find people. Now there are a couple of other things I'd like to ask your help on."

Nick, imitating VanSlack: "My help—oh yes—certainly."

Elsewhere in the house, other members of the household are being questioned separately.

In the living room a uniformed trooper is saying to Dudley Horn: "So you were asleep, huh? How long had you been asleep?"

Horn, who has put on some clothes, answers: "Half an hour— maybe three-quarters."

The Trooper asks: "What were you doing before that?"

Horn says: "Miss MacFay and I had taken a walk."

The Trooper says: "Miss MacFay, huh? The daughter?"

Horn says: "Yes. But if you'd stop wasting time here and start looking for Church—"

The Trooper interrupts him: "I got a *lot* of time to waste. Did MacFay know you and his daughter were out walking?"

Horn says: "Of course. I don't know. What different does that make? Miss MacFay and I are engaged."

Trooper: "Oh! So you're marrying the heiress? She *is* the heiress, isn't she?"

Horn says: "I suppose so. I don't actually know."

The Trooper says: "Hmm! A while back you said you used to work with this fellow Church. Are you and he still pretty close?"

Horn says: "We were never pretty close."

The Trooper says: "Oh! You didn't like each other much, huh?"

Horn says: "That's right."

The Trooper says: "Well, are you unfriends enough that it wouldn't make you mad to see him go back to the can or maybe to the chair?"

Horn stands up, saying indignantly: "If you're suggesting that I would frame him—"

The trooper puts a hand on Horn's chest and pushes him back into his chair, saying: "Don't get sore over a little thing like that. Wait'll you hear what I'm really going to suggest."

In another downstairs room, Mrs. Bellam, the housekeeper, is being questioned by a little, plump man in clothes that need pressing.

The Plump Man says: "Ain't that pretty late for a lady your age to be up?"

Mrs. Bellam: "I don't think so."

The Plump Man: "What time do you mostly go to bed?"

Mrs. Bellam: "Not often before two o'clock, and sometimes it's three or four."

The Plump Man: "Got things on your mind that worry you, keep you awake?"

Mrs. Bellam: "No, it's just that I don't sleep very much."

Plump Man: "What were you doing when you heard the shot?"

Mrs. Bellam: "Reading."

Plump Man: "Reading what?"

Mrs. Bellam: "The Bible."

Plump Man: "Oh!" then, after a pause: "Well, that's all right. How long had you been in your room?"

Mrs. Bellam: "I went up there about eleven o'clock."

Plump Man: "Were you undressed?"

Mrs. Bellam: "No."

Plump Man: "And you were in your room all the time from around eleven till you heard the shot?"

Mrs. Bellam: "That's right."

Plump Man: "And you didn't see or hear anything out of the ordinary till you got to his room and saw the others there?"

Mrs. Bellam: "Not a single thing except the shot."

Plump Man: "What did you think when you found out the old man had been killed?"

Mrs. Bellam: "I was sorry."

Plump Man: "You and the Colonel get along pretty well?"

She says: "Yes. I always know what to expect from Colonel MacFay and I never expected anything different."

The Plump Man thinks that over for a moment, then gives it up and asks: "Who gets the old man's money?"

She says: "I'm sure I don't know except I always thought it would go to Miss Lois."

He asks: "Will you get any of it?"

She answers: "I'd be mighty surprised if I did."

He says: "You've been working for the old man a long time, haven't you?"

Mrs. Bellam: "Sixteen years."

The Plump Man: "And you used to know this Sam Church when *he* worked for the old man?"

Mrs. Bellam: "Yes, indeed, I knew him."

The Plump Man: "All right, then, make yourself comfortable and we'll have a long talk about what you know about him."

In his bedroom, Freddie is being questioned by an elderly detective who from time to time jots down notes on pieces of paper he takes from various pockets, apparently never using the same piece twice.

The Detective says: "Now, son, when you left the old man in his room after midnight, what did you do?"

Freddie says: "I came here."

Detective: "Straight here?"

Freddie: "Yes, sir."

Detective: "You didn't hear or see anything until the shot came?"

Freddie: "That's right."

Detective: "Where were you when you heard it—in bed?"

Freddie: "No, sir."

Detective: "Where were you?"

Freddie: "Sitting at that table."

Detective: "Undressed yet?"

Freddie: "No sir."

Detective: "Well, you must have been doing something."

Freddie: "I—I had some work to do. I was writing."

Detective: "Writing what?"

Freddie stammers and finally says: "A play. I'm trying to write a play."

Detective, in a tone of slight surprise, says: "Oh, go on!" Then: "What's it called?"

Freddie: "'The Minute-Hand.'"

Detective: "Yes? Let me see it."

Freddie goes to the table and gives him a handful of manuscript pages written in longhand.

The Detective says: "You're a private secretary—how is it you don't write this on one of those typewriters?"

Freddie: "I only get a chance to work on it late at night and I was afraid the typewriter would disturb people. Besides, when you're writing your first play, you kind of don't like people to know about it."

The detective, puzzled by this, looks at Freddie for a moment, then begins to read the play.

Presently, the Detective puts the manuscript down on his knee and says: "So you write about murders, huh? Do you think much about murders?"

Freddie says: "It's a mystery play. Lots of people write mystery plays."

The Detective says: "They do? You wouldn't happen to make a hobby of what they call criminology?"

Freddie: "No sir."

Detective: "Well, I'll have to show this to VanSlack. He might think it kind of shows how your mind works—what they call psychology." He looks down at the manuscript. "This isn't all of it, is it?"

Freddie says: "No sir. I haven't finished the second act."

The Detective says: "Hmmm! And how many acts now would a play have?"

Freddie: "Three."

Detective: "Maybe you can write the rest of it while VanSlack's reading this. Who is MacFay's lawyer?"

Freddie: "Floyd Tanner."

Detective: "The one that's always in some jam with the income tax people?"

Freddie: "I don't know about that."

Detective: "When's the last time MacFay made a will?"

Freddie: "About seven months ago, I think."

Detective: "Well, who gets the money?"

Freddie: "I don't know whether I ought to—"

Detective: "This is a murder we're trying to clear up, lad, and the more you can tell us the better. So don't let's hang up over who's going to tell what."

Freddie: "According to the memorandum I typed, Miss MacFay was to get everything except a hundred thousand dollars. That went to Mrs. Bellam, the housekeeper."

Detective: "How much do you figure everything but a hundred thousand would amount to?"

Freddie: "I don't know. It would certainly be several million, but I don't suppose anybody but Colonel MacFay knew exactly what property he had."

Detective: "Where do these Charles people fit in?"

Freddie: "Why, they—they have money invested in some properties with the Colonel."

Detective: "And they never had any trouble with the Colonel over their money?"

Freddie: "No—nothing—nothing to pay any attention to. Of course not."

Detective: "What was there not to pay any attention to?"

Freddie: "Nothing. It was just a joke. He was laughing tonight about their wanting to examine the accounts for the first time and how he kept Mr. Charles up to his neck in figures for eight solid hours without Mr. Charles being able to tell a decimal point from a debit."

Detective: "How do you tell a—never mind. What came up that Charles wanted all of a sudden to examine the accounts?"

Freddie: "Nothing. It was just a joke. Even Colonel MacFay thought it was funny."

Detective: "A sense of humor. That's got men killed before."

Freddie: "But you can't—"

Detective: "Take it easy, lad. I'm going to give you a little rest now, but don't be going out of the house."

The detective goes down to the living room, where the uniformed trooper is still questioning Horn. The detective and the trooper whisper together for a moment in a corner of the room, then go back to Horn.

Trooper: "You been working for MacFay a long time; so has this Bellam woman. What's the connection?"

Horn: "Between her and me? None."

Detective: "She gets a hundred grand in his will."

Horn: "What's that got to do with me?"

Trooper: "You're marrying his daughter who gets the rest of his dough."

Horn: "What's that got to do with Mrs. Bellam?"

Detective: "It's a coincidence."

Trooper: "What makes Bellam rate a hundred gees?"

Horn: "It's none of my business, but I'll tell you. Years ago she was MacFay's girl. Then they drifted apart and she got married, and then after her husband died and left her without a nickel the old man took her in as housekeeper."

Trooper: "Just as housekeeper?"

Horn nods.

Detective: "That's kind of sweet."

Trooper: "He adopted this Lois: could she be Bellam's daughter?"

Horn: "No. He took Lois from an orphanage. Her mother's name was Shelley and she died when Lois was born. You can check that."

Detective: "We will. What's the tie-up between Charles and Church?"

Horn: "There's no tie-up! Church had threatened him, too."

Trooper: "Yeah? Well, do you think Charles is the type of man that might have killed the Colonel to frame Church?"

Horn stares open-mouthed at the trooper.

IN MACFAY'S OFFICE

VanSlack is keeping in touch with New York City and the surrounding country by telephone, meanwhile receiving information from and giving instructions to men who pass in and out of the room. Nick is sitting on a corner of the desk; a couple of VanSlack's men are lounging by the window.

Nick: "Did you people have a man watching Church?"

VanSlack: "No. The sheriff's office was keeping an eye on him in a way, but we didn't have anybody actually watching him. I suppose there will be a lot of complaining about that now. People will be saying we should have covered Church day and night after Colonel MacFay came to us, but I didn't see how we could have guessed it was going to turn out like this. You know yourself it was all pretty ridiculous in a way and could have turned out to be just a kind of bad practical joke. Couldn't it?"

Nick nods.

VanSlack: "Did you have any special reason for thinking we had a man on Church's tail?"

Nick says: "When I went down to see Church yesterday morning, there was a chap up on the hill keeping tabs on him with field glasses and, when I tried to strike up a conversation with him, he showed me a buzzer and told me to go chase myself."

VanSlack: "Really? What kind of looking man was he?"

Nick describes Vogel.

VanSlack looks questioningly at the other men in the room. They all shake their heads.

VanSlack says: "That's peculiar, because I don't know of anybody around here who looks like that."

Nick says: "I thought it was peculiar—I'd never seen a country cop with a new six-thousand-dollar coupe before, so I wrote the license number down."

VanSlack says: "That's splendid. Will you get it?"

Nick goes to his bedroom. Nick Jr. is asleep on one of the beds. Lois, sitting in a chair by the window, has recovered some of her composure. Nora is encouraging her to drink a cup of coffee.

They both turn to Nick as he comes in and Nora asks: "Have they found anything?"

Nick says: "They haven't found Church or his black man yet, if that's what you mean, but he can't have much of a start."

Lois says: "Do you suppose he did it?"

Nick looks at her in slight surprise, asking: "Don't you?"

She says: "Oh yes—he must have. Don't pay any attention to me."

Nick has crossed to a closet and is hunting through his coat for the paper on which he wrote the license number.

He asks: "Did you have your session with the police?"

Nora says: "Yes. They were very sweet. I think detectives' manners have improved since your day."

He finds his piece of paper.

Lois asks: "Could I—do you think they'd let me see Papa now?"

Nick shakes his head at Nora, who begins to explain to Lois why it is best not to see her father now, as Nick escapes.

In the hall, at the head of the stairs, Nick meets Freddie.

Freddie: "Is she all right?"

Nick says: "Lois? I think so."

Freddie: "Do you think she'd like to see me?"

Nick: "You could try."

Freddie: "Will these policemen be here long?"

Nick says: "Most likely. They tell me they don't often get a chance to play at being scientific detectives, so they'll probably make the most of it. Why? Do they bother you?"

Freddie: "No, but I wish they'd clear out."

Horn and the trooper who was questioning him come up the stairs together.

Nick, holding out the slip of paper with the license number on it to the trooper: "Will you give this to Mr. VanSlack for me and tell him I'm taking time out to dress?"

The Trooper, taking the paper: "Sure thing."

Horn, going over to Lois: "How are you now, darling?"

Lois: "I'm all right."

Freddie hovers over them, smiling an aimless smile that is meant to be cheering.

Nick moves between bedroom and bathroom, dressing.

Lois: "I think I would feel better if somebody told me whether Papa—did he die without—"

Horn: "There was no pain, dear; he died instantly."

Lois: "Where—where was he shot?"

Horn: "Your father fired that, at the murderer. Don't let's talk about it now."

Lois: "But I want to talk about it. I want to face it. I don't want to baby myself. Do you think the police are enough, or should we get somebody to help them?"

Horn, bitterly: "From my experience with them, I'd say they were being thorough enough anyway."

Lois: "Do you mean they questioned you?"

Horn: "They did everything but jail me, and that can still happen."

Lois: "Don't be unreasonable, dear. You know they have to suspect everybody."

Horn grumbles: "I don't know it. I think Church would be enough."

Lois: "Did they question you, Freddie?"

Freddie: "Yes. They haven't much respect for anybody's privacy, but I really didn't mind." He sits down on the baby.

Nick, Nora, Lois, and Horn all yell warnings at Freddie, but too late. Nora runs over to pick up the baby. Nick Jr. does not cry, but scowls unpleasantly at Freddie, and says: "Drunk."

Freddie: "I'm sorry! I'm—did I—"

The door bursts open and half a dozen detectives and troopers with guns in their hands come running in bawling: "What is it? What's the matter? What's going on here?"

Reporters try to crowd into the room behind the police.

Nora, indignantly: "How would you like somebody to sit on your baby?"

One of the troopers: "If you're talking about my baby, it would do her plenty of good."

The reporters, seeing Nick, begin to call: "There he is. Hello, Nick. These mugs didn't want to let us see you," etc.

The police herd the reporters out of the room as VanSlack comes in.

One of the detectives: "It's nothing, Van. They're just horsing around."

VanSlack, vaguely: "Is that so?" Then to Nick: "That license number belongs to a man named Vogel, a gambler-racketeer, and his description seems to fit the man you saw. The New York police think they can get hold of him for us. Do you—that is, I'm going in to see him and that Smith woman you told me about. Would you care to go along?"

Nick: "If you think I'd be any help."

Nora: "Then I'm going, too. I'm not going to keep Nicky down here with nothing but a lot of country pol—" She breaks off in consternation, staring at the country policemen around her, gulps, says, "country pol—" again while hunting desperately for an out, finds it, and finishes triumphantly "—country poultry to eat. You know he's on a diet."

Nick goes over and kisses her, saying: "Sweetheart, you are wonderful. I wouldn't have believed anybody could get out of that one."

Nora, with mock modesty: "It was nothing really."

One policeman to another: "How do you like them to do until a couple of real screwballs come along?"

VanSlack to Nora: "I can appreciate your feelings, Mrs. Charles. Naturally you think—with everything that's happened—I understand. But—well—we'd like to get away without attracting the attention of the newspaper men and we'll be in pretty much of a hurry. It might not be so comfortable for—and you'll be perfectly safe here with—or if you want you can follow us in as soon as you're ready and a couple of my men will ride in with you."

Nick, imitating VanSlack: "Yes, dear, you can—I think it would give you time—there's always another—and there you are."

A trooper comes in panting: "There's a dog running around outside with a knife in his mouth."

Nick and Nora exclaim: "Asta!" together.

Outside it is still night. With the help of lights that range in size from searchlights mounted on automobiles to flashlights carried in hands, policemen are trying to corner Asta, who, holding in his mouth a knife similar to the one seen in Dum-Dum's possession, dashes across an open space and disappears into darkness behind a row of shrubs.

At an upstairs window, Freddie and Mrs. Bellam can be seen looking down at the men chasing the dog.

As Nick and VanSlack come up, one of the troopers says: "We're going to have to shoot that mutt; we'll never catch him this way."

VanSlack: "First we'll see if Mr. Charles—it's Mr. Charles's dog—perhaps he can help us."

Nick: "Where did he find the knife?"

Trooper, pointing: "We don't know. He came around thataway with it."

Nick: "Where is he now?"

Trooper, pointing in the opposite direction: "We don't know. He went around thataway with it."

Nick whistles and calls to Asta, with no result.

Trooper: "A guy that can't make his dog mind ought to trade it in for goldfish or something."

Nick, pretending he hasn't heard the trooper, calls again, then says: "He's not going to come running up to a lot of strange men with lights. What do you think he is, a moth? Call your men back and give me a flashlight."

VanSlack sends a trooper to call back the men who are trying to corner Asta, and Nick, armed with a flashlight, whistling and calling as he goes, moves off into the darkness. Presently he finds Asta in the same folded beach umbrella in which the dog hid after the killing of Lois's collie.

As Nick takes the knife from Asta and straightens up, he hears somebody approaching stealthily. He switches off his light, moves a little to one side, and crouches there with his hand on his gun.

Lois's voice comes through the darkness, whispering: "It's Lois, Mr. Charles. I want to—"

Nick, as she comes up to him: "What are you doing running around out here?"

Lois: "I had to see you away from the police." She stands so that Nick, to face her, must turn his back toward a dark clump of bushes not far away. Then she starts as she sees the knife in Nick's hand, and asks: "Is that the—is that the one?"

Nick: "Probably."

Lois: "Oh, Mr. Charles, I've got a horrible question to ask you. Will you tell me the truth?"

Nick: "If I can."

Lois: "You've got to. There's nobody else I can turn to. I don't know what to—" Looking over Nick's shoulder, she sees a man with a gun in his hand emerge from the clump of bushes behind Nick. Lois gasps, "Look out!" and pushes Nick to one side as the man fires. (It must be obvious that she does save Nick from being shot.)

Nick, upset by the girl's push, yanks his gun out as he falls, and fires as the man near the bushes shoots a second time. The man staggers back into the bushes and from time to time fires again, with Nick, circling the bushes, returning his fire.

Police come running up, pouring bullets into the bushes. The grounds are flooded with lights again. Presently the firing stops, and Nick and the police force their way into the clump of bushes.

Dudley Horn is lying there dead, the ragged condition of his clothes suggesting that he has been nearly shot to pieces. The police stare at him in surprise.

Trooper: "Him! Can you beat that?" Then he suddenly looks sharply at Nick and demands: "Say, what were you shooting at him for?"

Nick: "Because he was shooting at me. What were you shooting at him for?"

Trooper, scratching his head: "Well, everybody else was."

VanSlack arrives, stares at Horn, says: "This is a surprise in a way. Do you mind telling me what—how it happened?

Nick: "I was taking the knife"—he hands the knife to VanSlack—"away from the dog when Lois MacFay came up and started to tell me something. Then she yelled and pushed me out of the way just as this fellow started snapping caps at me."

VanSlack: "Lois MacFay, hum? Do you—the question will surprise you no doubt—but do you think she might have been—you know?"

Nick: "Putting me on the spot? The first bullet would have caught me if she hadn't pushed me out of the way. I felt it go past."

VanSlack: "It was just a thought. Where is she?"

Nick looks around. "I don't know."

Police throw the beams from their lights across the grounds. Lois is lying on the grass back where Nick was first shot at, apparently unconscious, with blood staining her clothes.

Nick kneels beside her, feeling for a pulse, then says: "She's alive."

Another of the men says: "It's just her arm," and opens a knife to rip her sleeve.

Lois's eyes open. She sees Nick and asks: "Was it—Dudley?"

Nick: "Yes."

Lois shudders, then asks: "Did they catch him?"

Nick: "He's dead."

Lois shuts her eyes.

The man who has been examining Lois's arm says: "She'll be okay. The bullet only took a hunk of flesh out."

VanSlack: "Well, let's carry her up to the house. I want to talk to her when she comes to." Then to Nick: "What was it she started to tell you?"

Lois opens her eyes again and sits up, saying: "I'm not badly hurt. It was the shock. Oh, Nick, it was true then!"

Nick: "What was true?"

Lois: "What I tried to tell you, about Dudley." She begins to cry. "Oh, it can't be true. I loved him so."

Nick: "He killed Colonel MacFay?"

Lois: "That's what I wanted to ask you."

VanSlack: "I don't want to seem unkind, Miss MacFay, but surely you can see that all this might have been avoided if you had come to us with your suspicions, whatever they were."

Lois: "I know, but how could I believe it? I can't believe it now."

VanSlack: "It's not a matter of what you believe, Miss MacFay, it's more—well—what happened that you wanted to talk to Mr. Charles about?"

Lois: "It was about Dudley. He—it started right after Papa was killed. Dudley suggested that we say we were together at the time Papa was killed—so the police wouldn't bother me, he said. I told him we couldn't do that, but I didn't think anything of it until later when he began to act funny.

VanSlack: "Funny in just what way?

Lois: "Nothing that anyone who didn't know him so well would notice, but I noticed it. And then after that policeman said the knife had been found, and you and Mr. Charles went out, he acted still funnier, and when he went out of the room I followed him to ask him what was the matter, I saw him in his room putting a pistol in his pocket, and then I didn't know what to think except that I'd better find Mr. Charles as soon as possible and ask him what he thought."

(Those of Horn's actions which fit in with her story may be shown in their proper place if necessary, depending on whether it is thought better to bolster up her story than to keep the audience in doubt as to who Nick's assailant is until the last moment.)

* * *

Nick and VanSlack are together in the rear of a car being driven toward New York City. The sun is not yet up, though it is fairly light.

VanSlack: "It's amazing the obstacles one runs into in this work, isn't it?"

Nick: "Oh, quite."

VanSlack: "It's so unfortunate that your dog should have found the knife with nobody around to see where he found it. Now we'll probably never know."

Nick: "I'm apologizing. No fingerprints on the knife?"

VanSlack: "There'd hardly be, after the dog had been playing with it for nobody knows how long. Though there are plenty of his tooth prints on it. But I daresay we can safely assume it was the knife used for the murder. Don't you think so?"

Nick: "I think so." After a pause. "How do you fit Horn into all this?"

VanSlack: "I should ask you that. After all, you're the one who killed him."

Nick: "Maybe I am, maybe not. A lot of you people were shooting at him, too. All we know is that I am the one he was trying to kill."

VanSlack: "Doesn't that come to the same thing in a sense?" Looks at his watch. "Now that you have had time to think, perhaps you can remember something—something that happened or was said—that might have slipped your memory in the excitement . . . if you know what I mean."

Nick: "I know what you mean. You mean if I've been holding out on you, you'll make it easy for me to come clean now."

VanSlack: "Not at all, Mr. Charles. Well, not exactly. But perhaps Miss MacFay's story was not . . ."

Nick: "Miss MacFay may be a liar but that was a truthful bullet she pushed me out of the way of."

VanSlack, sighing: "I suppose it was, but it makes the whole thing more confusing, doesn't it?"

Nick, shrugging: "Maybe yes, maybe no. All we've got to find out is why Horn should try to kill me when I found the knife that killed MacFay and that belonged to Church's henchman."

VanSlack: "That's exactly it, and I must say that from my viewpoint everything would be clearer if it were not for your statements that Miss MacFay was with you and Mrs. Charles at the time of her father's murder and that she did save you from being killed by Horn."

Nick: "What do you want me to do? Confess that Horn killed me?"

VanSlack, his voice and manner for the first time cold and menacing: "What I want you to do, Mr. Charles, is to tell me the truth."

Nick stares at him a moment, then laughs. "You know, I am beginning to think you've really got hold of something, even if you don't know what it is or what to do with it. My guess is you are bouncing around not more than six inches away from the answer to the whole thing."

VanSlack looks down at the space between him and Nick on the seat of the car. The space is about six inches.

Back at MacFay's Lois is lying on her bed with her eyes shut. Mrs. Bellam sits in a chair beside the bed, placidly knitting.

Mrs. Bellam: "Whatever Mr. Horn did in this world, he is now answering for in the other world and it is not for us to judge him."

Lois, opening her eyes, sitting up: "But why did he kill Papa?"

Mrs. Bellam: "Lie down, dear. Men's hearts are incomprehensible."

Lois: "But Papa was so good to Dudley. He—"

Mrs. Bellam: "How are we, with our limited understandings, to say what is good and what is not good?" She pauses to count a row of stitches. "It would be easy for us in our worldliness to say that Colonel MacFay was the most wicked man that ever lived, but how can we look into his inner soul?"

Lois: "But nobody could say that. He wasn't. He wasn't."

Mrs. Bellam, quietly as before: "Only by human standards, my dear."

Lois: "But look how good he was to me, and to Dudley."

Mrs. Bellam: "Colonel MacFay was afraid of Dudley Horn. Dudley Horn knew too much about him, even knew how he was robbing that nice Mr. and Mrs. Charles."

Lois: "Oh, he wasn't!"

Mrs. Bellam, calmly nodding: "I'm only telling you that because I imagine it will come to light anyhow. Dudley Horn would most surely have taken the precaution of leaving a statement somewhere to be published in case he was killed. He would have thought that would tie Colonel MacFay's hands."

Lois: "But then why should Dudley have tried to kill Mr. Charles?"

Mrs. Bellam: "If Mr. Charles had discovered his losses in going over the accounts yesterday, the estate would have had to make them good, my dear."

Lois: "Go away, please, Mrs. Bellam." She turns over, burying her head in the pillow. "Go away."

Mrs. Bellam: "Try to rest, my dear." She gathers up her knitting, rises, and goes quietly out.

Freddie, listening outside the door, jumps back in confusion as Mrs. Bellam comes out of the room.

Mrs. Bellam smiles tranquilly at Freddie, shuts the door behind her, and goes upstairs.

Freddie stares after Mrs. Bellam for a moment, biting a fingernail, then looks at Lois's door in indecision, hears footsteps coming up the stairs from the ground floor, and goes off to his own room.

The man coming up the stairs is a detective. He goes into Nora's room, where she is being questioned by two detectives. Nick Jr. has gone to sleep holding Asta's tail. Asta is very uncomfortable, but afraid to try to pull away.

Detective: "One o'clock in the morning's a funny time to have a alibi down here in the country—unless you were expecting something to happen. Were you?"

Nora: "Of course not."

The Detective: "Nobody else had a alibi—just you and your husband and this Lois."

Nora: "It's a habit with Nick. He's had an alibi for everything that's happened since I married him."

Detective: "And a lot of things happen every place he goes, don't they?"

Nora: "Never a dull moment is what all our friends say."

Detective: "Wasn't there a killing in your family that he was mixed up in out on the Coast a year or two ago?"

Nora: "Do you mean wasn't there a killing that he solved while policemen were suspecting the wrong people?"

Detective: "You can put it any way you want, but he was mixed up in it; and there was another woman mixed up in it, too, wasn't there?"

Nora: "My cousin."

Detective: "I don't know anything about that. I just remember seeing her picture in the papers, and she was kind of young and pretty. Then he was mixed up in that Wynant murder last time he was in New York, and there was some women in that that he used to know before he was married, wasn't there?"

Nora: "Just what are you getting at?"

Detective: "Looks to me like every time he gets in with a gal the insurance companies take an awful beating. Say, that guy's deadlier than the Bourbon plague."

Nora: "But what has that got to do with Colonel MacFay's murder?"

Detective: "Lois. It's nice for a wife to trust her husband—in reason—but don't you ever get to wondering about him sometimes?"

Nora: "*Some*times?"

Detective: "We're not just dishing the dirt on your husband for the fun of it. We're trying to show you what you're up against. It ain't in the book that any man that's had that many numbers would settle down to one, and you are too fine a lady to get that kind of runaround."

Nora: "Was he really like that? I thought he was just bragging."

Detective: "I suppose you never heard about the coalman's widow in Cleveland that wanted to set him up in a detective agency of his own."

Nora, leading him on: "Was that Louella?"

Detective: "No, her name was Belle Spruce."

Nora, delighted: "I mustn't forget that one. Tell me more."

Detective: "Well, then there was a lighthouse keeper's daughter in—"

Nora: "A what?"

Detective: "A lighthouse keeper's daughter."

Nora: "What was her name?"

Detective, exasperated by her facetiousness: "What it all comes down to is this Lois. You're wrong to think there couldn't be anything between them. They're just making a monkey of you covering up for them."

A New Arrival: "Hey." The second detective turns to him. "Are you getting anywhere?"

Detective: "Naw, she's bats."

Second Detective: "I wouldn't mind my old lady being bats that way."

New Arrival to Nora: "There's a telephone call for you." He winks at the others.

First Detective to Nora: "Go ahead, take it. We're through with you."

Nora: "I'm sorry. You've no idea how interesting this sort of thing can be to a wife. Please tell me the lighthouse keeper's daughter's name."

As the three men go out, the Detective says, "Letty Finhaden," and slams the door.

Nora, happily, to the sleeping baby: "And Letty Finhaden. Isn't your papa going to be surprised at the things your mama knows?" She goes to the telephone.

In New York City Nick and VanSlack buy morning papers with screaming headlines—ANOTHER THIN MAN MURDER MYSTERY—LONG ISLAND MILLIONAIRE KILLED—NICK CHARLES GUEST OF SLAIN CAPITALIST—EX-CONVICT AND NEGRO SOUGHT BY POLICE, etc. Nick's photograph occupies the chief position on most front pages, with MacFay's and Church's (a rogues' gallery photograph) flanking it.

As Nick and VanSlack prepare to drive on, a bundle of extras is thrown to the newsdealer from a passing truck. They buy copies of the extras, whose headlines say—SECOND SLAYING IN LONG ISLAND THIN MAN MYSTERY—ENGINEER KILLED IN ATTACK ON NICK CHARLES, etc. There are more pictures of Nick, and one of Nora.

As they get out of their car in front of Smitty's apartment, they are joined by Lieutenant John Guild.

Nick: "Hello, Guild."

Guild, shaking Nick's hand warmly: "I'm glad to see you back with us. Say, things sure pop when you're in town, don't they? Remember last time when folks were being killed all over the—"

Nick: "Don't say that! I'm having enough trouble with VanSlack now. I've been on the wrong end of a third degree all morning."

VanSlack looks reproachfully at Nick.

Guild: "How are you, Mr. VanSlack? I came over as soon as I heard you were trying to get a line on Smitty. But if your killing was at one o'clock this morning, she's in the clear. We had a plant on this joint from before midnight till way after three and we know she was in it all the time."

VanSlack: "Are you sure she couldn't—"

Guild: "Dead sure. I saw her two-three times myself between twelve and three and it would take her easy an hour or an hour and a half each way to get down to MacFay's and back."

Nick, beginning to grin: "How did it happen you were watching her place?"

Guild: "It turned out to be a false alarm, but she phoned me yesterday—" He breaks off as Nick's grin widens. "Could she have been stringing me—using *me* to give her an alibi?"

Nick nods.

Guild, indignantly: "She can't do that to me!" He leads the way into the apartment building.

They go up to Smitty's apartment and knock on the door. After a little while it is opened by Smitty in pajamas and robe.

Smitty, yawning: "Good morning, Nick; good morning again, Lieutenant." Then to VanSlack: "Pleased to meet you." She yawns again. "Come on in and have some coffee before you tell me what Tip's been doing now."

Guild: "So you pick me to give you an alibi, huh? I've got to lose a night's sleep so you can duck a murder rap. Well, you're not ducking it. There's such a thing as complicity and—"

Smitty: "Murder?"

Guild: "What did you think was going to happen down at MacFay's after midnight?"

Smitty, holding up her right hand: "I never thought it was going to be murder."

VanSlack, edging in between her and the angry lieutenant: "But you did expect something to happen down there." Then, when she does not reply: "Where is Church?"

Smitty: "I don't know."

VanSlack: "When is he coming back?"

Smitty: "He isn't coming back. He said he was going to Cuba."

Guild, who has been looking in the closet, turns with a man's overcoat in his hand. "Who does this belong to?"

Smitty: "Sam."

Guild empties the contents of its pockets on the table. They are a handkerchief, a pair of gloves, crumpled package of cigarettes, and a book of paper matches. "What is his coat doing here if he ain't coming back?"

Smitty: "It's been here two or three weeks."

Guild, indicating the things he's taken from the coat pocket to Nick and VanSlack: "There's nothing else in it."

VanSlack to Smitty: "Where is his servant, Dum-Dum?"

Guild continues to look around the apartment, opening drawers, looking under cushions, etc.

Smitty: "I don't know. They went out of here around ten o'clock last night and that's the last I've seen or heard of them."

VanSlack: "Where were they going?"

Smitty: "I don't know."

VanSlack: "But they left together."

Smitty: "No. Dum-Dum left first, and Sam went out maybe ten or fifteen minutes afterwards." She turns to Nick. "Please tell me on the level—was MacFay murdered?"

VanSlack, before Nick can reply: "Why do you think MacFay was murdered?"

Smitty, holding up her right hand again. "I knew Sam was trying to get dough out of MacFay, but I never knew he meant to kill him."

VanSlack: "But you know it now, don't you?"

Smitty: "I don't know anything that's got anything to do with murders."

VanSlack: "Murders! Who else's murder was planned besides MacFay's?"

Smitty: "I don't know about anybody's murder being planned."

Guild: "You're psychic, huh? You get yourself alibis for murders you don't know are going to happen."

Smitty: "I'll never need an alibi for murder because I'll never have anything to do with any murder."

VanSlack: "You know Mr. Charles, don't you?"

Smitty: "Sure."

VanSlack: "Were you present at a meeting between Church and Mr. Charles yesterday morning?"

Smitty: "That's right."

VanSlack: "Exactly what happened at that meeting?"

Smitty looks at Nick in bewilderment.

Nick, cheerfully: "I'm a suspect, too. We must get together sometime and swap experiences."

Smitty: "What do you know about that? You cops don't even trust yourselves."

VanSlack: "What happened at that meeting?"

Smitty: "They didn't get along very well. There was a lot of talk about who ought to give Sam some money and about Nick's father-in-law, who's dead as far as I could make out, and it wound up with Nick slugging Sam."

VanSlack: "Why did he slug him?"

Smitty: "You know how men are."

VanSlack: "Did Church threaten Nick—and Nick's wife and kid?"

Smitty: "Nick seemed to think so—and I guess he was right. Sam's likely to say anything when he gets going: he's the loosest-talking man."

VanSlack: "How long have you known Church?"

Smitty: "Just since they sprung him. He was Tip's cellmate."

VanSlack: "It didn't take you long to tie up with him, did it?"

Smitty: "We weren't playing for keeps. He said he needed a girl to stooge for him. I'm small-time stuff and it wasn't costing him much, but I'm not fronting for murder. If he's innocent, he can come clean, and if he's guilty I'm getting out from under."

VanSlack: "Just what do you mean by stooging for him?"

Smitty: "There's a lot of rackets where it's handy to have a girl around."

VanSlack: "You mean in various blackmail rackets, for instance?"

Smitty: "I mean in a lot of kinds of rackets—except murder."

As VanSlack starts to ask his next question, the doorbell rings. Guild goes to the door and opens it.

Vogel, coming in: "What are you doing here, Guild?" He looks at Nick and VanSlack.

Guild: "Diamond-Back, I want you to meet Mr. Nick Charles and Mr. VanSlack, an assistant district attorney from the Island. This is Mr. Vogel." His manner toward Vogel is that of a policeman toward an influential politician whom he doesn't trust too much. "We were asking Smitty some questions."

Vogel: "About Church, huh? I always figured he was a wrong gee."

VanSlack: "What do you know about him?"

Vogel: "Me? Nothing except he was spending too much time hanging around Smitty." He scowls at the woman. "You haven't been unloading to these people yet, have you?"

Smitty, touching her knee: "Only from here up."

Vogel: "I ought to take a smack at you."

Smitty: "But I'll not be the goat for any—"

Vogel: "Shut up. Didn't you ever hear about talking through a lawyer? That's why mugs have got a slang name for them!"

VanSlack: "I may as well tell you, Mr. Vogel, that the lady has told enough to justify us holding her as a material witness at the very least."

Vogel: "Okay, hold her as long as you want, ask her all the questions you want, but let's have her lawyer there; and if you want to let her out on bail afterwards, make it any amount you want, but let's do it regular."

VanSlack: "Just what is your relationship to the people involved?"

Vogel: "None. Call me a friend of the family."

VanSlack, to Nick: "Is this the man you saw watching Church's house?"

Nick: "Yes."

Smitty to Vogel: "Why, you big ape!"

VanSlack: "Well, what's the matter?"

Vogel: "It won't get you very far. Tip's married to this baby and you know how it is when a guy's hanging on the wall upstate—he gets to worrying about things. So I been kind of keeping an eye on her for him. Well, I hear Church is going away and for all I know this cluck might think she's going away with him."

VanSlack: "Suppose she had gone away with Church."

Vogel: "That's supposing too much."

VanSlack: "You mean you would have stopped her? But just as a friend of the family."

Vogel: "Listen, chum. So Tip's a crummy little coffee-and-doughnut crook, but when I hit this town strickly on my insteps ten years ago he was the only guy in it that would give me a stake. Well, that boy can call on me for anything I got—money, time, or the gun." He jerks a thumb at Guild. "He can tell you I got a permit to carry *that*."

VanSlack clears his throat and begins to slip back into his former vagueness: "I think I can understand your feelings. Now in the course of—uh—watching over Mrs. Smith, just what did you learn about Church that might help us?"

Vogel: "Just nothing. You can get whatever you want to know out of Smitty—as soon as she gets her lawyer."

Smitty to Vogel: "So that's the way it's been."

Vogel: "What did you think was going on? Did you think I was hanging around because I was nuts about you?"

Nick: "Don't let's quarrel with one another. The police are our natural enemies."

VanSlack looks reproachfully at him again.

There is a noise from the direction of the kitchen. Guild dashes toward the kitchen, with the others following him, except for Nick, who stands looking after them. Through the open door Dum-Dum can be seen running down the service entrance. Guild and VanSlack dash out in pursuit of him with Smitty and Vogel following them more slowly.

Nick walks over to the table where Guild put the articles taken from Church's coat pocket, pokes at them with a finger, picks up the paper of matches, reads the advertisement on it—"West Indies Club"— tosses it back on the table, picks up his hat, and goes out.

He pauses at the top of the back stairs, looks down the well at a landing several floors below where Guild and VanSlack have caught Dum-Dum and are searching him. Guild finds the wooden-handled knife in his waistband.

VanSlack, staring at it in amazement, says: "This is the knife Mac-Fay was killed with, dog's tooth prints and all. It can't be."

Nick smiles and turns away to descend by the other staircase.

Nick walks up a street in the Latin American section of Harlem. It is now broad daylight and the street is almost empty except for eight or ten men planted in doorways watching the West Indies Club. These men are obviously detectives, but Nick gives no sign that he notices them.

Nick goes into the West Indies Club, a not too Broadwayish establishment fairly full at this hour; its patrons are chiefly Latin American, with a sprinkling of New York underworld characters. On the small dance floor a West Indian boy and girl are singing and dancing a beguine to the music of a noisy native orchestra. Many of the customers are reading the newspaper accounts of MacFay's murder and discussing them: Church and Dum-Dum are well-known habitués of the place. At a large table a group of men is extremely interested in something that is hidden from us and from Nick by their backs.

As Nick appears in the doorway, one of the men looking at the newspapers sees him, nudges his neighbor, points to Nick's picture in the paper, then at Nick. Others recognize him by the same means.

The proprietor goes over to Nick, bowing, saying: "Ah, Mr. Nick Charles, is it not? And you are alone?"

Nick, accepting recognition as his due: "The good are often alone."

The proprietor, smiling: "I fix it so you will not be good long."

He leads Nick to a table near the orchestra where two or three girl entertainers are seated. Nick is welcomed with that special cordiality reserved for liberal spenders in Harlem late-spots.

The beguine over, one of the girls at the table signals the orchestra and gets up to do a special number for Nick. While she is working at it a waiter brings Nick a note, which reads:

Darling Nickie,

    If you still remember poor little me and my little coal-yard in Cleveland, and can tear yourself away from your charming little playmates, won't you come over and have a little drinkie for old times' sake.

Adoringly,
Belle Spruce

Nick, to the waiter: "Where did this come from?"

Waiter indicates the table men are crowded around.

Nick, seeing nothing but men: "Is there a lady there?"

Waiter, enthusiastically: "A lady? What a lady! If I didn't have to work for a living carrying drinks to these pigs!" He throws a kiss toward the hidden lady.

Nick, rising, straightening his tie, eluding the detaining hands of his tablemates: "Well, well, old Belle Spruce." He crosses to the crowded table, pats the shoulder of one of the men standing in his way, and, when the man steps aside, is face-to-face with Nora.

Nora, brightly: "Why, Nickie, are you looking for somebody?"

Nick, looking at her, speaking as if with carefully controlled anger: "Tonight, two nights ago, three times last week. How much longer did you think I was going on believing you had to sit up with your sister's sick baby?" Then sharply: "Which is the man?" Then craftily, as he begins to look in turn at each of the men at the table: "They tell me he limps a little."

Each man, as Nick looks at him, walks away from the table with exaggerated agility, or firmness, or gracefulness, to show he is not lame. Nick quickly sits down at the table and says to the waiter: "Take the rest of those chairs away and bring us two Bacardis and a menu. I'm starving."

Nora, looking regretfully at her departed admirers: "They were such nice men, Nick. One of them promised to teach me a new dance. And another was telling me how much I'd like Buenos Aires."

Nick: "With a blond wig? What are you doing here anyhow?"

Nora, putting a finger up beside her nose: "I have a clue."

Nick, with complete loss of interest: "Oh, well, if that's all it is."

Nora: "I oughtn't to tell you."

Nick, agreeably: "Go ahead and don't." Then, as the waiter arrives with their drinks and menus: "What do you want to eat?"

Nora, sulking: "I don't care. Anything you want."

Nick, to the waiter: "Two more Bacardis, two orders of oysters on the half shell, two . . ." etc., etc. He orders two enormous and complicated meals. The waiter goes away.

Nora: "You're going to feel very silly if you don't solve this mystery just because you were too smart-alecky to listen to my clue."

Nick: "Don't get mad—I'll listen."

Nora: "You don't have to listen. Just give me the fourteen dollars and seventy-five cents."

Nick: "What fourteen dollars and which seventy-five cents?"

Nora: "For the man."

Nick, patiently: "What man?"

Nora: "The man who phoned me."

Nick: "Let's get this straight. A man phoned you and—"

Nora: "No, he phoned *you*."

Nick: "A man phoned me and I promised him fourteen dollars and seventy-five cents?"

Nora: "Yes. I did. You weren't there."

Nick: "I wasn't where?"

Nora: "You're just trying to get me mixed up. At MacFay's, after you left, a man phoned you, a man with an accent, and when you weren't there he talked to me, and he said he'd seen in the paper that you were hunting for Church and Dum-Dum and he could tell you where to find Dum-Dum if you met him here. He said not to bring the police because he was not a stool-pigeon and he only wanted fourteen dollars and seventy-five cents because that was what Dum-Dum owed him and wouldn't pay and the whole thing was between gentlemen. He kept saying the whole thing was between gentlemen."

Nick: "That must have made you feel pretty much an outsider. Where did he say Dum-Dum is?"

Nora: "He didn't say."

Nick: "Is that why we're going to give him fourteen dollars and seventy-five cents?"

Nora: "No. He hasn't had a chance to speak to me yet. All those nice men came over and began to talk to me, so there wasn't much privacy."

Nick, as the waiter brings their fresh drinks and the oysters: "I'm sorry I chased them away. For fourteen seventy-five they can come back."

Nora, rising as the orchestra begins to play again: "They don't have to. I'm going to dance with my new teacher." She goes over to one of the men who had been at her table, and they dance.

The girl entertainer who had done a number for Nick, now seeing him alone, comes over to his table. Her face lights up when she sees the two orders of oysters in front of him and she asks: "What are you doing later?"

Nick starts to answer her, then breaks off as he sees Dum-Dum coming into the Club. Dum-Dum is making a smiling entrance, bowing to acquaintances right and left, and when he sees Nick he comes straight to his table.

Dum-Dum, to the entertainer: "Mr. Charles my friend. You sharpen the teeth someplace else. Scram, scram."

The girl goes away.

Nick: "Make out all right with the police?"

Dum-Dum: "Always I do. Last night I get drunk and go to sleep in a vestibule and they lock me up until a couple hours ago I get sober. Those policemen from Long Island, they don't believe me, but they believe policemen in station-house when I take them there."

Nick: "How about Church? Is he making out all right?"

Dum-Dum, shaking his head: "That I come to ask you. I do not know."

Nick: "Where do you think he is?"

Dum-Dum: "I do not know."

Nick: "Think he killed MacFay?"

Dum-Dum, grinning: "Does any man say he think his friend killed?"

Nick: "MacFay was killed with a knife just like yours."

Dum-Dum: "The police tell me that. I think they tell lie to trick me. I never see another knife like that up here."

On the dance floor, Nora has just begun to learn the new step when, each time she comes around close to the orchestra, she is thrown off by one of the musicians going, "ps-s-s-s!" in her ear. She doesn't succeed in learning which musician it is, or why he is "ps-s-sing" in her ear until the music stops. Then, as she moves off the floor, one of the musicians catches her eye and makes a double gesture—indicating Dum-Dum with a jerk of his thumb, rubbing the fingers of his other hand with that thumb to say "Pay me."

Nora nods and goes back to her table, accompanied by her dance partner. Thus encouraged, the other men who had been at her table begin to drift back to it, bringing chairs with them.

Nora, whispering to Nick: "The man wants his money."

Nick: "All men want money. Greed, greed! It's the curse of the age."

Nora: "But he did help us find Dum-Dum."

Nick: "If he helped you, you pay him." He turns to find his table is crowded with Nora's admirers, most of them busy just now ordering drinks on him of course.

Nora takes advantage of Nick's preoccupations with his guests to pick his pocket.

Sitting opposite Nick is a fat man the others call Cookie. He is very tight and talkative and none of the others seems to like him.

Cookie: "I could tell you right now who killed most of the guys that get themselves killed in this man's town. A fellow that gets around as much as I do and keeps his eyes open and can put two and two together don't have to wait to read things in newspapers."

One of the men, contemptuously: "Okay, big lard, who knocked off A. R.?"

Cookie: "Don't think I don't know, but you don't have to think I'm putting the finger on guys. Listen, I could . . ." As he goes on, the orchestra begins to play again; one of the men at the table rises and bows to Nora, who gets up and goes off with him to dance, the money she took from Nick wadded in one hand. Dancing past the musician who had signaled her, she drops the money into his instrument.

Back at the table, Cookie is telling Nick: "And I could tell you plenty about Sam Church, too. Many's the bottle him and me killed in this joint and over in that gal's flat he run around with, too."

Nick: "What girl? Smitty?"

Cookie: "No—Linda Mills—the one he ditched, or got ditched by, before he took up with Smitty. A cute-looking kind of doll, I guess, under all that war-paint, but too plenty tough for me. Too plenty tough, I guess, for most guys—the way she didn't hold on to any of 'em very long. Lives over in the Chestevere Apartments."

Nick: "He must move around fast. I thought he'd only been back from Cuba ten days or so."

Cookie: "If you call this Cuba. He's been around these joints ever since he got out of stir. Say, you don't know no more about him than the police; and it's a cinch they're plenty wrong about him if they say Sam was mixed up in anything down on the Island last night. I seen him going in Vogel's at—"

Dum-Dum suddenly jumps up, reaches for his knife, which is not in its usual place at his waistband, then hits Cookie in the face with his fist. A waiter swings his tray high in the air with both hands and bangs it down on Cookie's head. As Cookie falls down on all fours another man hits him with a bottle, and then half a dozen are making flying leaps at him as the lights go out.

The orchestra, in the manner of a well-trained orchestra in a joint, continues, playing a little louder than usual. When the lights go on,

Nora is one half of the only couple still dancing. Nick is the other half of the couple. Nora's former partner is coming out from under a table. Police are coming into the place. Cookie has disappeared.

Nick: "Shall we rejoin our guests, Mrs. Charles?"

Before Nora can reply, her former partner comes up to her holding one side of his jaw, saying: "Are you all right? Something bumped into me something terrible."

Nick looks down at the knuckles of his right hand, but does not say anything.

They return to their table. Their uneaten dinner is a smeary mess. The police are trying to find out what happened.

Dum-Dum: "It is that Cookie. Always he want to start something—always a fight."

Nick: "I didn't see him do anything."

Waiter: "Aw, you can't wait till he does anything. It's too late then. You got to get the jump on him."

Another man: "That's right. It's a kind of look he gets in his eye."

Nick gives it up. He and Nora start to leave. Nick gets his hat and they start down the stairs.

Nora, stopping: "Oh, Asta. I checked Asta."

Nick returns to the hatcheck room and gets Asta, who has been sleeping on a pile of coats. When Asta gets up from them the hatcheck girl calmly begins to pick them up one at a time to hang them carefully on hangers.

As Nick and Nora go downstairs, Nick: "Before we get outside, darling. We have a baby—remember? You didn't check that, did you?"

Nora: "I left Nicky home with the policemen."

Nick, as they go into the street: "Oh, the policemen, of course. What policemen?"

Nora: "That Lieutenant Guild sent up to the hotel to guard him. Oh, there's the park. Let's give Asta a little run in it before we go home."

Nick, as they walk toward the park: "Did you have a chance to count the policemen?"

Nora: "I counted both of them."

Nick: "I'm glad there are only two."

Nora: "So am I, because they said they were going to stay with us till things quieted down if it took six months, and that they wouldn't be any trouble at all—we could just treat them like members of the family."

They turn Asta loose in the park and sit down wearily on a bench, where Nora immediately falls asleep. Nick is thinking. He makes up his mind, calls Asta, ties him to the bench, gets up quietly, and leaves Asta and Nora there.

At the Chestevere Apartments Nick knocks on Linda Mills's door. There is the sound of movement in the apartment, but nobody opens the door. Nick knocks again.

The Chestevere landlady comes out of another apartment. She is a frowsy, middle-aged woman with the sniffles. In one hand she carries a newspaper, in the other a handkerchief.

Landlady: "At this time of morning, mister, she's either asleep or ain't home yet."

She peers sharply at Nick, then down at the newspaper in her hand.

Nick cranes his neck to see his picture in the paper, then strikes the pose shown in the picture.

Landlady, all agog: "Say, you're him, ain't you?"

Nick bows.

Landlady, dabbing her nose with her handkerchief: "Well, I declare. What are you—" She lowers her voice to a noisy whisper. "Say, is she involved?"

Nick: "Who?" he whispers. The next seven lines are spoken in whispers that would be audible at a distance of twenty feet or more.

Landlady, gesturing toward the door with her handkerchief: "Mills."

Nick: "What makes you think she might be—involved, as you put it?"

Landlady: "You being here—and then that friend of hers."

Nick: "What friend?"

Landlady, raising paper to show Church's picture—rogues' gallery picture: "Him."

Nick: "Do you know him?"

Landlady: "I seen him coming in and out."

Nick: "When's the last time you seen him?"

Landlady: "I don't know. Maybe a couple of weeks. But that don't mean nothing. Sometimes I don't see my tenants for that long—them that ain't behind in their rent."

Nick: "What does Linda Mills do for a living?"

Landlady: "What do you think these girls do? I don't run no Y.M.C.A. She's been here a couple of years and she's good pay. That's all I care about. That's what I tell some of the others when they kick about her throwing noisy parties sometimes and having fights in her flat."

Nick: "How's chances of finding out whether she's in now?"

Landlady: "I'll see."

She knocks on the door, then knocks louder, calling in an unnaturally sweet voice: "Miss Mills. Miss Mills. It's me, Mrs. Dolley."

There is no answer. She dabs her nose with the handkerchief and takes a bunch of keys from her belt, unlocks the door, sticks her head in, and calls again: "Miss Mills." Then to Nick: "I guess she ain't in all right."

Nick, stepping into the apartment, pushing the door back against the wall and standing with a heel against it, holding it there: "That's too bad. Will you do me a favor?"

Landlady: "What?"

Nick: "I left the district attorney sitting out front in my car. Will you ask him to come up?"

Landlady, impressed: "Yes, sir." She hurries away.

Cookie comes out sheepishly from behind the door. He has a black eye, a swollen ear, and his clothes are torn.

Cookie: "I can explain everything if you just give me a chance."

Nick: "That's dandy. How about explaining that bag of nails at the West Indies."

Cookie: "Oh, that! Those guys get too excited."

Nick: "I agree with you, but the point is, what was it they got too excited about this morning?"

Cookie: "I don't know—unless maybe they thought I hadn't ought to dragged Linda's name in."

Nick: "You mean they're old-fashioned gentlemen who think a woman's name shouldn't be bandied about a pub?"

Cookie: "No, not exactly, but—I don't want to do the gal no harm. She and Sam Church don't pal around no more, so I don't see how I was tying her up in anything. That's what I came over here for after they threw me out of that dump—to tell her about it and see what she said."

Nick: "And?"

Cookie: "No soap. She ain't home."

Nick: "How did you get in?"

Cookie: "The door's unlocked. Try it yourself."

Nick tries the door, finds it unlocked.

Nick: "I've misunderstood the whole thing. I thought the boys ganged up on you when you mentioned Vogel's name.

Cookie: "Vogel? What Vogel?"

Nick, patiently: "You said Church wasn't down on the Island last night because you saw him going into Vogel's. And then the shindig was on."

Cookie: "Oh, sure, I remember now. I started to say I saw Sam going in Vogel's Delicatessen down on Third Avenue last night and he told me he was catching a 'leven o'clock train south, so I knew he couldn't have been down on Long Island way around one."

Nick: "Unless he was lying to you."

Cookie, earnestly: "But why would he lie to *me*?"

Nick: "I give up. What Vogel is this that has the delicatessen?"

Cookie: "Do I know? Sol Vogel or something."

Nick: "Not Diamond-Back Vogel?"

Cookie: "You mean the gambler? What would he be doing with a delicatessen?"

The Landlady comes back, saying: "I couldn't find no car out front with or without a district attorney."

Nick: "I'm sorry. He's such a restless fellow. Have you met Cookie?"

Landlady: "I seen him somewhere, but I never met him."

Nick: "Cookie's a friend of Linda Mills."

Landlady: "Maybe. I seen him somewhere."

Nick: "Mind if I look around?"

He goes into the living room without waiting for the landlady's reply, then into the kitchen, and finally into the bedroom. The apartment is not dirty, but there are signs that Linda Mills is a careless housekeeper. The landlady complains about cigarette burns on a table and when she touches them, she gets dust on her fingers. The bed has not been made; its two pillows are on a chair beside the bed.

Nick notices an unfaded rectangle of wallpaper the size and shape of a nearby picture, looks behind the picture, and sees that the wallpaper behind it is faded the same shade as the uncovered paper—except where a small patch of white paper has been pasted over a small hole.

He goes over to the bed. On the floor beside the bed there is a scorched spot on the rug.

Nick: "How long since either of you have seen this Mills girl?"

Cookie: "Oh, I'd say ten days anyways, maybe longer."

Landlady: "I ain't seen her in a couple of weeks, but that ain't unusual. I don't see my people much most of the time—them that ain't behind with their rent."

Nick: "What does she look like?"

The landlady and Cookie collaborate in giving him a description that would fit either Lois MacFay or the nurse, Ella Waters, with allowances for heavy makeup, flashy clothes, a tougher manner, etc.

Nick, wandering around, opening drawers: "She get much mail?"

Landlady: "Not that I know anything about."

Nick stops by a small table and, as if idly, thumbs the phone directory there.

Cookie, coming over to him, eagerly helping him turn the pages: "See, there is Sol Vogel, the delicatessen on Third Avenue. See, I didn't lie to you. See."

Nick, skeptically: "I see it's in the book and I believe it's on Third Avenue, but I don't know how much further I can go with you."

Cookie begins long-winded protestations of his trustworthiness, which continue while Nick leaves the apartment and walks down the street. Cookie trots along beside him, chattering away until they are in front of an electrical appliance shop.

(Nick then drops back, the CAMERA PANNING WITH COOKIE until he suddenly realizes he is alone, turns to look back, cannot see Nick, and, crestfallen, goes on alone.)

Presently Nick comes out of the electrical appliance shop, saying "A million thanks" to someone inside, and goes off down the street.

When Nick returns to Nora and Asta in the park, she is still asleep. He starts to rouse her, then sits down beside her, starts once more, hesitates, his eyelids drooping, lifts his hand a couple of inches in another attempt, and goes to sleep beside her.

When they are finally awakened it is early afternoon.

In their suite at the Normandie, Nick and Nora find Nick Jr.'s guards—Detectives Dan Schultz and Red Jensen—playing cards. Nick Jr. is sitting under the table playing with a pistol.

Nora cries out in consternation.

Jensen: "It's all right, lady. I took the bullets out. He can't hurt anything."

Nick Jr. bangs the pistol down on Jensen's foot.

Schultz falls out of his chair laughing, gasping between laughs: "That kid's a humdinger. I never seen anything like him." He points at the child, who is staring with calm interest at Jensen holding his injured foot, and goes off into further roars of laughter.

Nora picks up Nick Jr., separates him from the pistol, and goes toward the bedroom. Asta grabs the pistol and heads for the kitchen with it, Jensen running after him.

Nick, to Schultz: "We live like this." He follows Nora into the bedroom, where he takes the child from her and begins to play with it.

Nora: "Sh-h-h. You'll wake her up."

Nick: "Who?"

Nora, indicating door opposite the one they came in through: "Didn't I tell you I brought Lois up with me?"

Nick: "No, you didn't. Are you telling me now?"

Nora: "But, Nick, I couldn't leave her down there alone with all those terrible things happening." She puts a finger to her lips and goes over to open the other bedroom door. Nick goes with her.

In the next room Lois is lying in bed apparently asleep. There are no pillows on the bed.

As Nora softly shuts the door a commotion breaks out in the living room, that door opens, and Schultz sticks his head in.

Schultz: "Hey! Gangrene's setting in out here."

They go into the living room. The corridor door is open. Jensen is blocking the doorway, trying to keep out Creeps, Whacky, and six or eight of their friends, each with a child of some sort in tow.

Nora: "The baby party!"

AN HOUR LATER, WITH THE BABY PARTY IN FULL BLAST. THE SCENE:

1. Creeps and Whacky tend the door, insisting that "You can't come in unless you got a kid."

2. Gilbert Wynant is slugged when Mimi tries to pass him off as a kid.

3. Bootleg business in kids being passed out at service chute at a dollar a head to be used as tickets of admission. Nick Jr. used for this purpose, as his guards have trouble telling one child from another and are satisfied to be guarding any child that is about the same age and size as Nick Jr.

4. Children of Nora's more social friends, some terrified by the thugs' brats, some delighted.

5. Mrs. Bellam and Freddie come to see Lois, but are drowned in party before they see her. She is still asleep.

6. Assortment of gifts brought for Nicky, ranging from costly dolls to homemade blackjacks.

7. Creeps, with his collection of keys to fit every door in the hotel, throws open adjoining suites to the guests as Nick and Nora's suite

becomes crowded. A very dainty young girl from one of the higher social levels follows him around in admiration, and when, in one of the suites they open, a man sits up in bed, she snarls at him: "Nick Charles has brought his mob on from the Coast and we're taking the dump over for a little while, but you'll be okay if'n you stay in bed with your head under the covers." The man quickly takes her advice.

8. A drunk staring at the party in two layers—bending down, he sees a room full of children, playing, squabbling on the floor, with everything above them a hazy blur; standing erect he sees a riotous adult party, with the children blotted out by the haze.

9. Creeps and a thug near a telephone. Nick comes to phone, says to operator: "Hello, darling, will you get me . . . .'s candy store." Then: "This is Nick Charles at the Normandie Hotel. Can you send me over [some candy suitable for children] right away? Thanks." He hangs up, starts away from phone, then remembers something, and says: "Creeps, will you phone the drugstore and order some . . ." Creeps says: "Sure, Nick," picks up the phone and tells the operator: "Sweetheart, will you get me the drugstore?" Then: "Will you send . . . to Nick Charles at the Normandie Hotel?" The Thug, curiously: "What do they do, send it up C.O.D.?" Creeps: "No, these rich people don't have to bother about things like that. They pay for it downstairs and put it on the bill." The Thug: "Say, that ain't bad." He picks up the telephone and says: "Snooky, will you get me Tiffany's jewelry store?" Creeps takes the phone away from him.

FLASHES:

1. Smitty at her phone, saying heatedly: "He's gone to the Normandie? He can't get away with that." (It should seem that she may be speaking threateningly, though she is not.)

2. Dum-Dum, at drugstore phone, speaking to Smitty, saying softly but menacingly: "Maybe you're right, but you stay away from there." He hangs up, thinks for a moment, then leaves the store, steps into a taxi, and says to the driver: "Drop me around the corner from the Normandie, Ted."

3. Smitty getting up from phone, grabbing hat and coat, and leaving apartment.
4. Nick Jr.'s nurse walking up and down the street opposite the Normandie, starting toward it, then walking on a little way.
5. Vogel getting out of a car in front of the Normandie.
6. Church, his hat pulled down over his face, walking swiftly toward the Normandie.

Nora, in her bedroom, picks up the telephone and asks the operator: "Will you ring my living room, please?"

In the living room, Nick answers the phone. The ensuing conversation is interrupted from time to time by one or another of his guests falling over him, etc.

Nora, in a disguised voice: "Mr. Charles?"

Nick: "Yes."

Nora: "Oh, Nickie. Guess who this is."

Nick: "Oh, hello! It's good hearing your voice again. I didn't recognize it for a moment. How have you been?"

Nora: "Who is it, then?"

Nick: "Now you don't think I'd ever forget your voice."

Nora: "Yes, I do. Who am I?"

Nick: "Okay, who are you?"

Nora: "Oh, Nickie, to think you'd forget poor little me in just a few years."

Nick: "I know your voice as well as I do my own, but I just can't place it at the moment."

Nora: "It's Letty, Nickie!"

Nick: "Who?"

Nora: "Letty Finhaden. Don't you remember? My papa used to have a lighthouse."

Nick: "Of course . . . This connection is so bad and there is so much noise I can hardly hear you. How are you, darling?" He takes the Belle Spruce note from his pocket and nods at it.

Nora: "I'm fine, but you had forgotten me completely."

Nick: "No, no. It's all this noise. I often think about you. How is your father?"

Nora: "He's all right, except that he gets a little giddy climbing up and down those ladders. Can you meet me for lunch, Nickie?"

Nick: "Not today, honey. I've been up all night and—"

Nora: "How about tomorrow?"

Nick: "Well, you'd better phone me in the morning. I've been so—"

Nora: "I know what's the matter. That awful rich woman you married won't let you out. Tell me, Nickie, is she really as ghastly as everybody says?"

Nick: "She's not as ghastly as *everybody* says."

Nora, after a moment's struggle to stay in character: "Hold the line a minute, Nickie. I hear Papa coming in his rowboat and I know he'd love to talk to you." She hangs up gently.

In the living room, Nick makes a face at the telephone and hangs up, then goes over to straighten out a disagreement between a couple of his guests, after which he goes into the bedroom.

Nora, at the telephone, is saying: "Will you ring my living room again, please?"

Nick: "Who are you this time? That cooch dancer I used to run around with in Juarez? You have to do that with a Greek accent."

Nora puts the phone down and turns toward him, then gasps and looks over his shoulder. Nick spins around.

Church is coming into the room from the fire-escape, one hand in his coat pocket as if pointing a pistol at Nick.

Church: "I got no time to waste. Get your hands up."

Nick puts them up, backing away until he is against the door leading to Lois's room. Church walks over to him.

Church: "I missed connections and need getaway money. Come across."

Nick, somewhat loudly: "How much do you need, Church?"

Church: "I'll take what you've got." He runs his hand over Nick's clothes, finds his wallet, and takes it. He is very careless, giving Nick ample opportunity to grab him, but Nick makes no move in that direction.

Nora, watching her husband in proud anticipation at first, begins to look puzzled as he makes no attempt to disarm Church, even when Church's attention is centered on counting the money in the wallet.

Church, too, seems puzzled. He stands there awkwardly for a moment, until it is apparent that Nick is not going to grab him; then he says: "If you're smart, you'll wait five minutes before you blow any whistles," and goes out the window and up the fire-escape.

Nick, still standing with his back to Lois's door, says in a clear voice: "I never saw anybody trying so hard to get caught as this Sam Church. And now look at the clown, going *up the fire-escape in broad daylight.*"

Nora, who has been looking at Nick with almost tearful disillusionment, asks: "But why would anybody want to get caught?"

Nick: "Maybe because he thinks he could beat the rap now—and then he couldn't be tried again no matter what came out later."

Nora: "But—"

Nick: "That's the law. What fooled all of us was our not thinking there was anything serious between him and Smitty, that they were just playing around." Nick is sweating.

Nora: "But what's—"

Nick: "They're a couple of no-goods, but what I've got hold of now shows they're certainly two people in love with each other, if two people ever were. Wait till he gets off the fire-escape. I'll show you a—"

There is a sound of a shot from outside.

Nick starts and goes to the window. Nora goes with him. On the sidewalk below, Church is lying dead. Not far from him stands Smitty, staring at him. Near her on the sidewalk is a pistol. Dum-Dum is running away; as he reaches the corner a policeman jumps out and grabs him.

As Nick and Nora see these things from the window, Lois joins them, asking: "I heard a shot—what is it?"

Nora leads Lois away from the window, then exclaims, "Nickie!" and the three of them go into the living room.

There is a mad scramble of departing guests; thugs are grabbing their ticket-kiddies and hurriedly departing. Vogel, coming in, is caught in a jam of departers, and his glasses are knocked off and broken. He takes another pair from an inner pocket and puts them on.

Schultz and Jensen are standing guard over a child sleeping on a sofa. Nick and Nora do not see the child's face, though Lois does. Jensen assures them: "This is our job and we're sticking with it, no matter who gets killed where."

Police begin to come in, bringing Smitty, Dum-Dum, and Ella Waters. VanSlack and Guild arrive. Vogel does not try to leave. Mrs. Bellam and Freddie try to go, but are detained.

VanSlack takes Nick into the bedroom and, after a bit of preliminary hemming and hawing, says: "Look here, Mr. Charles. You kidded me unmercifully about suspecting you, but I want to tell you right now that if Church did come here to make good his threats in connection with your wife and child and you killed him, I don't think any jury in the world would or should convict you."

Nick: "Let's go back with the others. They'll think we're talking about them." He returns to the living room, followed by VanSlack.

Guild is questioning Smitty: "What were you doing around here anyhow?"

Smitty: "I knew Sam was coming to see Nick Charles and I wanted to head him off."

Guild: "Why?"

Smitty: "I knew Sam would be up to some trick too slick for his own good and I knew he'd wind up in trouble—but I never expected this."

Guild: "How'd you know he was coming here?"

Smitty: "Dum-Dum told me."

Guild turns to Dum-Dum, who has been crying since he came in. He does not sob and his face is not contorted; it's simply that tears keep running down his cheeks.

Guild: "Come on—talk."

Dum-Dum: "Mr. Church told me he coming here. He did not say why. I did not ask. When Miss Smitty ask me, I tell her, and then I am sorry when she get excited, and I afraid she come over and butt in maybe, so I come to maybe stop her."

Guild: "And then what?"

Dum-Dum: "I just had seen her and was going cross the street to talk to her—a truck get in my way—and when it pass I see her—and Mr. Church."

Guild: "Didn't you hear the shot?"

Dum-Dum: "No, sir. I am dodging noisy truck."

Guild, to Smitty: "What did you see?"

Smitty: "I heard the shot, I think, though I didn't know what it was at the time."

Guild: "I didn't ask you what you heard. What did you see?"

Smitty: "Just—I looked up and there was Sam falling down right in front of me. I didn't know who it was at the time. I—I don't think I knew until the copper grabbed me."

Guild: "Oh, you didn't? And you didn't know about the gun you dropped?"

Smitty: "I didn't drop that gun. I heard it fall right after he fell, but I didn't drop it."

Guild turns to Ella Waters: "And what's your unlikely story, Hilda?"

Ella, turning to Nick and Nora: "My name's really not Ella Waters. I took that after I got out of jail for shoplifting, but I was honestly trying to go straight, but I knew the police wouldn't believe it after Colonel MacFay was killed, and would find out from my fingerprints who I was, so I ran away; but I felt bad about it and was coming back to tell you about it, because I knew you'd understand, when there was all that excitement downstairs and a policeman that knew me grabbed me and brought me up here, but I—"

Guild stops her by putting a hand over her mouth, growling: "You still talk more and say less than anybody I ever ran into." He turns to Vogel: "And what were you here for, Diamond-Back?"

Vogel: "I had a couple of questions I wanted to ask Charles."

Guild: "Such as for instance?"

Vogel: "Is that monkey Church really dead?"

Guild: "He'll never be any deader. Somebody shot him off the fire-escape from below with a .38, and if the slug hadn't done the job, the fall would—he must've dropped twenty stories."

Vogel: "Okay. I didn't trust that guy, and when it looked like he was going out of his way to do folks a favor I thought I'd better come over and see what I could angle out of Charles."

Guild: "Could you come to the point now—you can fill in the details afterwards."

Vogel: "You're getting it all. I got a place I run uptown that gets a high-class trade that wouldn't want their connections to know they're there. Get what I mean? Or do you want me to wait till I can talk through a lawyer?"

Guild: "I get it. You don't admit you run gambling joints."

Vogel: "That's right. Last night there was—say—a bank vice-president in my place and a couple of other customers like that—big and respectable—and Sam Church comes in and sits in with them for an hour or two—including the time MacFay was being killed down on the Island. Well, when I see in the morning papers that coppers are hunting for him, I don't feel so good about it, and I don't think my customers are going to feel so hot either—having to give him that kind of alibi. And just when I'm stewing about it, he phones and says tell them not to worry. He knows what it'll cost them to come to the front for him, and he says even if he's picked up and things look pretty black, he won't call on them unless it's only that between him and the chair—so they can sleep pretty, because he don't think things'll ever get that far."

VanSlack: "I don't understand. Do you mean he had an alibi—a genuine one?"

Nick: "That's what he means. And he didn't want to use it—yet. A man who saw Church going into Vogel's last night was slugged all over Harlem by Church's friends for trying to tell me about it."

VanSlack: "That's incredible."

Nick: "Not as incredible as if Church *had* killed MacFay, after going to all that trouble before and after to advertise himself as the murderer and coming here trying to get himself pinched."

VanSlack: "But if he were innocent—"

Nick: "I didn't say he was innocent. I'm saying—drew all the attention to himself while his accomplice did the dirty work—and when the accomplice thought Church was working a double cross, the accomplice killed Church."

Dum-Dum draws a deep breath, stops crying, smiles as if to himself.

VanSlack, looking at Smitty and Dum-Dum: "But they have alibis, too."

Nick: "So then they didn't kill MacFay, huh? Maybe Dum-Dum's knife that didn't do the killing had Asta's tooth prints in it from when he pulled it out of the wall of the cottage yesterday—huh?"

Guild: "All right. Who did it?"

Van Slack: "Yes, who?"

Nick, aside to Nora, indicating VanSlack and Guild: "A couple of schoolboys," then: "Didn't you think it was funny that nobody heard any sounds of a struggle before the shot at MacFay's—in spite of the signs of a row in which a lamp had been upset and his arm broken—though all of us had heard noises of people moving around afterwards?"

VanSlack: "I don't know. That is—what do you mean?"

Nick: "Let me show you a trick." He sets up the electric-cord-gun-paper-water trick as it was used by the murderer, saying as he arranges it: "I figured this out by myself, but I had an electrician check up the details for me. Lend me a gun, somebody . . . Will you switch on the lights . . . Get me a glass of water, etc."

The trick works perfectly, even to blowing out the fuses. Nick takes a bow as they all stare at him.

Dum-Dum, who has been held tightly by a policeman up to this point, takes advantage of the policeman's attention being on the trick to suddenly dive across the floor after the pistol that has been hurled into a corner by the recoil, grab it, and begin shooting. Nick has leapt upon Dum-Dum, grappling with him, so that the bullets go wild. As he succeeds in disarming Dum-Dum, a policeman knocks the Cuban cold.

VanSlack, bewildered: "But he had an alibi."

Nick: "Then he's still got it. All he was trying to do just now was to kill the accomplice that killed his Mr. Church."

VanSlack: "And who is that?"

Nick looks at VanSlack and at the others who are impatiently awaiting his reply.

Nick: "You people haven't been paying any attention to what I'm saying or doing. Listen to me now. There was no struggle in Mac-Fay's room. He was stunned—probably with a blow from the hilt of the knife—then his throat was cut and his wrist broken, and it's easy enough to break a dead man's wrist—to pretend there was a struggle in which the lamp and stuff was upset. The trick I just showed you gave the murderer between five and ten minutes to get an alibi before the water soaked through and set the gun off. Get it?"

Nora: "But who, Nick?"

Nick: "Who is the only person that used that particular alibi?"

Nora stares at Nick in bewilderment.

Nick, answering his own question: "Lois, of course. Everybody else had real alibis or none at all." He steps close to Lois, speaking swiftly:

"Church, the engineer, planned it, and you carried it through; that's why he needed Smitty to stooge for him, so folks wouldn't suspect him of being mixed up with any other woman. You were friends with Church and Dum-Dum; that's why your dog was friends with them and let them come and go on the grounds as they wanted, and that's why your dog stood up with his paws on his killer's shoulders—as the prints showed—and let his throat get cut."

Lois: "But why should I kill Papa?"

Nick: "For money. But don't interrupt the maestro when he's exposing criminals. I don't get the Horn killing exactly, unless he had found out you killed MacFay and you told him I had you cold or would have when I came back from getting the knife from the dog. He'd have covered you up and would have tried to kill me for those millions he would have when he married you. You had to get him going quick, because once he saw it was Church's knife you'd used, he'd have seen through you. So you put me on the spot, even moving around so I had to turn my back toward where he was standing, and then pushed me off the spot so there was nothing for me to do but kill him in self-defense."

Lois: "But Papa gave me everything I wanted. He—"

Nick: "That wasn't your kind of life and he looked good for years. Your kind of life was the Linda Mills life you had been leading ever since you got old enough to sneak out after the folks went to bed."

Lois: "Linda Mills?"

Nick: "Yes—L. M. for Linda Mills and Lois MacFay. Linda Mills, the girl whose description fits you with allowance for makeup and flashy clothes. Linda Mills, who sleeps without pillows, just as you do. Linda Mills, in whose apartment there is a scorched spot beside the bed and a bullet hole in the wall where the lamp-trick was rehearsed. Linda Mills, who disappeared a couple of weeks ago when you and Church started planning MacFay's murder."

Lois stares stonily at him.

Nick: "This is going to be easy enough to prove, you know. We'll make you up for the people who knew you as Linda Mills and see what they say. Or maybe you'd rather be left alone with Dum-Dum after he comes to."

Lois: "But he can't think I killed Sam Church. They said he was shot from the street."

Nick: "Nonsense. They said he was shot from below. Well, he ran *up* the fire-escape from here, and you leaned out the window and shot him from below, and dropped the gun down after him."

Lois: "But why?"

Nick: "Why? I'm still hoarse from standing close to your door bellowing that he was trying to get himself arrested and tried, so he would be in the clear forever after, and in a spot to shake you down if he wanted to double-cross you; and telling you how nuts he was about Smitty and—"

Smitty: "That's a lie and you know it."

Nick: "I don't know anything. Anyhow I thought it would sound good at the time. I didn't know how sweetness here would kill Church, but I wanted to stir her up as much as I could."

Lois, horrified: "Sam wasn't—" Then she pulls herself together, shrugs slightly, says: "Can I talk to you and Nora alone?"

VanSlack and Guild look at Nick, who nods.

Guild: "Okay, but slap her down if she gets funny."

Nick, Nora, and Lois go into the bedroom and shut the door.

Lois to Nick, coolly: "You're right. I'm Linda Mills at heart. I hated having to play Little Red Riding Hood to that horrible old man. So when Sam was fooling around trying to find a way of getting money out of him and picked me up, we found out we talked the same language. I'm not sorry for any of it—except your lying to me about Sam and Smitty—it was a chance and I took it. Having to get rid of Horn that way—and you guessed it right—made things tough—gummed the works pretty bad—but what could I do? Then when I thought Sam was crossing me up for that big tramp—well, I let him have it. I'd always figured he was safe because he was nuts about me, but—oh, well, I still think you gave me a raw deal on that, but the chances are he was playing me for a sap anyway, even if not with Smitty. So far, so good or bad, whichever way you look at it. What I'm getting at is, I'll make a deal with you."

Nick: "What'll you give us? The moon?

Lois, calmly: "You like that brat of yours, don't you?"

Nick and Nora stare at her, alarmed.

Lois: "Let me walk out of here and I'll send the kid back in an hour."

Nick and Nora start for the door together, then Nick checks himself and says to Nora: "You look. I'll stay here with angel."

Nora goes into the living room and looks at the sleeping child. It is not Nicky. Paying no attention to the others in the room, she runs back to Nick, leaving the door open. She cannot speak, but one look at her tells Nick the child is gone. He grabs Lois by the shoulders.

Lois, wincing, but smiling coolly: "Now you know. Make up your minds. Try to send me to the chair, or get your child back all in one piece. Whichever you like best."

As the others start to come in from the living room, there is a terrific pounding on the corridor door. A policeman opens it.

Into the room comes an enormous unkempt woman carrying Nick Jr. under one arm, holding one of Creeps's friends by the ear with her other hand.

Woman, loudly and angrily: "My beautiful Raphael. Give me back my beautiful Raphael and take this toad-frog you try to palm off on me. Where is my lovely boy?"

Nora runs to her and takes Nick Jr., while the woman, spying the child who has been awakened by the noise and is sitting up on the sofa, goes over and gathers him into her arms, crooning over him: "Mama's darling. Did they try to swap that awful hideous dwarf for Mama's darling? Never again will your mama lend you to go to a party."

Raphael is a truly, deeply, and offensively ugly child.

Jensen and Schultz stare at each other, Schultz muttering: "Kids are like Chinamen—how can you tell 'em apart?"

Lois says philosophically to Nick: "Oh, well, all you can do is try to play the breaks as far as you get them."

THE END

ANOTHER THIN MAN

Afterword

On November 25, 1939, eight days after the release of *Another Thin Man*, the headline on a brief notice in the *Los Angeles Times* announced, "Thin Man of Film Fame Gone but Title Lives On." Dashiell Hammett's original Thin Man was an eccentric inventor named Clyde Wynant, who was, as the *Times* notes, "killed and buried beneath his laboratory floor, thus providing a mystery for Detective Nick Charles in the initial picture." Yet the title character refused to die. "Through a quirk on the public's part, the character of the Thin Man was shifted from its original owner to William Powell. Faced with this widespread belief, the studio decided to title the picture *Another Thin Man*, to fit both Powell and William Poulsen, the eight-month-old infant, who plays Nick Charles Jr." The *Times* report suggests that MGM was happy to trade on movie fans' misconceptions.

Dashiell Hammett played his part in the confusion, as well, first by posing on the dust jacket of Knopf's first edition of *The Thin Man* novel. Hammett was lean and stylish as any film star. He was also a master of observation and wordplay who claimed credit for the film's title. Hammett told his daughter Jo that MGM's filmmakers had gone round and round, unable to discover a suitably artful moniker for the third of the *Thin Man* films, and that he had suggested what seemed the obvious solution—*Another Thin Man*. The title was simple and straightforward on its face, subtle in its implications. Little Poulsen joined Wynant, Hammett, and Powell as another of the "thin men." Nick and Nora launched another episode of merry mayhem. And Hammett and the Hacketts were caught up again, against their better judgments, in yet another *Thin Man* filmmaking ordeal.

While Albert Hackett and Frances Goodrich failed to kill off the *Thin Man* film franchise with Nora's pregnancy, the arrival of Nick Jr. did alter *Another Thin Man*'s trajectory. Nick and especially Nora are more temperate. Nick talks about wanting a drink more often than he gets one. Nora rarely imbibes, as is fitting for a young mother. After reviewing the Hacketts' initial screenplay submission, the Breen office made only a general request to minimize the "display of liquor and drinking." A few scenes depicting violence or sexuality drew specific objections. Body parts, whether bloody or alluring, were frowned upon. Innuendo-laden dialogue was censured, though not eliminated. *Another Thin Man* is tame by comparison with the first two films. Nick and Nora recapture their smart and sassy relationship and the film maintains what one reviewer called "that agile, faintly sardonic quality." But, whether influenced by the Charleses' transformation into parents, Hammett's accommodation to the *Thin Man*'s formula, or the Hacketts' pragmatic modifications, the film is more domestic than decadent.

Hammett fulfilled his screenwriting obligation to MGM in mid-May 1938. He was hospitalized in New York ten days later, again leaving the Hacketts to shape his crime-fiction story line into its final filmable form. As in *After the Thin Man*, they pruned, juggled, and appended Hammett's story elements. They compressed the time line by a day, curbed some of the characters' rougher interactions, and reshaped some ancillary action. The Hacketts inject new complications as well, so that Mrs. Bellam professes motherly concern for Lois and Colonel MacFay distrusts Dudley Horn to the extent that he threatens to disinherit his daughter if the two were wed. These were the Hacketts', not Hammett's modifications and while they are generally helpful, the film's plot and resolution remain complicated.

The final filmed version of *Another Thin Man* also shows changes to Hammett's cast of supporting characters. Hammett's original thieving bellboy, "a youngish man with a small, cheerful, wizened face" named "Face" Peppler, is supplanted by "Creeps" Binder—who is similarly young and cheery, but without the improbably aged face. Interesting, Hammett and the Hacketts used the name "Face" Peppler for entirely different characters in *The Thin Man* novel and film. Mrs. Dolley's role is more subtly altered. Hammett describes the landlord of Linda Mills's apartment building as a "frowsy, middle-aged woman with the sniffles. In one hand she carries a newspaper, in the other a handkerchief." Marjorie Main plays Dolley, as gruff as Hammett imagined. But Main is a tough not tawdry character, who carries no damp handkerchief and delivers her lines in tones that minimize potential for innuendo. Changes to her role might be attributed to Production Code censors, who had objected to implications that the building was a "house of assignation, or that the landlady is a madam." The breed of the murdered dog undergoes more conspicuous transformation, beginning in Hammett's "Farewell Murder" as an Airedale pup, becoming in his screen story a collie, and ending in the film as an Irish wolfhound—big enough to leave paw prints on a man's shoulders.

Two other supporting roles deserve attention. The first is Assistant District Attorney VanSlack. In Hammett's screen story VanSlack is an unlikeable character who toggles between incompetence and authoritarian insolence. Hammett described him as "a tall, stooped colorless young man with a vague face; the same vagueness characterizes his words and manner." Hammett's VanSlack is ambiguous, tentative, and unsure how to assert himself and enact his obligations. In *Another Thin Man*, the role is played by Otto Kruger, a veteran stage and film actor who was fifty-four when he received an urgent casting call from MGM and rushed back to the studio from a family vacation. Kruger's VanSlack is cryptic—even vague—but he offers none of the moral vacillation suggested by Hammett's younger version. The character still works, and works well, but Hammett's subtleties are lost in translation.

The final character of note is Nick Charles Jr., described in Hammett's screen story as "a fat, year-old boy who is interested in very little besides eating and sleeping." He eats anything and sleeps anywhere. His basic vocabulary consists of "'Drunk' for things he does not like and 'Gimme' for things he does." Nick Jr. rarely laughs, never cries, and is not amused by his fun-loving parents. "He ordinarily regards them with the same sort of mild curiosity or tolerant boredom with which he regards the rest of the world," wrote Hammett. Bored babies don't play well on the big screen, however, so while William Poulsen's infant character is docile, he is hardly the dullard child that Hammett bestowed on the Charleses in *Another Thin Man*'s screen story. Hammett's littlest Thin Man was tubby, vapid, and humorless—the opposite of everything Nick and Nora represented and a fitting Parthian shot for Hammett's last piece of long fiction.

J. M. R.

SEQUEL TO THE THIN MAN

Headnote

Hammett's final contribution to the *Thin Man* film franchise was an eight-page story that was neither developed nor produced. He was fed up with the project—and it showed. Hammett's slapdash invention of the "Sequel to the Thin Man" may in fact have been a signal to producer Hunt Stromberg to give up, to recognize that Hammett wanted nothing more to do with his Hollywood stepchild.

Evidence within the text suggests Hammett based his 1938 "Sequel" on an early story idea for the second of the *Thin Man* films, *After the Thin Man*, released in 1936. The train station and surprise party descriptions, in particular, are nearly parallel in both stories. Those scenes had been settled upon long before the script for *After the Thin Man* took its final shape. Hammett's description of Dancer and his Chinatown nightclub are also suggestive, since they are introduced as if for the first time, as though the first sequel did not exist. Morelli, Georgia, Macaulay, and other supporting roles reprised from the novel and original film go unexplained. Nick Jr., from *Another Thin Man*, is absent. And, in a move that would have satisfied producer Hunt Stromberg's earliest demands, most of the original cast of characters from *The Thin Man* reappears. From the very beginning Stromberg had advocated for the Charleses' return to New York for the second film "because it would give us the opportunity to bring back all those swell characters of the original." Hammett does not set his "Sequel" in New York. Instead he transports the troupe to San Francisco for a madcap adventure.

Hammett's "Sequel to the Thin Man" features a merry pastiche of bantering romance, eccentric encounters, greed, and crime. While not a recipe for a true screwball comedy, it would have complemented contemporary popular releases like *Holiday* (directed by George Cukor, starring Cary Grant and Katharine Hepburn) and *Bringing Up Baby* (directed by Howard Hawks, also starring Grant and Hepburn, with Asta cast as her dog George), both released in 1938. Hammett's blend of mystery and comedy was in vogue, but in this instance he may have pushed his literary license beyond what MGM could bear. Reluctant screenwriters, an unenthusiastic leading lady, and an indisposed leading man spelled troubles enough for the film franchise. The potential for public distaste for the sour turn of a sympathetic character might have been anticipated as beyond the pale. A scribbled annotation on a draft of the "Sequel" ("what is audience reaction to . . . being murderer . . .") suggests that the dénouement in Hammett's final *Thin Man* offering gave MGM one more reason to reject the story.

J. M. R.

"SEQUEL TO THE THIN MAN"

Metro Goldwyn Mayer Script Dept.
December 7, 1938

Nick, Nora, Tommy, and Dorothy arrive in San Francisco and are met by reporters who want to know about "new developments" in the Macaulay case. Nick ignores their questions as he has ignored the telegrams he has been receiving en route. They are driven to his house and have settled down with signs of relief at being in a quiet place once more when a mob of surprise party guests comes out from behind furniture at them.

While the party is going on, Mimi phones from New York to say that Macaulay has escaped and she is afraid he will kill her, since she was the chief witness against him. Nick, uninterested, hangs up and tells Nora it was a man trying to sell him something.

Nick and Nora are asleep when Mimi—fresh from a plane—crashes their bedroom to demand Nick's protection. She is followed by Gilbert, complaining about the cost of taxis in San Francisco. He has become a miser since inheriting money. Nick and Nora unwillingly tell them they can stay.

In New York, Macaulay—disguised as a middle-aged woman—learns Mimi has gone to San Francisco and dashes for a plane, being helped aboard by Guild, who is at the airport hunting for him.

Next day Mimi phones Chris in New York, begging him to come out. He pretends indifference until his first wife, Georgia, comes in, overhears the conversation, and starts a quarrel, saying she will never let Mimi have him unless she gets some money out of it. Chris laughs at her threats and leaves for the West. Georgia goes out to keep a date with Morelli, who has been in love with her since Nick's dinner, and tells him about the dirty deal she is getting. He is having the first "clean" love affair of his life and thinks this slut is Joan of Arc. He offers to take her to San Francisco and see that her wrongs are righted.

In San Francisco Nick and Nora have been leading dogs' lives for a couple of days. In addition to Mimi—who keeps complaining about Gilbert's stinginess—and Gilbert—with his complaints about her extravagance—they have an antique uncle and aunt of Nora's visiting them, people who never trusted Nick very much and now suspect him of everything down to being Mimi's lover and Gilbert's father.

Chris arrives on the Coast and phones a man called Dancer—a man of Chris's type but much more dangerous—who tells Chris, "Yeah, I remember you," and hangs up. Chris calls him back and with promises of easy money persuades Dancer to meet him.

Nick and Nora, fed up with their guests, sneak out the back way, run into Tommy and Dorothy doing the same thing, and they all set out for a peaceful evening somewhere away from home.

In a Chinatown joint Chris tells Dancer he knows he can get a lot of money from Mimi, because she is crazy about him, but he is afraid of Nick, Georgia, Morelli, etc., as well as having no local connections. Dancer is skeptical, especially since Chris has no cash now. Nick and his party come in, are greeted warmly by the proprietor, and Dorothy sees Chris; she's angry at his having followed Mimi to San Francisco and tells him so. When Chris starts to tell her what he thinks of her, Tommy hits him, and as much riot as we want is on—winding up with Chris and Dancer out on the sidewalk. Dancer says: "If you're on the level, now's your chance. Let's go up and see the dame while these people are here and collect." Chris agrees to call on Mimi.

Across the street from Nick's house Macaulay, still in disguise, sees Morelli and Georgia arrive and go in.

Inside Mimi and Georgia have a grand row, Georgia demanding money for giving up Chris, Mimi saying she wouldn't give her a cent if it meant losing him forever, throwing threats at each other and at Chris—"Even if I can't have him, you won't," etc.

Chris and Dancer arrive and after a bit of five-handed quarreling Chris gets Mimi aside and tries to get some money out of her but she is too afraid Georgia will get some of it, so she gives him very little. He tells her she has till the next morning to make up her mind and they rejoin the others for another battle-royal that lasts until Nick arrives and puts Chris, Dancer, Morelli, and Georgia out.

Macaulay follows Chris and Dancer down the street and waits outside when they go into a saloon. When they come out Dancer says to Chris: "If the idea is for me to keep you from being hurt maybe it's better I stick a little ways behind you," so he follows Chris while Macaulay follows him. Meanwhile Nick and Nora have gone to bed; Mimi, after trying to get Chris on the phone, has sneaked out of the house, shadowed by the ever-spying Gilbert; and downtown, Morelli and Georgia, making lame excuses and a date for later, have separated and each is headed for Chris's hotel.

At Chris's hotel—a small one in a dark and now foggy street—Mimi is told that he has not come in yet. She leaves the hotel. Morelli and Georgia arrive separately, neither aware of the other's presence, and conceal themselves in darkness. (For reasons that will be obvious the audience should not know too much about their positions in relation to the hotel; they should simply be hiding in darkness.)

As Chris, walking down the street, approaches a dark alley on one side of the hotel, Dancer silently moves up closer behind him. Macaulay is half a block down the street. A policeman standing on that farther corner hears two shots and turns toward the hotel. Dancer dashes into the dark alley and there are scuffling sounds, his voice grunting in surprise, the sound of running feet in the alley. Macaulay, scampering down the street, trips himself on his skirts and falls, losing hat and wig.

The approaching policeman grabs him, drags him up to the entrance of the alley next to the hotel, and turns his light down on Chris, who lies dead on the sidewalk.

In an all-night lunchroom Morelli and Georgia keep their date and immediately each knows the other was at the scene of the killing. They leave to find a place to hide.

In the morning Guild and some local detectives call on Nick and tell him about Chris's murder and Macaulay's arrest. Nick tells them of the meeting between Chris, Dancer, Morelli, Georgia, and Mimi the previous night and arrangements are made to try to pick up Dancer, Morelli, and Georgia. Then Guild asks, "And how about this Mimi?" Nick says he thinks she is out of it—she was in the house. Guild says the clerk at Chris's hotel described a woman like her calling for Chris not half an hour before he was killed. Nick sends for Mimi, who comes in followed by Gilbert. When asked about her whereabouts she says she was at home of course but Gilbert interrupts her. He tells her it is silly to lie at a time like this; he knows she went to Chris's hotel because he shadowed her there and back again to Nick's. Questioned, he places the time of her return early enough to make it impossible for her to have been in the neighborhood of the hotel at the time of the shooting, though the police do not altogether believe him.

Macaulay is brought in and questioned again. He says he accidentally ran into Chris on the street, was surprised to know he was in the city, and shadowed him in an attempt to learn where he lived so he could avoid that part of town until he could board a boat for the Orient. He said he heard the shot and ran because as an escaped convict he could not afford to be around trouble, but he did not see the flash and could not tell whether the man walking behind Chris had killed him or not.

Dancer phones Mimi, saying: "This is the fellow who was with your boyfriend. Can you meet me now?" She says she can and he gives her careful instructions. When she goes out a detective shadows her, with the result that both she and the sleuth have walked a couple of inches off their heights before Dancer can safely pick her up in his car.

Later that afternoon, in a room behind drawn blinds, Morelli and Georgia see their pictures in an afternoon paper, with WANTED over them; Dancer looks at his as he leans carelessly against a police-call box on crowded Market Street.

Morelli suggests that now her husband's dead, Georgia should marry him so neither can be made to testify against the other in case they are caught, but she thinks it is simpler for them just to lie, and besides how could they walk into the City Hall with their faces spread over all the papers? Morelli has to go out, his only explanation being that he's "got a job to do."

At cocktail hour Nick and Nora, with Mimi, Gilbert, Dorothy, and Tommy, are drinking in a front room in his house when somebody firing through the window from the street shoots a glass out of his hand. Nick digs the bullet out of the wall and takes it to headquarters, where the expert says it was from the same gun Chris was shot with.

Dancer comes into headquarters and gives himself up, saying he had just seen in the papers that he was wanted. He tells of the proposition Chris made him, but said he had no intention of getting hurt, at least until Chris paid him something, which is why he walked behind Chris—he didn't want to stop a bullet meant for the other fellow. He didn't see the flash and as soon as he saw Chris fall he ran up the alley and away from there, taking no chances on being next. Nobody can prove he ever owned a gun or had the slightest reason for killing Chris, whom he had never known well and had not seen for years. Macaulay sends for Nick and makes a complete confession to having shot Chris over Dancer's shoulders, involving Mimi in both the murder and his escape from prison. Nick says: "Hooey! Just a fellow who'd rather stall through a long, drawn-out murder trial here than go back to be burnt in a few days," and tears the confession up.

"Having," as he says, "not only been shot at, but also insulted by yaps," Nick decides to go to work. He goes down into Chinatown and gets a line on Dancer's friends and habits and digs into them; he combs the waterfront; he has practically exhausted the city before he, also exhausted, returns home looking fairly satisfied with himself.

Meanwhile Morelli, returning from his "job," has arrived in the neighborhood of his hideout just in time to see Georgia being taken away by the police, so later that night he comes calling on Nick again, asking him to help save the little woman. Grilled, he admits that both of them were near the hotel when Chris was shot but swears both are innocent and didn't even see the flash.

Nick makes Morelli a proposition. He says he's got everything he needs to convict Dancer except an eyewitness. If Morelli and Georgia can find it in their hearts to change their testimony just a little bit, even if only enough to swear there was nobody except Dancer within ten feet of Chris when he was killed (he was shot under one ear and there were plenty of powder-marks), Nick will promise to save them. Morelli balks; he would never frame anybody and he hadn't thought Nick would. Nick insists that it's not really framing to add a little needed evidence against a man you're positive is guilty and keeps talking about "saving the little woman" until Morelli agrees.

The next day Nick assembles everybody and goes to work on Dancer. He has a mob of witnesses: a bellboy to swear Dancer had a gun for years; a longshoreman to swear he saw him throw what looked like a gun off a dock the previous afternoon; a newsboy to swear he had seen him running from the direction of Nick's house right after the shot had been fired through the window; a pool-room attendant to swear he had once told him when drunk that there was one guy in the world he wanted to get, a guy named Chris Something. He has more witnesses, but the most effective are Morelli and Georgia, who now almost remember seeing the gun in Dancer's hand.

Dancer gives up. "All right," he tells Nick, "you win. I'll take what's coming to me but I don't want a murder rap. It was all just as I told you till we got to the alley. I was closing in then, wanting to get some few pennies anyway from Chris before he went in his hotel, and then that gun came out and was almost under my nose when it went off, and I didn't want to be the next on the list, so I grabbed it and then I see what I've got besides the gun. Real dough, if what Chris said was right. So I helped in the getaway and the next day I called her [nodding at Mimi] up and—"

Mimi screams: "That's a lie, you double-crossing—" and a copper grabs her and puts handcuffs on her wrists.

Dancer shakes his head coolly and goes on talking: "Not her, you mug. I went to her and told her if she wanted the kid kept off the gallows I'd have to be fixed up regular and so—after a little trouble: she was kind of tough at first—we made the deal." He scowls at Nick. "And a fine deal you turned it into."

Nick says excuse me and goes out to pay off his witnesses, one of whom suddenly looks up and asks: "Mister, was it just a joke like you said?" Nick assures him it was and goes back into the room where Gilbert was assuring the detectives very seriously that he *did* feel that now he was the head of the house he had a right to protect his mother from ravenous males, and after all the money she would waste on Chris was actually *his* money, since it was doubtful if she would get anything out of his father's estate, and . . .

THE END

THE END